THE PONIARD'S HILT

THE FULL SERIES OF

Ⓣⓗⓔ Mysteries of the People

:: OR ::
History of a Proletarian Family Across the Ages

B y   E   U   G   E   N   E   S   U   E

Consisting of the Following Works:

THE GOLD SICKLE; or, *Hena the Virgin of the Isle of Sen.*
THE BRASS BELL; or, *The Chariot of Death.*
THE IRON COLLAR; or, *Faustine and Syomara.*
THE SILVER CROSS; or, *The Carpenter of Nazareth.*
THE CASQUE'S LARK; or, *Victoria, the Mother of the Camps.*
THE PONIARD'S HILT; or, *Karadeucq and Ronan.*
THE BRANDING NEEDLE; or, *The Monastery of Charolles.*
THE ABBATIAL CROSIER; or, *Bonaik and Septimine.*
THE CARLOVINGIAN COINS; or, *The Daughters of Charlemagne.*
THE IRON ARROW-HEAD; or, *The Buckler Maiden.*
THE INFANT'S SKULL; or, *The End of the World.*
THE PILGRIM'S SHELL; or, *Fergan the Quarryman.*
THE IRON PINCERS; or, *Mylio and Karvel.*
THE IRON TREVET; or, *Jocelyn the Champion.*
THE EXECUTIONER'S KNIFE; or, *Joan of Arc.*
THE POCKET BIBLE; or, *Christian the Printer.*
THE BLACKSMITH'S HAMMER; or, *The Peasant Code.*
THE SWORD OF HONOR; or, *The Foundation of the French Republic.*
THE GALLEY SLAVE'S RING; or, *The Family Lebrenn.*

Published Uniform With This Volume By
THE NEW YORK LABOR NEWS CO.
28 CITY HALL PLACE   NEW YORK CITY

THE PONIARD'S HILT

:: :: OR :: ::

KARADEUCQ AND RONAN

A Tale of Bagauders and Vagres

By EUGENE SUE

TRANSLATED FROM THE ORIGINAL FRENCH BY
DANIEL DE LEON
NEW YORK LABOR NEWS COMPANY, 1907

INDEX.

TRANSLATOR'S PREFACE

The invasion of Gaul by Clovis introduced feudalism in France, which is equivalent to saying in Europe, France being the teeming womb of the great historic events of that epoch. It goes without saying that so vast a social system as that of feudalism could not be perfected in a day, or even during one reign. Indeed, generations passed, and it was not until the Age of Charlemagne that feudalism can be said to have taken some measure of shape and form. Between the Ages of Clovis and Charlemagne a period of turbulence ensued altogether peculiar to the combined circumstances that feudalism was forced to struggle with two foes—one internal, the disintegrating forces that ever accompany a new movement; the other external, the stubborn and inspiring resistance, on the part of the native masses, to the conqueror from the wilds of Germania. Historians, with customary levity, have neglected to reproduce this interesting epoch in the annals of that social structure that is mother to the social structure now prevalent. The task was undertaken and successfully accomplished by Eugene Sue in this boisterous historic novel entitled *The Poniard's Hilt; or, Karadeucq and Ronan,* the sixth of his majestic series of historic novels, *The Mysteries of the People; or, History of a Proletarian Family Across the Ages.* The leading characters are all historic. It required the genius, the learning, the poetry, the tact, withal the daring of a Sue to weave these characters into a fascinating tale and draw a picture as vivid as the quartos, from which the facts are gathered, are musty with old age.

DANIEL DE LEON.

January, 1908.

PART I

THE KORRIGANS

CHAPTER I.

ARAIM.

Occasionally they are long-lived, these descendants of the good Joel, who, five hundred and fifty years ago and more lived in this identical region, near the sacred stones of the forest of Karnak. Yes, the descendants of the good Joel are, occasionally, long-lived, seeing that I, Araim, who to-day trace these lines in the seventy-seventh year of my life, saw my grandfather Gildas die fifty-six years ago at the advanced age of ninety-six, after having inscribed in his early youth a few lines in our family archives.

My grandfather Gildas buried his son Goridek, my father. I was then ten years old. Nine years later I lost my grandfather also. A few years after his demise I married. I have survived my wife, Martha, and I have seen my son Jocelyn become, in turn, a father. To-day he has a daughter and two boys. The girl is called Roselyk, she is eighteen; the elder of the two boys, Kervan, is three years his sister's senior; the younger, my pet, Karadeucq, is seventeen.

When you read these lines, as you will some day, my son Jocelyn, you will surely ask:

"What can have been the reason that my great-grandfather Gildas made no other entry in our chronicles than the death of his father Amael? And what can be the reason that my grandfather Goridek wrote not a line? And, finally, what can be the reason that my own father, Araim, waited so long—so very long before fulfilling the wishes of the good Joel?"

To that, my son, I would make this answer:

Your great-grandfather had no particular liking for desks and parchments. Besides, very much after the style of his own father Amael, he liked to postpone for to-morrow whatever he could avoid doing to-day. For the rest, his life of a husband-man was neither less peaceful nor less industrious than that of our fathers since the return of Schanvoch to the cradle of our family, after such a very long line of generations, kept away from Armorica by the hard trials and the slavery that followed in the wake of the Roman conquest. Your great-grandfather was in the habit of saying to my father:

"There will always be time for me to add a few lines to our family's narrative; besides, it seems to me, and I admit the notion is foolish, that to write 'I have lived', sounds very much like saying 'I am about to die'—Now, then, I am so happy that I cling to life, just as oysters do to their rocks."

And so it came about that, from to-morrow to to-morrow, your great-grandfather reached his ninety-sixth year without increasing the history of our family with a single word. When he lay on his deathbed he said to me:

"My child, I wish you to write the following lines for me in our archives:

" 'My grandfather Gildas and my father Goridek lived in our house quietly and happy, like good husbandmen; they remained true to their love for old Gaul and to the faith of our fathers; they blessed Hesus for having allowed them to be born and to die in the heart of Britanny, the only province where, for so very many years, the shocks that have elsewhere shaken Gaul have hardly ever been felt—those shocks died out before the impregnable frontiers of Breton Armorica, as the furious waves of our ocean dash themselves at the feet of our granite rocks.' "

That, then, my son Jocelyn, is the reason why neither your grandfather Goridek nor his father wrote a line themselves.

"And why," you will insist, "did you, Araim, my father,

why did you wait so long, until you had a son and grand-children, before you paid your tribute to our chronicle?"

There are two reasons for that: the first is that I never had enough to say; the second is that I would have had too much to write.

"Oh!" you will be thinking when you read this. "His advanced age has deranged old Araim's mind. He says in one breath that he had too much and too little to say. Is that sensible?"

Wait a moment, my son; be not in a hurry to believe that your old father has fallen into his second infancy. Listen, and you will discover how it is that I have at once too much and not enough to write upon.

As to what concerns my own life, being an old husbandman, I have been in the same predicament as my ancestors since Schanvoch—there never was sufficient matter for me to write about. Indeed, the interesting and charming narrative would have run somewhat after this fashion:

"Last year the autumn crop was richer than the winter crop; this year it is the reverse."

Or, "The large black cow yields daily six pints of milk more than the brindled cow."

Or, "The January sheep have turned out more woolly than the sheep of last March."

Or, "Last year grain was so dear, so very dear, that a 'muid' of old wheat sold at from twelve to thirteen deniers. The price of cattle and poultry is also on the upward tack: we now pay two gold sous for a draft ox, one gold sou for a milch-cow, six gold sous for a draft horse."

Or, "Will not our descendants be delighted to know that in these days a pig, if good and fat, fetches twelve deniers in autumn, which is neither more nor less than the cost of a bell-wether? And will they not rejoice to learn that our last coop of one hundred fat geese was sold last winter at the market of

Vannes for a full pound of silver by the weight? And imagine how well posted they will feel when they learn that the
day-laborers whom we hire during harvest time are paid by us
one denier a day."

That would hardly be considered either a charming or a thrilling narrative.

On the other hand, would our descendants feel more elated
if I were to tell them:

"That in which my pride lies is the knowledge that there is
no better field-laborer than my son Jocelyn, no better housekeeper than his wife Madalen, no sweeter creature than my
grand-daughter Roselyk, no handsomer and more daring lads
than my two grandsons, Kervan and Karadeucq—especially the
latter, the youngest of the set, my own pet!—a very demon for
deviltry, bravery and attractiveness. One should see him, at
seventeen years of age, break in the wild colts of our meadows,
dive into the sea like a fish, not lose an arrow out of ten when
he shoots at the sea-gulls on the wing, along the beach, during a
storm—or handling the 'pen-bas,' our redoubtable Breton stick!
Five or six soldiers armed with lances or swords would find
more sores than pleasure if they rubbed against my Karadeucq
with his 'pen-bas.' He is so robust, so agile, so dexterous! And
then, he is so handsome, with his beautiful blond hair cut round
and falling over the collar of his Gallic blouse; his eyes of the
blue of heaven, and his stout cheeks tanned by the wind of the
fields and the breeze of the sea!"

No! By the glorious bones of old Joel. No! He could not
have been prouder of his three sons—Guilhern the field-laborer,
Michael the armorer, and Albinik the mariner; or of his daughter Hena, the Virgin of the Isle of Sen—a now deserted island
that, at this moment, looking out at the window, I see yonder,
far away, almost in the open sea, veiled in mist. No! The good
Joel could not be any prouder of his family than I, old Araim,
am of my grandchildren! But the sons of Joel either fought

valiantly for freedom or remained dead on the battlefield; and his daughter Hena, whose saintly and sweet name is sung to this day and has come down from century to century, disinterestedly laid her life on the altars of Hesus for the welfare of her country, while the children of my son will die, obscure like their father, in this corner of Gaul. At least they will die free! The barbarous Franks have twice dashed forward as far as the frontiers of our Britanny, but never dared to enter it; our impenetrable forests, our bottomless marshes, our inaccessible and rocky mountains, above all our sturdy men, quickly up and in arms in response to the call of our ever-beloved druids, the Christian as well as the non-Christian druids, have rolled back the Frankish marauders, who, however, have rendered themselves masters of our other provinces since nearly fifteen years ago.

Alas! After nearly two centuries, the gloomy prophecy of the foster sister of our ancestor Schanvoch has been verified. Victoria the Great predicted it but too accurately. Long ago did the Franks pour over our frontier of the Rhine; they have since spread themselves over the whole of Gaul and subjugated the land—except our Breton Armorica.

These are the reasons why old Araim believed that neither as a father nor a Breton did his obscure happiness deserve to be chronicled in our family records, and these are the reasons why, alas! he had too much to write as a Gaul. Is not the account of the defeat, the shame, the renewed slavery of our common country, too much to write about, although we here in Britanny are ourselves free from the misfortunes that overwhelm our brothers elsewhere?

"But," meseems I hear you, my son Jocelyn, still insist, "why should old Araim, who has too little or too much to say, why should he begin his narrative to-day, rather than yesterday, or why did he not postpone starting to write until to-morrow?"

This is my answer, my son:

Read the narrative that I am now writing on that winter's evening when you, your wife and your children will gather by the fire in the large hall of our farmhouse and await the return of my pet Karadeucq, who left for the chase early in the morning promising to bring home a stag. Read this narrative, it will recall to your mind the family gathering of the previous evening, my son Jocelyn—it will also inform you of something that you do not know. You will not thereafter ask again:

"Why did good Araim start this narrative to-day, and not yesterday?"

CHAPTER II.

FAIRIES AND HOBGOBLINS.

The January snow and hail are falling in torrents; the wind moans; at a distance the sea roars and dashes inshore as far as the sacred stones of Karnak. It is only four o'clock in the afternoon, and yet it is night to all intents and purposes; the warmly stalled cattle are locked in; the gates of the farmyard are closed tightly out of fear of prowling wolves; a large fire shoots up its flames in the fireplace of the hall; old Araim is seated in his armchair, at the chimney-corner, with his large grey dog, its head streaked with the white of old age, stretched out at his feet. The old man is at work on a net for fishing; his son Jocelyn is fashioning a plough handle; Kervan is adjusting new thongs to a yoke; Karadeucq is sharpening the points of his arrows on a flint-stone. The tempest will last till morning if not longer, because the sun went down like a ball of fire behind thick black clouds that wreathed the isle of Sen like a dense fog. Whenever the sun sets in that fashion and the wind blows from the west the tempest lasts two, three, sometimes four and five days. The next morning Karadeucq will be out on the beach to shoot sea-gulls while they graze with their wings the still raging waves. It is the lad's amusement—my pet is such a skilful and expert archer!

The sea roars from the distance like rumbling thunder; the house rocks in the gale; the hail is heard clattering in the chimney. Roar, tempest! Blow, sea gale! Drop, both snow and hail! Ah! How good it feels to hear the ice-laden blast thunder, when one sees his family merrily gathered in the house around a blazing fireplace! And then, the young lads and their sister whisper things to one another that make them shiver and smile at once. For it does, indeed, look as if during the last century all the hobgoblins and all the fairies of Gaul have taken refuge in Britanny. Is it not a positive pleasure to hear tell during a tempest and by the fire those wonders to which one gives a lingering credence if one has not seen them himself, and more so if one has seen them?

This is what the young folks are saying to one another. My grandson Kervan starts the ball rolling as he shakes his head:

"The traveler who has lost his way and who should happen to pass to-night by the cavern of Pen-March will hear the hammers clang—"

"Yes, the hammers that beat in time while the devilish hammerers themselves sing their song, the burden of which ever is: 'One, two, three, four, five, six, Monday, Tuesday, Wednesday—'"

"And it is said they even add 'Thursday,' 'Friday' and 'Saturday,' but never 'Sunday,' the day of the mass—of the Christians."

"And the traveler may prize himself happy if the little Dus do not drop their false coiners' hammers and start to dance, compelling him to join in their reel until death closes upon him."

"What dangerous demons those Dus must be, dwarfs no taller than barely two feet high! Meseems I see them, with their hairy and shriveled faces, their cats' claws, their goats' hoofs and their eyes flashing fire. The bare thought of them is enough to make one shiver."

"Look out, Roselyk! There is one under the bin. Look out!"

"How imprudent you are, brother Karadeucq, to sport in that way over the Dus! Those hobgoblins are spiteful things. I tremble when I think of them."

"As for me, were I to come across a band of these customers, I would capture two or three brace of them, I would tie them together by the legs like partridges—and off I would make with them—"

"Oh! You, Karadeucq, are not afraid of anything."

"Justice should be done the little Dus. Although they do coin false money in the cavern of Pen-March, they are said to be excellent blacksmiths, and matchless in the shoeing of horses."

"Yes, you may rely on that! From the moment a horse has been shod by those devilish dwarfs, he shoots fire out of his nostrils; and as to running—as to running without ever stopping for breath—either night or day—to even take a look at his rider—"

"Children, what a tempest! What a night!"

"Fine night for the little Dus, mother! They love storms and darkness! But it is a bad night for the poor little Korrigans, who love only the mild nights of the month of May."

"Certes, I am dreadfully afraid of the hairy and clawy dwarfs with their purses full of false coin dangling from their belts and their blacksmith's hammers on their shoulders. But I would be still more afraid if I were to run across a Korrigan, only two feet high, combing her hair, and looking at herself in some secluded fountain, in the clear water of which she is admiring those blonde tresses that they are so proud of."

"What! Afraid of those pretty little fairies, brother Kervan! I, on the contrary, have often tried to meet one of them. It is said positively that they assemble at the fountain of Lyrwac'h-Hen, which lies in the thickest of the large oak forest that shades several druid stones. I have gone thither three times—and all the three times I saw nothing—"

"Luckily for you that you saw nothing Karadeucq, because it is said that the Korrigans never meet for their nocturnal dances except near the sacred stones. Woe to him who sees them!"

"I gather that they are expert musicians and that they sing like nightingales."

"It is also said of them that they like to pilfer food like cats. Yes, Karadeucq, you may laugh—but you should believe me; I am no fibber," observed his sister indignantly. "I have heard the rumor that at their nocturnal feasts they spread upon the sward, but always near a fountain, a cloth white as snow, and woven of the dainty thread that we find in summer on the meadows. In the very center of the cloth they place a crystal cup that shines so brightly, so very brightly, that it serves the fairies for a torch. People add that a single drop of the liquid in the cup would make one as wise as God."

"And what do the Korrigans eat on that table cloth as white as snow? Do you know, Karadeucq, you who love them so much?"

"The dear little darlings! It can not be costly to nourish their rosy and transparent bodies that are hardly two feet high. Sister Roselyk says they are gourmands. What is it they eat? The juice of night flowers, served upon gold grass blades?"

"Gold grass blades? That superb grass that, if you step upon it, puts you to sleep and imparts to you the knowledge of the language of birds—"

"And what do the Korrigans drink?"

"The dew of heaven in the azure shell of wrens' eggs—what boozers they are! But at the slightest sound of human feet— off they vanish. They vanish into the fountain and return to their crystal and coral palace at the bottom of the water. It is to the end of being able to escape quickly the sight of men that they always stay near the water. Oh, the pretty little fairies! I would give my best bow and twenty arrows, I would give all my fishing nets, I would give ten years, twenty years of my life to see a Korrigan!"

"Karadeucq, my son, make not such impious vows on such a stormy night as this—it may bring ill luck—I have never heard the enraged sea roar like this—it sounds like thunder—"

"Good mother, I would brave murky darkness, tempest and thunder to see a Korrigan!"

"Hold your tongue, rash boy, hold your tongue—do not say such words!"

"What a bold and venturesome lad you are, my boy!"

"Grandfather, you should join us in scolding my brother Karadeucq instead of encouraging him in his dangerous wishes. Do you not know—"

"What, my blonde Roselyk?"

"Alas! grandfather, the Korrigans steal the children of poor mothers and put little monsters in their place. The song so has it—"

"Let's hear that song, my little Roselyk."

"It runs this way, grandfather:

"Mary is very sad; she has lost her little Laoik; the Korrigan snatched him away.

"As I went to the spring for water I left my Laoik in his cradle; when I came back to the house, my little one was gone far away.

"And in its place the Korrigan left me this monster—with a face as red as a toad's; he scratches and bites.

"And all day he wants to be nursed, and yet he is seven years old—and yet he wants to be nursed.

"Mary is very sad; she has lost her little Laoik; the Korrigan snatched him away!

"That is the song, grandfather. And will brother still want to meet the wicked things, these Korrigan fairies who snatch away babes?"

"What have you now to say in defense of your fairies, my pet?"

"Grandfather, my sweet sister Roselyk has been imposed upon by evil tongues. All mothers with ugly urchins for children declare that the Korrigans substituted a little monster for their darling."

"Well answered, my grandson!"

"And, on my part, I maintain that the Korrigans are, on the contrary, sweet and serviceable. Do you know the valley of Helle?"

"Yes, my dare-devil."

"One time the finest hay in the world was to be got in that valley—

" 'Hay from Helle, perfumed hay.' "

"Well, that was thanks to the Korrigans—"

"Indeed? Tell me how—"

"When the time for mowing and haymaking came around, the Korrigans arrived and camped on the crests of the rocks around the valley to watch over the meadow. If during the day the sun parched the grass too much, the Korrigans caused a plentiful dew to drop. When the grass was mowed, they scattered the clouds that might have interfered with the making of hay. A foolish and wicked bishop wanted to chase away the pretty and kind fairies. He caused a large heather fire to be kindled early one night all over the rocks; when these were sufficiently hot, the ashes were all carefully removed. At their regular hour, and suspecting nothing, the dear Korrigans came to hold watch over the meadow, but they instantly burned their feet on the hot rocks. They then wept and cried: 'Oh! Wicked world! Oh! Wicked world!' Since then they never more returned to the place, and as a consequence, ever since, the hay has been either rotted by the rain, or burned by the sun in the valley of Helle. That is what comes of being unkind to the Korrigans. No, I shall not die happy if I do not see at least one of them—"

"Children, children, put no faith in such witcheries; above all never wish to witness any. It brings bad luck—"

"What, mother, simply because I desire to see a Korrigan, some misfortune will befall me? What kind of misfortune?"

"Hesus only knows, wild boy! I wish you would keep still; your talk frightens me."

"What a tempest! The house shakes!"

"And it is on such a night that Karadeucq dared to say he would give his life to see a Korrigan."

"Come, dear wife, your fears only show weakness."

"Mothers are weak and timid, Jocelyn. We must not tempt God—"

Old Araim stops working for a moment at his net; his head drops on his chest.

"What is the matter, folks? You seem to be in a brown study! Do you fear, like Madalen, that danger may threaten Karadeucq just because, on such a tempestuous night as this, he wishes to see a Korrigan?"

"I am not thinking of the fairies; I am thinking of this frightful storm, Jocelyn. I read to you and your children the narrative of our ancestor Joel, who lived about five hundred and odd years ago, if not in this very house, at least in the neighborhood of where we now are. I was thinking that on a somewhat similar stormy night, Joel and his son, both greedy after stories like the inquisitive Gauls that they were—"

"Did the trick of stopping a traveler at the pass of Craig'h, binding him fast, and carrying him home to tell stories—"

"And the traveler happened to be the Chief of the Hundred Valleys—a hero!"

"Oh! Oh! How your eyes sparkle as you speak, Karadeucq."

"If they sparkle, grandfather, it is because they are moist. Whenever I hear you speak of the Chief of the Hundred Valleys tears come to my eyes."

"What is the matter with Erer, father? The dog growls between his teeth and pricks up his ears."

"Grandfather, do you hear the watchdog bark?"

"Something must be going on outside of the house—"

"Alas! If it is the gods who wish to punish my son for his

audacious wishes, their anger is swift—Karadeucq, come near me."

"What! Madalen—there you are weeping and embracing the boy, as if really misfortune threatened him. Come, be more sensible!"

"Do you not hear the dogs barking louder and louder? And there is Erer now running to the door. There is something wrong going on outside—"

"Fear not, mother; it is some wolf prowling about. Where is my bow?"

"Karadeucq, you stay here—"

"Dear Madalen, be not in such fear for your son, nor you my sweet Roselyk for your brother. Perhaps it is better not to challenge the hobgoblins and fairies on a stormy night, but your fears are idle. There is no wolf prowling about here; if there were, Erer would long ago have bitten off the panel of the door and rushed to the encounter of the unwelcome guest—"

"Father is right—it may be a stranger who lost his way."

"Come, Kervan, come brother, let's to the gate of the yard."

"My son, you stay here by my side—"

"But, mother, I cannot allow my brother Kervan to go out alone."

"Hark! Hark! It seems to me I hear a voice calling—"

"Alas! mother, some misfortune threatens our house—you said it—"

"Roselyk, my child, do not add fuel to your mother's fright. What is there astonishing in a traveler calling from without to have the door opened to him—"

"His cries are not human—I am frozen with fear—"

"You come with me, Kervan, seeing that your mother wishes to keep Karadeucq near her. Although this is a quiet neighborhood, hand me my 'pen-bas,' and take yours along, my boy."

"My husband, my son, I conjure you, do not go out—"

"Dear wife, suppose some stranger is outside in such weather as this! Come Kervan!"

"Alas! I tell you the cries that I heard are not human. Kervan! Jocelyn! They will not listen—they are gone—Alas! Alas!"

"My father and brother go out to face danger, and I remain here—"

"Do not stamp your feet that way, bad boy! You are the cause of all this evil with your impious wishes—"

"Calm yourself, Madalen—and you, my pet, do not put on, if you please, the air of a wild colt that seeks to snap his reins; just obey your mother."

"I hear steps—they are drawing near—Oh! grandfather!"

"Well, my dear Roselyk, why tremble? What is there frightful in the steps that are approaching? Good—do you hear them laughing aloud? Are you now at ease?"

"Laughing!—on such a night!"

"It is frightful to hear, is it not, my sweet Roselyk, especially when the laughers are your own father and brother? Well—here they are. Well, my children?"

"The misfortune that threatened our house—"

"The cries that were not human—"

"Will you be done laughing? Just look at them! The father is as crazy as the son! Will you speak?"

"The great misfortune is a poor peddler who lost his way—"

"The voice that was not human was his voice—"

And father and son laughed merrily, it must be admitted, like people who are happy to find their apprehensions unfounded. The mother's fears, however, were not so quickly allayed; she did not join the laughter; but both the boys, the girl and even Jocelyn himself, all cried out joyously:

"A peddler! A peddler!"

"He has pretty ribbons and fine needles."

"Iron for arrows, strings for bows, scissors to clip the sheep."

"Nets for fishing, seeing that he comes to the seashore."

"He will tell us the news of outlying places."

"But where is he? Where is the good peddler that Hesus sends to us to help enliven this long winter's night?"

"What a happiness to be able to see all his merchandise at one's ease!"

"But where is he? Where is he?"

"He is shaking off the ice that his clothes are frozen stiff with."

"Good mother, now see the misfortune that threatened us because I wished to see a Korrigan!"

"Be still, son! To-morrow rests with God!"

"Here is the peddler! Here he is!"

CHAPTER III.

HEVIN THE PEDDLER.

The man who stepped into the house gave at the threshold a last shake to his traveling boots, which were so covered with snow that he seemed to be clad in white hose. He was of a robust frame, but squat and square, in the full strength of manhood, jovial and of an open yet determined face. Still uneasy, Madalen did not take her eyes from him, and twice she made a sign to her son to return to her side. Removing the hood from his thick, ice-pearled coat, the peddler laid down his bulky bale, a heavy burden that, however, seemed light to his sturdy shoulders. He then removed his cap and stepped towards Araim, the oldest member of the household:

"Long life and happy days to hospitable people! This is Hevin the Peddler's wish to yourself and your family. I am a Breton. I was going to Falgoët, when the night and the tempest overtook me on the beach. I saw the light of this house from a distance; I came, I called, and the door was opened to me. Thanks to you all, thanks to hospitable people!"

"Madalen, what gives you that absent and pensive look? Do not the peddler's pleasant face and kind words set you at ease?"

"Father, to-morrow rests with God—I feel all the more uneasy since the stranger's arrival.

"Speak lower, lower still, dear daughter. The poor fellow might overhear you and be grieved. Oh! these mothers! these mothers!"

And addressing the stranger:

"Draw near the fire, you sturdy peddler. The night is rough. Karadeucq, while we wait for supper, fetch a pot of hydromel for our guest."

"I accept, good old man! The fire will warm me from without, the hydromel from within."

"You seem to be a gay stroller."

"So I am. Joy is my companion; however long or rough my road may be, joy never tires of following me."

"Here—drink—"

"Your health, good mother and sweet girl; to the health of you all—"

And clicking his tongue against the roof of his mouth: "This is the best hydromel I ever tasted. A cordial hospitality renders the best of potions still better."

"Do you come from afar, gay stroller?"

"Do you mean since I started this morning or since the beginning of my journey?"

"Yes, since the beginning of your journey."

"It is now two months since I departed from Paris."

"From the city of Paris?"

"Does that surprise you, good old man?"

"What! Cross half Gaul in such times as these, when the cursed Franks overrun the country?"

"I am an old roadster. For the last twenty years I have crossed Gaul from end to end. Is the main road hazardous, I take the by-path. Is the plain risky, I go over the mountain. Is it dangerous to travel by day, I journey by night."

"And have you not been rifled a hundred times by those thievish Franks?"

"I am an old roadster, I tell you. Accordingly, before entering Britanny, I bravely donned a priest's robe, and painted on my pack a big cross with flames red as hell-fire. The Frankish thieves are as stupid as they are savage; they fear the devil, whom the bishops frighten them with in order to share with them the spoils of Gaul. They would not dare to attack me, taking me for a priest."

"Come, supper is ready—to table," said old Araim; and addressing his son's wife, who continued to give signs of pre-occupation, he said to her in a low voice:

"What is the matter, Madalen? Are you still thinking of the Korrigans?"

"This stranger who disguises himself in the robe of a priest without being one will bring misfortune over our house. The tempest's fury seems to have redoubled since he came in."

It is an impossible thing to allay a mother's apprehensions once they are aroused.

The family and the guest sat down to table, ate and drank. The peddler drank and ate like a man to whom the road imparts a good appetite. The jaws did their ample duty; teeth and tongues played their parts well; the family was in good spirits. It is not every long winter's night that one has a peddler from Paris in his company.

"And what is going on in Paris, brave roadster?"

"The most satisfactory thing that I have seen in the city was the burying of the King of the cursed Franks!"

"Ah! Is their King dead?"

"He died more than two months ago—on the 25th of November of last year, of the year 512 of the 'Incarnation of the Word,' as the bishops say who blessed and gave sepulchre to the crowned murderer in the basilica of the Holy Apostles at Paris."

"Ah! He is dead, that Frankish King! And what was his name?"

"He had a devil of a name, Hlode-Wig."

"It must choke one to pronounce it—"

"Hlode-Wig was his name. His wife, whom they call the Queen, is no less happily endowed—her name is Chrotechild—and her four children are named Chlotachaire, Theudeber—"

"Enough! Friend peddler! A truce of those savage names! Those who wear them are worthy of them."

"Right you are, as you may judge by the deceased Hlode-Wig, or Clovis, as he is popularly pronounced; and his family bids fair to surpass even him. Imagine gathered in that monster, whom St. Remi baptised a son of the Church—imagine gathered in that one monster the cunning of the fox and the cowardly ferocity of the wolf. To enumerate to you the murders that he committed with his dagger or his axe would take too long. I shall only mention some of the leading ones. An old Frankish chief, a hunchback named Sigebert, was King of Cologne. This is the way these bandits become Kings: they pillage and ravage a province at the head of a band, massacre or sell like so many heads of cattle men, women and children, reduce the rest of the inhabitants to slavery, and then they say: 'Here we are Kings'; the bishops echo back: 'Yes, our friends the Franks are Kings here; we shall baptize them into the Church; and you, people of Gaul, obey them or we will damn you!'"

"And has there never been found any courageous man to plant a dagger in the heart of such a King?"

"Karadeucq, my pet, do not heat yourself in that manner. Thanks to God, that Clovis is dead. That is, at any rate, one less. Proceed, good peddler!"

"Well, as I was saying, Sigebert the hunchback was King of Cologne. He had a son. Clovis said to him: 'Your father is old—kill him and you will inherit his power.' The son sympathized with the idea and killed his father. And what does Clovis do but kill the parricide and appropriate the kingdom of Cologne!"

"You shudder, my children! I can well imagine it. Such are the new Kings of Gaul!"

"What, you shudder, my hosts, at so little? Only wait. Shortly after that murder, Clovis strangled with his own hands two of his near relatives, father and son, named **Chararic,** and plundered them of what they themselves had plundered **Gaul** of. But here is a still worse incident: Clovis was at war with another bandit of his own royal family named Ragnacaire. He ordered a set of necklaces and baldrics to be made of imitation gold, and sent them through one of his familiars to the leudes who accompanied Ragnacaire with the message that, in exchange for the present, they deliver to him their chief and his son. The bargain was struck, and the two Ragnacaires were delivered to Clovis. This great King thereupon struck them both down with his axe like oxen in the slaughter house; he thus at one stroke committed two crimes—cheated the leudes of Ragnacaire and murdered their chiefs."

"And yet the Catholic bishops preach to the people submission to such monsters?"

"Certes, seeing that the crimes committed by these monsters are the source of the Church's wealth. You can figure it out for yourself, good old man, the murders, fratricides, parricides and acts of incest committed by the great Frankish seigneurs yield more gold sous to the fat and do-nothing bishops than all the lands, that your hard and daily toil fructifies, yield deniers to you. But listen to another of Clovis' prowesses. In the course of time he had either himself despatched or ordered others to massacre all his relatives. One day he gathers around him his forces and says with a moan:

" 'Woe is me! I am now left all alone, like a traveler among strangers; I have no relatives left to help me in case adversity overtake me.' "

"Well, so at last he repented his many crimes—it is the least of the punishments that await him."

"He repent? Clovis? He would have been a big fool if he had, good old man! Do you forget that the priests relieve him of the burden of remorse in consideration of good round pounds of gold or silver?"

"And why, then, did he use those terms; why did he say:
'Woe is me! I am now left all alone, like a traveler among
strangers; I have no relatives left to help me in case adversity
overtake me?'"

"Why? Another trick of his. No, in the language of a
bishop himself who chronicled the life of Clovis, it was not that
Clovis grieved over the death of all the relatives whom he had
caused to be put to death; no, it was a ruse on his part when
he held that language, malefactor that he was; he only wished
thereby to ascertain whether there was any relative left, and
then to kill him."

"And yet was there not a single man resolute enough to
plant a dagger in the monster's breast?"

"Keep quiet, bad boy! This is the second time that you have
given vent to those sentiments of murder and vengeance! You
only do so to frighten me!"

"Dear wife, our son Karadeucq is indignant, like anyone
else, at the crimes of that Frankish King. By my father's
bones! I who am not of an adventurous disposition, I say myself—it is a shame to Gaul that such a monster should have
reigned fourteen years over our country—Britanny fortunately
excepted."

"And I, who in my trade of peddler have crossed Gaul
from end to end, and seen the country's wretchedness and the
bloody slavery that oppresses it, I say that the people's hatred
should fall as heavily upon the bishops! Was it not they who
called the Franks into Gaul? Was it not they who baptised
the murderer a son of the Roman Church? Did they not propose to canonize the monster with the title of 'Saint Clovis?'"

"God in heaven! Is it craziness or cowardly terror on the
part of those priests?"

"It is unbridled ambition and inveterate cupidity, good old
man. At first, allied to the Roman emperors from the time that
Gaul became again a Roman province, the bishops succeeded by

underhanded means to secure large endowments for themselves and their churches and to occupy the leading magistracies in the cities. That did not satisfy them; they counted upon being better able to dominate the barbarous Franks than the civilized Romans. They betrayed the Romans to the Franks. The latter came; Gaul was ravaged, pillaged and subjugated, and the bishops shared the plunder with the conquerors whom they speedily placed under their thumb through the fear of the devil. And so it happens that these sanctimonious men have become richer and more powerful under the Frankish than under the Roman rule. Now old Gaul has become their quarry jointly with the barbarians; they now possess vast domains, all manner of wealth, innumerable slaves—slaves that are so well chosen, trained and docile to the whip that an 'ecclesiastical slave' generally fetches twenty gold sous in the market, while other slaves fetch only twelve sous. Would you form an idea of the wealth of the bishops? This identical St. Remi, who baptised Clovis in the basilica of Reims, and thus approved him a worthy son of the holy Roman Church, was so fatly remunerated that he was able to pay five thousand pounds of silver by the weight for the domain of Epernay."

"Oh! Thus to traffic in the blood of Gaul! It is horrible! It is shocking!"

"Oh! That is still nothing, good father. Had you traveled as I have done over regions that were once so flourishing, and seen them now, ravaged and burned down by the Franks! Had you seen the bands of men, women and children, bound two by two, marching among the cattle and wagons heaped with booty of all sorts, that the barbarians drove before them after they conquered the country of Amiens, which I then happened to cross—had you seen that, you would have felt your heart bleed as mine did."

"And where did they take those men, women and children whom they carried away as slaves?"

"Alas! good mother, they took them to the banks of the Rhine, where the Franks keep a large market of Gallic flesh. All the barbarians of Germany who have not yet broken into our unhappy country, repair thither to supply themselves with slaves of our race—men, women and children."

"And what becomes of those who remain in Gaul?"

"The men of the fields are enslaved and made to cultivate under the rod of the Franks their own ancestral estates that King Clovis divided with his leaders, his old comrades in pillage and massacre, and whom he since has made dukes, marquises and counts of our country. But there are still some drops of generous blood left in the veins of old Gaul. Even if the rule of the Franks and the bishops is to endure, they will, at least, not enjoy their conquest in peace."

"How so?"

"Did you ever hear of the Bagaudy?"

"Certainly, and praisefully, too."

"What is the Bagaudy, grandfather?"

"Let me first answer our friend the peddler—it will be information to you also. My grandfather Gildas told me that he heard from his father that, a few years after the death of Victoria the Great, the first Bagaudy took place, not in Britanny, but in the other provinces. Irritated at seeing herself again reduced to the level of a Roman province, as a result of the treason of Tetrik, and of being obliged to pay heavy imposts into the empire's fisc, Gaul rose in rebellion. The uprisings were called 'Bagaudies.' They threw the emperor Diocletian into such consternation that he hurried an army into Gaul to combat them; at the same time, however, he remitted the imposts, and granted almost everything that the Bagauders demanded. As you see, it is only a question of knowing how to present one's demand to kings and emperors. Bend your back and they will load it to the breaking point; show your teeth and they remove the load—"

"Well said, old father—beg them with clasped hands, and they laugh; make your demand with clenched fists, and they yield—that was another good feature of the Bagaudy."

"Well, there were so many good features about it, that, towards the middle of last century, it was started against the Romans anew. That time it spread as far as Britanny, to the very heart of Armorica. But we only talked about it, there was no occasion for serious action. The time was well chosen; if my memory serves me right, I was one of those who accompanied our venerated druids to Vannes, to the curia of that town which consisted of Roman magistrates and officers. To them we said:

"'You govern us Breton Gauls in the name of your emperor; you lay rather heavy imposts upon us, always in the name and for the benefit of the same emperor. For a long time we have found that very unjust. We enjoy, it is true, our freedom and citizen rights. Nevertheless our subjection to Rome galls us. We think the hour has come for us to emancipate ourselves. The other provinces are of the same mind, seeing that they are rebelling against your emperor. Accordingly, it now pleases us to become free once more, as independent of Rome as we were before the Conquest of Caesar, as we were at the time of Victoria the Great. Accordingly, ye Roman officials and tax-gatherers, pack yourselves off. Britanny will henceforth keep her silver and gold to herself, and will govern herself without your help. A happy journey to you, and do not come back again; if you do, you will find us in arms ready to receive you with our swords, and, if need be, our scythes and forks.'

"The Romans went, their garrisons along with them. Without troops to enforce their decrees, the magistrates took their departure, and never returned. The Bagaudy in Gaul and the Franks on the Rhine kept their hands full. This second Bagaudy, like the first, had its good effect, in our province even better than elsewhere, seeing that the bishops, having joined the

Romans, succeeded in imposing themselves upon the other provinces of Gaul, but were prevented by the Bagaudy from making
their weight felt as heavily as in former years. As to ourselves, of
Breton Armorica, Rome never sought to resubjugate us. From
that time on, and obedient to our ancient custom, each tribe
chooses its own chief, and these choose a chief of chiefs who
governs the land. He is kept if he does well, he is removed if
he does not give satisfaction. It has continued so to this day,
and I hope will ever be, despite the doings of the cursed Franks
outside of Britanny. The last Breton will have died before our
Armorica shall be conquered by the barbarians as they have done
the rest of Gaul. And now, friend peddler, I understand you
to say that the Bagaudy is again raising its head, now against
the Franks? So much the better! They will, at least, as you
say, not enjoy their conquest in peace, if the new Bagauders
are worthy of the old."

"They are, good old man; they are; I have seen them at
work."

"The Bagauders are, then, numerous armed troops?"

"Karadeucq, my pet, do not excite yourself—listen without
interrupting."

"Bad boy, he can only think of battles, revolts and adventures!"

And the poor woman added in a low voice in Araim's ear:

"Was there any occasion for the peddler to mention such
matters before my son? Alas! I told you so, father, it is an
ill wind that blew this man into our house."

"Do you think him in league with the Dus and Korrigans,
Madalen?"

"What I believe is, father, that a misfortune threatens this
house. I wish this night were over, and it were to-morrow!"

And the alarmed mother sighed while the peddler answered
Karadeucq, who hung upon the stranger's words:

"The new Bagauders, my brave lad, are what the old ones were. Terrible to the oppressors, kind to the people."

"Do the people love them?"

"Whether they love them! Aëlian and Aman, the two chiefs of the first Bagaudy who were put to death nearly two centuries ago in an old Roman castle near Paris, at the confluence of the Seine and the Marne—Aëlian and Aman are to this day loved by the people as martyrs!"

"Ah! Theirs is a happy fate! To be still loved by the people after two centuries! Did you hear that, grandfather?"

"Yes, I did, and so did your mother—see how sad she looks."

But the "bad boy," as the poor woman called him, already seeming in thought to be running the Bagaudy, cast inquisitive and ardent looks at the peddler, and asked:

"Did you ever see the Bagauders? Were there many of them? Had they already run any raids against the Franks and bishops? Is it long since you saw them?"

"Three weeks ago, on my way hither, as I crossed Anjou. One day I missed my road in the forest. Night fell upon me. After having walked a long, long while, and going astray ever deeper in the woods, I noticed at a distance a bright light that issued from a cavern. I ran thither. There I found about a hundred lusty Bagauders. They were resting around a fire with their Bagaudines, because you must know that they are generally accompanied by determined women. A few nights before, they had made a descent upon some Frankish seigneurs, our conquerors, and attacked their 'burgs' as the barbarians term their castles. The Bagauders fought furiously and without neither mercy or pity; they pillaged churches and episcopal villas, exacted ransom from the bishops, hung from the trees the most perverse of the priests who fell into their hands, rifled the coffers of the royal tax-collectors, and slew whatever Frank came in their way. But, as fast as they took from the rich, they gave to the poor. They generously distributed among these the plunder of the rich prelates and Frankish counts, and set free all the chained slaves whom they found. Ah! By Aëlian and Aman, the patrons of the Bagauders, the life of those gay and brave fellows is a noble and happy one. Had I not been on my way to Britanny in order to see my old mother once more, I would have then and there joined them in running the Bagaudy in Anjou and the contiguous provinces."

"And what must one do in order to be admitted into the ranks of those intrepid people?"

"The first thing to do, my brave lad, is to sacrifice one's skin in advance; you have to be robust, agile, courageous; you must love the poor, swear eternal hatred for the Frankish counts and the bishops; feast by day and bagaude by night."

"And where are their haunts?"

"You might as well ask the birds of the air where they perch, the beasts of the wood where they lie down. Yesterday on the mountain, to-morrow in the woods, marching ten leagues during the night, hiding for days in succession in the nearest cave— the Bagauder knows not to-day where he will be to-morrow."

"It must, then, be a lucky accident that would make one run across them?"

"A lucky accident for good people, an unlucky one for counts, bishops or tax-collectors!"

"Was it in Anjou that you met that troop of Bagauders?"

"Yes, in Anjou—in a forest about eight leagues from Angers, whither I was then bound—"

"Do you notice my pet Karadeucq? Look at him! See how his eyes sparkle and his cheeks burn. Truly, if he does not dream of little Korrigans to-night, he will surely dream of Bagauders. Am I wrong, my lad?"

"Grandfather, what I say is that the Bretons and the Bagauders are and will be the very last Gauls. Were I not a Breton I would indeed run the Bagaudy against the Franks and the bishops."

"And it is my opinion, my grandson, that you will surely run it to-night with your head upon your pillow. I wish you pleasant dreams of the Bagaudy, my pet. Now go to bed, it is late; you are making your mother feel unnecessarily uneasy."

CHAPTER IV.

OFF TO THE BAGAUDY!

I broke off this narrative three days ago.

I began writing it on the afternoon of the day when the peddler, after having spent the night under our roof, proceeded on his journey. When he appeared at the hall the next morning the tempest had subsided. After the peddler left the house, before he disappeared at the turning of the road, and as he waved us a last adieu, I said to Madalen:

"Well, now, you silly thing! You poor frightened mother— did the angry gods punish my pet Karadeucq for having wished to see the Korrigans? Where is the misfortune that this stranger was to bring down upon our house? The tempest has blown over, the sky is serene, and the sea is calming down and looking as blue again as ever! Why is your mien still preoccupied? Yesterday, Madalen, you said: 'To-morrow rests with God.' Here we are at yesterday's to-morrow. What evil has befallen us? Nothing, absolutely nothing."

"You are right, good father, my forebodings have proved

false. And yet, I do not feel at ease. I still am sorry that my son spoke the way he did of the Korrigans."

"Turn around, here is your Karadeucq with his hunting dog in the leash, his pouch on his back, his bow in his hand, his arrows at his side. How handsome he is! How handsome! How alert and determined his mien!"

"Where are you going, son?"

"Mother, yesterday you said to me that it was two days since we have had any venison in the house. This is a good day for the purpose. I shall endeavor to bring down a doe in the forest of Karnak. The chase may take me long; I am carrying some provisions along—bread, fruits and a bottle of our wine."

"No, Karadeucq, you shall not go hunting to-day; I shall not allow it—"

"And why not, mother?"

"I do not know. You might lose your way and fall into some pit in the forest."

"Mother, do not feel alarmed; why, I know all the paths and pits in the forest."

"No, no; you shall not go hunting to-day. I forbid you to leave the house."

"Good grandfather, intercede for me—"

"Willingly. I delight in eating venison. But you must promise me, my pet, that you will not go on the side of the spring where you may encounter the Korrigans."

"I swear to you, grandfather!"

"Come, Madalen, let my skilful archer depart for the chase —he swears to you that he will not think of the fairies."

"Is it really your wish that he go, father?"

"I beg you; let him go; see how crossed he looks."

"Well, let it be as you wish—it is against my wish, how-ever!"

"A kiss, mother!"

"No, bad boy, leave me alone!"

"A kiss, good mother; I beg you—do not deny me a caress—"

"Madalen, see those big tears in his eyes. Would you have the courage to refuse him an embrace?"

"Kiss me, dear child—I felt sorrier than you. Be gone, but come back early."

"One more kiss, good mother—good-bye—good-bye!"

Karadeucq left, wiping his tears. Three or four times he turned around to look at his mother—he then disappeared behind the trees. The day passed. My favorite did not return. The chase must have carried him far away. He will be here in the evening. I started to write this narrative that sorrow interrupted. It grew dark. Suddenly someone burst into my room. It was my son Jocelyn, closely followed by his wife. He cried.

"Father! Father! A great misfortune."

"Alas! Alas! father. I told you that the Korrigans and the stranger would be fatal to my son. Why did I yield to you? Why did I allow him to depart this morning? Why did I allow my beloved Karadeucq to go away! It is done for him! I shall never more see him again! Oh! unhappy woman that I am!

"What is the matter, Madalen? What is the matter, Jocelyn? What makes you look so pale? Why those tears? What has happened to Karadeucq?"

"Read, father, read this little parchment that Yvon the neatherd has just brought me—"

"Oh! A curse! A curse upon that peddler with his Bagaudy! He bewitched my son—the Korrigans are the cause of this misfortune—"

While my son and his wife wrung their arms in desolation I read what my grandson had written:

Good father and good mother—when you will read this I, your son Karadeucq, will be very far away from our house. I have told Yvon the neat-herd, whom I met this morning in the fields, not to put this parchment into your hands until night, to the end that I may have twelve hours the lead, and may thus escape your efforts to overtake me. I am going to run the Bagaudy against the Franks and bishops. The times of the Chiefs of the Hundred Valleys, the Sacrovirs and Vindexes are past. But I could never remain quiet in a corner of Britanny, the only free section of Gaul, without avenging, if but upon one of the sons of Clovis, the slavery of our beloved country. Good father, good mother, you have left beside you my elder brother, Kervan, and my sister Roselyk. Be not angry with me. And you, grandfather, who love me so much, obtain my pardon and keep my dear parents from cursing their son—Karadeucq."

Alas, all efforts to recover the unhappy boy were futile.

I started this narrative because the conversation of the peddler impressed me deeply. I talked long with the stranger, who for twenty years had been traveling over all parts of Gaul and who thus had exceptional opportunities to observe events. He solved to me the mystery—how our people, who had known how to emancipate themselves from the powerful Roman yoke, fell and remained under the yoke of the Franks, a people whom our own surpass a thousandfold in courage and in numbers.

I had meant to insert here the stranger's answer. But the departure of that unhappy boy who was the joy of my old days, has broken my heart. I lack the courage to continue this narrative. Later, perhaps, if some good news from my pet Karadeucq should revive the hope of seeing him again, I shall finish what I meant to say. Alas! Shall I ever hear from him? Poor boy! To leave all alone, at the age of seventeen, to run the Bagaudy!

Can it be true, after all, that the gods punish us for wishing to see the malign spirits? Alas! Alas! I now also say, with the poor mother, who incessantly runs to the door demented in the hope that she may be able to see whether her son is coming back:

"The gods have punished Karadeucq, my pet, for having wished to see the Korrigans!"

*　　*　　*　　*　　*　　*

My father Araim died of a broken heart shortly after the departure of my second son. He left me the family archives.

I write these lines ten years after my father's death, and have never had any tidings of my poor son Karadeucq. He probably met his death in the adventurous life of a Bagauder. ,

Britanny preserves her independence, the Franks dare not attack us. All the other provinces of Gaul have remained under the yoke of the bishops and the sons of Clovis. The latter, it is said, surpass their father in ferocity. Their names are Thierry, Childebert and Clotaire; the fourth, Chlodomir, is said to have died this year.

How many years of life are left to me and what events are in store for me? I know not. But I wish this day to bequeath to you, my eldest child, Kervan, the chronicles of our family. I bequeath them to you five hundred and twenty-six years after our ancestress Genevieve witnessed the death of Jesus of Nazareth.

*   *   *   *   *   *

I, Kervan, the son of Jocelyn, who died seven years after he bequeathed to me our family archives have this to add:

The narrative that follows was brought to me here, at my house, near Karnak, by Ronan, one of the sons of my brother Karadeucq, who left our house to run the Bagaudy, the year after the death of Clovis. These two narratives contain the adventures of my brother Karadeucq and of his two sons Loysik and Ronan. The first portion of the narrative brought to me by Ronan, and which I here subjoin, entitled "The Vagres," and "The Burg of Neroweg," was written by Ronan himself in the ardor of youth, and in a style and form that differ greatly from those of the previous narratives of our family chronicle; the second, which I have entitled "Ghilde," I wrote from the word of mouth account that Ronan left with me, and which I think should not be lost.

Britanny, still in peace, governs herself by chiefs of her own choice. The Franks have not dared to penetrate into our fast-nesses. But in the course of my nephew's narrative, our descendants will find the secret of that mystery that my grandfather Araim had not the courage to put in writing:

"How the Gallic people, who had known how to emancipate themselves from the powerful Roman yoke, fell and remained under the yoke of the Franks, whom they surpass a thousand-fold in courage and in numbers."

May it please the gods that it may not some day be in Brittany as in the other provinces of Gaul! May it please the gods that our country, the only one that to-day remains free, may never fall under the domination of the Franks and the bishops of Rome. May our druids, both the Christian and the non-Christian, continue to inspire us with a love for freedom and with the virile virtues of our ancestors.

PART II

THE VAGRES

CHAPTER I.

"WOLVES' HEADS."

" 'The devil take the Franks! Long live the Vagrery and Old Gaul!'
Such is the cry of all Vagres. The Franks call us 'Wand'ring Men,'
'Wolves,' 'Wolves' Heads.' Let us be wolves!

"My father ran the Bagaudy, and I now run the Vagrery, but both
to the one cry—'The devil take the Franks!' and 'Long live Gaul!'

"Aëlian and Aman, Bagauders in their days, as we in ours are
Vagres, in revolt against the Romans, as we against the Franks—Aëlian
and Aman, put to death two centuries ago in their old castle near
Paris, they are our prophets. We take communion with the wine, the
treasures and the wives of the seigneurs, the bishops and rich Gauls
who made common cause with the Frankish counts and dukes to whom
King Clovis gave our old Gaul. The Franks have pillaged us, they
massacred and burned down; so let us do likewise—pillage, massacre
and burn! And let us live in joy—'Wolves,' 'Wolves' Heads' and 'Wan-
d'ring men!' Vagres that we are! Let us live in summer under the green
foliage, and in winter in caverns warm!

"Death unto oppressors! Freedom to the slave! Let us take from
the seigneurs! Let us give unto the poor!

"What! A hundred kegs of wine in the master's cellar, and only the
water of the stream for the wornout slave?

"What! A hundred cloaks in the wardrobe, and only rags for the
toiling slave?

"Who was it planted the vine? Who harvested the grape and pressed
it into wine? The slave! Who should drink the wine? The slave!

"Who was it that tended and sheared the sheep and wove the cloth
and made the cloak? The slave!'

"Who should wear the cloak? The slave!

"Up, ye poor and oppressed! Up! Revolt! Here are your good
friends the Vagres! They approach! Death to the seigneurs and the
bishops!

"Six men united are stronger than a hundred divided: Let us unite!
Each for all, and all for each! 'The devil take the Franks! Long live
the Vagrery and Old Gaul!' "

Who sang this song? Ronan the Vagre. Where did he
sing it? On a mountain path that led to the city of Clermont

in Auvergne, that grand and beautiful Auvergne, land of magnificent traditions—Bituit, who gave Roman legions to his pack
of hounds for breakfast in the morning; the Chief of the Hundred Valleys! Vindex! and so many other heroes of Gaul,
were they not all sons of Auvergne? of the beautiful Auvergne,
to-day the prey of Clotaire, the most odious, the most ferocious
of the four sons of Clovis?

Other voices answered in chorus to the song of Ronan the
Vagre. They had met on a mild summer's night; there were
about thirty Vagres gathered at the spot—gay customers, rough
boys, clad in all styles, but armed to the teeth, and all carrying
in their caps a twig of green oak as the emblem of their solidarity.

They arrive at a place where the roads fork—one road leads
to the right, another to the left. Ronan halts. A voice is
heard—the voice of Wolf's-Tooth. What a Titan the man is!
He is six feet high, with the neck of a bull and enormous hands;
only the hoop of a barrel could encircle his waist:

"Ronan, you said to us: 'Brothers, arm yourselves!' We
armed ourselves. 'Furnish yourselves with torches of straw!'
Here are the torches. 'Follow me!' We did. You halt; and
we have halted."

"Wolf's-Tooth, I am considering. Now, brothers, answer
me. Which is to be preferred, the wife of a Frankish count or
a bishopess?"

"A bishopess smells of holy water—the bishop blesses; a
counts' wife smells of wine—the count, her husband, drinks
himself drunk."

"Wolf's-Tooth, it is exactly the contrary: the wily prelate
drinks the wine, and leaves the water to the stupid Frank."

"Ronan is right!"

"To the devil with the holy water, and long live wine!"

"Yes, long live the wine of Clermont, with which Luern,
the great Auvergnan chief of former days, used to fill up the

ditches wide as ponds, in order to refresh the warriors of his tribe."

"That would have been a cup worthy of you, Wolf's Tooth! But, brothers, do answer me; to whom shall we give the preference, to a bishopess or to a count's wife?"

"To the bishopess! To the bishopess!"

"No, to the count's wife!"

"Brothers, so as to please all, we shall take both—"

"Well said, Ronan!"

"One of these roads leads to the burg of Count Neroweg, the other to the episcopal villa of Bishop Cautin."

"We must carry off both the bishopess and the countess— we must pillage both burg and villa!"

"With which shall we start? Shall we start with the prelate, or shall we start with the seigneur? The bishop spends more time over his cup; he loves to roll the sweet morsels over his tongue, and to taste the wine leisurely; the seigneur drinks larger quantities; he gulps them down like a toper—"

"Ronan is right!"

"Consequently, at this hour of the night, midnight, the hour of the Vagres, Count Neroweg must be full as a tick, and snoring in his bed; his wife or some concubine, lying beside him, must be dreaming with eyes wide open. Bishop Cautin, on the other hand, will be leaning with both his elbows on a table, and face to face with a bowl of old wine and one of his favorite boon companions, cracking jokes."

"First to the count; he will be in bed."

"Brothers, let us first call on the bishop; he will be found up; there is more sport in surprising a prelate at his wine than a seigneur at his snores."

"Well said, Ronan! The bishop first!"

"March! I know the house!"

Who was it that said this? A young and handsome Vagre of about twenty-five years of age. He went by the name of

"Master of the Hounds." There was no more accurate marks-
man than he with his bow and arrow. His arrow simply traveled as he wished. Once the forester slave of a Frankish duke,
he was caught in an amour with one of the women of his seigneur's household, and escaped death by flight. He thereupon
ran the Vagrery.

"I know the episcopal house," repeated the daring fellow.
"Feeling it in my bones that some day or other we would be
holding communion with the bishop's treasury, like a good
master of the hounds, I went one day and took observations
around his lair. I saw the dear old man there. Never did I
see a buck with blacker or more fiery eyes!"

"And the house, Master of the Hounds, the house; how is
it arranged?"

"Bad! The windows are high; the doors heavy; the walls
strong."

"Master of the Hounds," replied Ronan the Vagre, "we
shall reach the heart of the bishop's house without crossing
either the door, the windows or the walls—on the same principle that you reach your sweetheart's heart without penetrating
by her eyes—the night is favorable."

"Brothers, to you the treasures—to me the handsome bishopess!"

"Yours, Master of the Hounds, be the bishopess; ours, the
booty of the episcopal villa! Long live the Vagrery!"

CHAPTER II.

BISHOP AND COUNT.

In the summer season Bishop Cautin inhabited a villa situated not far from the city of Clermont, the seat of his episcopacy. Magnificent gardens, crystalline springs, thick arbors, green lawns, excellent meadows, gold harvests, purpled vines, forests well stocked with game, ponds well supplied with fish, excellently equipped stables—such were the surroundings of the holy man's palace. Two hundred ecclesiastical slaves, male and female, cultivated the church's "vineyard," without counting the domestic personnel—the cup-bearer, the cook and his assistants, the butcher, the baker, the superintendent of the bath, the shoemaker, the tailor, the turner, the carpenter, the mason, the master of the hounds, besides the washerwomen and the weavers, most of the latter young, often handsome female slaves. Every evening one of these girls took to Bishop Cautin, who lay softly tucked on a feather bed, a cup of warm and highly spiced wine. Early in the morning another girl took in a cup of creamy milk for the first breakfast of the pious man. And thus lived that good apostle of humility, chastity and poverty!

And who is that portly, handsome and still young woman, who resembles Diana the huntress? With her bare neck and arms, clad in a simple linen tunic and her long black hair half undone, she leans on her elbows over the balcony that crowns the terrace of the villa. At once burning and languishing, the eyes of this woman now rise towards the starry sky, now seem to peer through this mild summer's night, under shelter of which, with the stealthy step of wolves, the Vagres are wending

their way towards the bishop's residence. The woman is Fulvia, Cautin's bishopess, whom he married when, still a simple
friar, he did not yet aspire to a bishopric. After he was pro-
moted to the higher office that he now fills in the hierarchy,
he piously calls her "my sister," agreeable to the canons of the
councils.

"Woe is me!" the bishopess was saying. "Woe to these summer nights during which one is left alone to inhale the perfume
of the flowers, to listen to the murmur of the nocturnal breezes
in the foliage of the trees, murmurs that so much resemble the
stolen kisses of lovers! Oh! I always fear the unnerving heat
of these summer nights! It penetrates through my whole
frame! I am twenty-eight years of age. I am now twelve years
married, and I have counted these conjugal years with my tears!
A recluse in the city, a recluse in the country by the orders of
my lord and master, my husband, Bishop Cautin, who spends
his time in the women's part of the house among my female
slaves, whom the profligate debauches while pleading the canons of the councils that, he says, order him to live chastely
with his wife—such is my life—my sad life! My youth is ebb-
ing away without my enjoying a single day of love or of freedom. Love! Freedom! Shall I grow old without knowing
you? Woe is me!"

And the handsome bishopess rose, shook her black hair to
the night breeze, puckered her black eyebrows and cried defiantly:

"Woe to violent and debauched husbands! They hurl women
into perdition! Loved, respected, treated, if not as wife, at
least truly as his sister by the bishop, I would have remained
chaste and gentle. But disdained and humiliated before the
lowest of the domestic slaves, I have grown to be wrathful and
vindictive. From the height of this terrace, and often my
cheeks mantling with shame, I follow with distracted gaze the
young slaves of the field when they go out to work in the morning and return in the evening. I have struck my husband's con-

cubines with my hands—and yet, poor wretches that they are, they do not yield to the lover who begs, but to the master who orders. I struck them in anger, not in jealousy. Before that man became odious to me, I was indifferent to him. Nevertheless, I might have loved him, had he wished it—and as he willed. 'Sister-wife' of a bishop—it looked attractive! How much good could not be done! How many tears could not be dried! But I have had only my own to dry, soon finding myself degraded and despised. The measure overflows; I have wept enough; I have moaned enough; I have sufficiently resisted the temptations that devour me! I shall flee from this house, even at the risk of being captured and sold as a slave! Can it be called to live, this dragging of my days in this opulent villa, a gilded grave? No! No! I wish to leave this sepulchre! I wish to breathe the free air! I wish to see the sun! I wish to move free in space! I crave a single day of love and freedom! Oh! If I could only see again the young lad, who more than once went by this terrace early in the morning! What warm and loving glances he shot at me! What a beautiful and fearless face looked from under his red headcover! What a robust and graceful build did not his Gallic blouse reveal with the belt of his hunting knife! He must be some forester slave of the neighborhood! A slave! What does it matter! He is young, handsome, nimble and amorous! My husband's concubines also are slaves! Oh! Shall I never enjoy a day of love, of freedom?"

In the meantime, what is the bishop doing while his bishopess, lost in revery on the balcony over the terrace, contemplates the stars, sighs into the darkness, and breathes her sorrows and her devilish hopes upon the midnight breezes? The holy man is drinking and conferring with Count Neroweg, who happens on this night to be his guest. The banquet hall in which they are seated is built after the Roman fashion. It is a spacious room, ornamented with marble pillars, and decked with gilded work and fresco paintings. Gold and silver vases are ranged on ivory sideboards. The floor is slabbed with rich mosaics that are pleasing to the eye. But still more pleasing to the eye is the large table loaded with drinking cups and half-emptied amphoras. The leudes, Neroweg's companions in arms and his equals in time of peace, have gone to play at dice with the bishop's clerks and familiars in the vestibule, after having partaken of supper at the same table with the count, as is the custom. Here and there along the walls the rough weapons of the leudes are stacked up—wooden bucklers, iron-rimmed staves, 'francisques' or double-edged axes, 'haugons' or demi-pikes furnished with iron grappling hooks. The count's buckler is illumined with a painting that represents three eagle's talons. Left alone at table with his guest, the prelate induces Neroweg to drain cup after cup. At the lower 'end of the table sits a hermit laborer. He drinks not, neither does he speak. At times he seems to listen to the conversation of the two topers. Oftener, however, he is steeped in thought.

The Frank, Count Neroweg, has the appearance and emits the odor of a wild-boar in spring; his face resembles a bird of prey, with his beaked nose and restless little eyes that alternately assume a savage and then a sleepy look; his coarse yellow hair, tied over his head with a leather thong, falls back over his neck like a mane; the coiffure of these barbarians remained unchanged during the last two centuries. Neroweg's chin and cheeks are closely shaven, but his long reddish moustache droops down to his chest, which is covered by a doe-skin jacket, shines with grease, and is dotted with wine spots. Long leathern straps criss-cross over his lower hose from his coarse iron-spiked shoes up to his knees. He has removed his heavy sword from his broad and loosely hanging baldric and laid it upon a seat nearby, beside a stout holly club. Such is the convivial guest of the prelate, such is Count Neroweg, one of these new masters of the old lands of Gaul.

Bishop Cautin resembles a large, fat, ruttish fox—lascivious and sly eyes, red ears, a mobile and pointed nose, hirsute hands. He prinks in his violet robe of fine woven silk. And what a paunch! One would say there was a barrel under the gown.

As to the hermit-laborer—all respect for that priest, a worthy disciple of the young man of Nazareth! He is thirty years of age at the most. His face is pale, and it is at once mild and firm; his beard is blonde, his head is prematurely bald; his long brown robe, made of some coarse material, is here and there frayed by the brambles on the lands that his toil has cleared. The man's bearing is rustic, his hands are strong, the plow and the hoe-handle have made them horny.

The bishop again fills another large cup to the Frank, saying:

"Count—I repeat it—the twenty gold sous, the meadow lands and the little blonde female slave—either I must have them, or you get no absolution!"

"Bishop! I shall fall upon your house with all my leudes and sack it; I shall roast you over a slow fire—and you will give me absolution—"

"Impious man! Sacrilegious blasphemer! Pharaoh! Hog of profligacy! Reservoir of wine! How dare you hold such language to your bishop! And you a son of our apostolic Church!"

"You shall give me absolution, will ye, nill ye!"

"Oh! The beast! Is it that you are itching to fall into the very bottom of hell? Is it that you are itching to remain for centuries in succession broiling in pails full of burning pitch! You seem to be itching after a thorough trouncing with the forks of the devils! Devils with toads' heads, rams' horns, serpents for their tails, elephants' trunks for arms, and cloven hoofs—aye archcloven!"

"Did you see them?" queried the Frank with a savage and yet frightened mien. "Did you, bishop? Did you see those demons?"

"Whether I saw them! They brought before me in a cloud

of bitumen and sulphur Duke Rauking, who, the sacrilegious wretch! struck Bishop Basile with his cane!"

"And did the devils carry off Duke Rauking?"

"They threw him into the bottomless pit! I counted them; there were thirteen of them; a large red devil, that was Lucifer, led them. Such a fate is in store for you, if I refuse you absolution."

"Bishop, you may be saying all that only to frighten me out of my twenty gold sous, the fine meadow lands, and the pretty blonde slave!"

The prelate rang a bell; one of his confidential servants stepped in; the holy man said to him a few words in Latin while with his eyes he indicated a spot on the mosaic floor. The servant went out again. The hermit-laborer thereupon addressed the bishop, also in Latin:

"What you propose to do is an unworthy trick! It is a sacrilegious fraud!"

"Hermit, is not everything allowed to the clergy of our holy Church in order to terrify these brutes of Franks into subjection?"

"Fraud never is allowed—"

Cautin shrugged his shoulders, and addressing the count in the Frankish tongue—the prelate spoke the language like any of the barbarians—he said:

"Are you a Christian and a Catholic? Did you receive holy baptism?"

"Bishop Macaire, twenty years ago, ordered me to step naked into the stone tank of his basilica; he then threw a handful of water upon my head and mumbled some Latin words."

"You are a Catholic—a son of our holy Church—by reason of which you must respect and obey me as your father in Christ!"

"Bishop, you are trying to confuse me by such language, but I will not be duped by you. Our great King Clovis conquered and subjugated Gaul at the head of his brave leudes. My father Gonthram Neroweg was one of his warriors, and—"

"You lie, count! It is to the bishops that your King owed his conquest; it was they who ordered the people to submit to Clovis; without them, your great King would have remained only a chief of brigands. Never forget that, barbarian! You may now proceed with what you had to say, and speak respectfully."

"When Theodorik lived, the son of Clovis who had Auvergne as one of his kingdoms, he allotted to me vast domains in this region—lands, people, cattle and houses, and he sent me here as his representative. He made me what is called 'graf' of this country, and what we Franks call 'count'; and he authorized me to preside together with the chief bishop of the city and the magistrates of the city of Clermont."

"What are you driving at with that long digression?"

"I wish to prove, first of all, that King Clovis committed many more crimes than I did, and that his crimes did not prevent him from entering paradise, as the bishops themselves declare."

"True enough, brute that you are! But you seem to forget what that paradise cost him. St. Remi, who baptized him, was so richly endowed by him that the holy prelate was able to buy an estate in Champagne that cost him five thousand pounds of silver by weight."

"I then meant to say that if you are bishop, I am count of the conquered country, and I can force you to give me absolution!"

"Ah! You blaspheme!" and the bishop struck under the table with his foot. "Ah! You dare to defy the anger of the Lord! You—soiled with execrable crimes!"

"Well! Yes! Is it perchance an unpardonable crime to kill a brother? I confess that I murdered my brother Ursio! Give me absolution!"

"You seem to forget the murder of your concubine Isanie, and of your fourth wife Wisigarde, whom you married when two previous ones were still alive, and you then took a fifth wife, Godegisele—"

"And did you not give me absolution for all those sins? By the faith of the Terrible Eagle, my glorious ancestor! It cost me five hundred acres of the best stretches of my forest, thirty-eight gold sous, twenty slaves, together with the superb cloak of Northern marten skin in which you strutted about last winter, and which King Clovis presented to my father!"

"You have been absolved of those first crimes—as to them you are as white as the pascal lamb, but for the fresh crime of your brother's murder."

"I did not kill Ursio out of hatred, I only killed him for his part of our inheritance."

"And what else should you have killed your brother for, beast? To eat him up?"

"Did not the great Clovis also kill all his relatives for their heritage, and yet you declare that he entered paradise. I also wish to go there, and I have killed fewer people. If you do not promise paradise to me on the spot and without any further payments, if you refuse to give me absolution, I shall have you torn into pieces by four horses, or hacked to pieces by my leudes."

"And I tell you that if you do not expiate your fratricide by a gift to the Church, you shall go to hell, like a new Cain who killed his brother."

"What you are after is my hundred acres of meadow land, my twenty gold sous, and my pretty little blonde slave."

"What I am after is the salvation of your soul, unhappy man! What I aim at is to save you the torments of hell, the very thought of which should make you shudder with terror."

"You are always talking of hell. Where is hell?"

Bishop Cautin again struck the floor with his feet under the table.

"Count, do you smell that odor of sulphur?"

"I do feel a pungent odor."

"Do you see the smoke that is coming up from between those stone slabs?"

"Whence does that smoke proceed?" cried Neroweg affrighted, rising from the table and jumping back from a near place where a thick black vapor was curling upward. "Bishop, what magic is this? Come to my help!"

"Oh, Lord God! You have heard the voice of your unworthy servant!" said Cautin clasping his hands and falling upon his knees. "You wish to manifest yourself to this barbarian!" And turning his head toward Neroweg: "You asked where hell was? Look at your feet—see the abyss—see that sea of flames, all ready to engulf you!"

As the bishop spoke, one of the mosaic slabs sank below the floor, drawn down by an artful contrivance of ropes and weights; a large gap was thus left open, and out of it a whirl of flames leaped up, spreading a suffocating odor of sulphur.

"The earth is opening!" cried the terrorized Frank. "Fire! Fire! My feet burn! Help! Help!"

"It is the everlasting fire," said the bishop rising and striking a threatening attitude, while the count, dropping on both his knees, hid his face in his hands. "Ah! You asked me where hell was, impious, blaspheming brute!"

"Father! Good father—have pity upon me!"

"Do you hear those underground cries? It is the devils; they are coming for you. Listen! Do you hear them cry: 'Neroweg! Neroweg! The fratricide! Come to us! Cain, you are ours!'"

"Oh! Those cries are frightful. Good father in Christ, pray to the Lord that he forgive me!"

"Ah! Now you are on your knees, pale and distracted, with hands clasped, your eyes closed with terror! Will you still ask where is hell?"

"No! No! Holy bishop! Holy Bishop Cautin! Absolve me of the death of my brother; you shall have the meadow lands, the twenty gold pieces—"

"And the pretty blonde slave?"

"Oh! You want my pretty blonde slave also?"

"I have a donation deed ready made out. You shall order one of your leudes to come in and sign the parchment as your witness—yonder hermit shall be my witness, and you will sign the document in their presence. The donation will then be in order and binding."

"I consent to everything—have pity upon me. Order the devils back. Order them back! Oh! good father, order them away! Keep them from dragging me to hell!"

"They will certainly drag you thither if you fail in your promise."

"I shall keep all my promises."

"Seeing that you are no longer in doubt of the power of the Lord," the bishop proceeded to say while he again stamped on the floor with his foot, "you may rise, count, open your eyes, the abyss of hell is closed again"; the slab had in the meantime been raised and adjusted in its former place. "Hermit, bring the parchment to me and writing materials. You shall be my witness."

"I decline, seigneur bishop, to aid in the accomplishment of such a sacrilegious knavery," the hermit-laborer answered in Latin, "but if I reveal your trick to that barbarian he will put you to death! I shall not be the means of your death. God will one day judge you! In the meantime I shall raise my voice against your unworthy comedies."

"What! Would you be capable of abusing your influence over the masses in order to incite them to a rebellion in my diocese? Is it a declaration of war that you make to me? Do you not know that the officers of the Church must stand by one another? Or is it some favor that you mean to draw from me through intimidation? Answer!"

"To-morrow, before proceeding upon my journey, I shall tell you what I demand of you—"

Cautin, who stood in awe of the hermit, rang a bell while the count, who remained upon his knees, still trembled at every limb, and mopped the cold sweat that inundated his forehead. At the bishop's call, the confidential servant appeared. The holy man said to him in Latin:

"The hell was very satisfactory. Have the fires put out!"

And he added in the Frankish tongue:

"Order one of the count's leudes, one who can write, to step in. You shall come back with him; I shall need your services."

The servant left, and the bishop addressed the kneeling Frank:

"You have believed, you repent—you may now rise!"

"My good father, I am afraid of returning to my burg to-night. The devils might come for me on the road and take me to hell. I am terror-stricken. Keep me in your house to-night!"

"You shall be my guest until to-morrow. But I want the pretty blonde slave to be delivered to me this very evening. I promised her to my bishopess, who was once my wife according to the flesh, and is to-day my sister in God. She needs a young girl for her service—and I promised her that one. The sooner she has her, all the better pleased will she be."

"And so, bishop," said the count scratching himself behind his ear, "you must have that blonde slave?"

"Will you dare to break your engagement?"

"Oh, no! No, father! One of my leudes shall take horse, ride to my burg, and bring the slave to you on the crupper."

The deed of the donation was signed and duly witnessed by the bishop's servant and one of the count's leudes. It provided that Neroweg, count of the King of Auvergne and the city of Clermont, donated to the Church, represented by Cautin, and in remission of his sins, a hundred acres of meadow land, twenty gold sous, and a spinner female slave, fifteen years old, named Odille. After the ceremony of signing was concluded the bishop gave the Frankish count absolution for the murder of his brother and offered him three full cups of wine to comfort him.

"Sigefrid," said the count to his leude, smothering a last sigh of regret, "be a good friend to me; ride to my burg; take Odille the spinner girl on the crupper of your horse and bring her here."

CHAPTER III.

AT THE CHAPEL OF ST. LOUP.

The Vagres arrived near the episcopal villa.

"Ronan, the gates are solid, the windows high, the walls thick—how shall we penetrate into the place and reach the bishop?" asked the Master of the Hounds. "You promised to lead us to the very heart of the house. As for me, I'm off to the heart of the bishopess."

"Brothers, do you see yonder, at the foot of the hill, that little structure surrounded by pillars?"

"We see it—the night is clear!"

"That building was formerly a warm water bath. The warm spring lay in the mountain. The bath is reached from the villa by a long underground gallery. The bishop had the stream turned away, and transformed the former bath into a chapel that he consecrated to St. Loup. Now, then, my sturdy Vagres, we will penetrate to the very heart of the episcopal villa by that underground gallery, without need of boring holes through walls or breaking doors or windows. If I promised, did I keep?"

"As always, Ronan! You promised and kept!"

The troop entered the former warm water bath, now chapel of St. Loup. It was dark as a pocket. A voice was heard saying:

"Is that you, Ronan?"

"I and mine. Lead, Simon, you good servant of the episcopal villa! Lead on, we follow."

"We shall have to wait."

"Why delay?"

"Count Neroweg is still with the bishop, with his leudes."

"All the better! We shall capture a fox and a wild-boar at once! A superb hunt!"

"The count has with him twenty-four well armed leudes."

"We are thirty! That is fifteen Vagres more than enough for such a raid. Lead on, Simon, we follow."

"The passage is not yet free."

"Why is not the passage free that leads underground into the banquet hall?"

"The bishop prepared a miracle for this evening, in order to frighten the Frankish count with hell. Two clerks carried into the apartment under the banquet hall large bales of hay, bundles of fagots and boxes of sulphur. They are to set them on fire and yell like devils possessed; then one of the mosaic slabs of the flooring in the hall will sink down; it drops by means of the same contrivance that used to remove it in order to descend to this gallery for the warm baths."

"And the stupid Frank, imagining he sees one of the mouths of hell yawning wide, will make some generous donation to the holy man—"

"You guessed it, Ronan. So, then, we shall have to wait until the miracle is over. When the count is gone and the villa slumbering you and your men can come in safely."

"The bishopess for me!"

"To us the iron money-chest, the gold and silver vases! To us the bishop's full money-bags—and then we shall scatter alms among the poor who have not a denier!"

"To us," cried another set, "the full wine pouches and bags of grain—to us the hams and smoked meats! Alms, alms to the poor who hunger!"

"To all of us the wardrobes, the fine clothes, the warm robes —and then alms, alms to the poor who suffer with cold!"

"And then, fire to the episcopal villa—and to the sack!"

"Freedom to the slaves!"

"We shall take with us the young girls, who will follow us gladly!"

"Long live love and the Vagrery!" cried Ronan, saying which he struck up the song:

"My father was a Bagauder, and I a Vagre am; born under the green foliage as any bird in May.

"Where is my mother? I do not know, forsooth!

"A Vagre has no wife.

"The poniard in one hand, the torch held in the other, he moves from burg to burg and villas kept by bishops; he carries off the wives or concubines of bishops and of counts, and takes the belles along into the thickest of the woods!

"And first they weep and then they laugh. The jolly Vagre knows the art of love. In his strong arms the loving belles forget full soon the cacochymic bishop or the brutified duke!"

"Long live the Vagre's love!"

"You are in rollicking mood—"

"Aye, Simon, we are about to put a bishop's house to the sack!"

"You will be hanged, burned, quartered!"

"No more nor less so than Aman and Aëlian, our prophets, Bagauders in their days as we are Vagres in ours. For all that, the poor say: 'Good Aëlian!' 'Good Aman!' May they some day say: 'Good Ronan!' I would die happy, Simon!"

"Always living in the recesses of the woods—"

"Verdure is so cheerful!"

"At the bottom of caverns—"

"It is warm there in winter, cool in summer!"

"Always on the alert; always on the run over hill and valley; always wandering without hearth or home—"

"But always living free; old Simon. Yes, free! free! instead of leading a slave's life under the whip of some Frankish master or some bishop! Join us, Simon!"

"I am too old for that!"

"Do you not hate your master, Bishop Cautin, and the whole seigniory?"

"One time I was young, rich and happy. The Franks invaded Touraine, my native country. They slew my wife after violating her; they dashed my little girl's head against the wall; they pillaged my house; they sold me into slavery, and from master to master, I have finally fallen into the hands of Bishop Cautin. So you see, I have every reason to execrate the Franks; but worse than them, if possible, I execrate the Gallic bishops, who hold us Gauls in bondage, and sanctify the crime of our foreign oppressors. I would hang them all if I could!"

"Who goes there?" cried Ronan noticing a human form on the outside, creeping on its knees and approaching the door of the chapel in that posture. "Who goes there?"

"I, Felibien, ecclesiastical slave of our holy bishop."

"Poor man! Why do you crawl on your knees in that style?"

"It is in obedience to a vow that I took. I come on my knees —over the stones of the road—to pray to St. Loup, the great St. Loup, to whom this chapel is dedicated. I come at night so that I may be back at dawn when I must start to work. My hut is far from here."

"But why do you inflict such a punishment upon yourself, brother? Is it not hard enough to have to rise with the sun, and to lie down upon straw at night worn out with fatigue?"

"I come upon my knees to pray St. Loup, the great St. Loup, to request the Lord to grant a long and happy life to our seigneur, the bishop."

"To pray for a long and happy life for your master is to pray for a lengthening of the whip of the superintendents who flay your back."

"Blessed be their blows! The more we suffer here below, all the happier will we be in paradise!"

"But the wheat that you sow is eaten by your bishop; the wine that you press is drunk by him; the cloth that you weave, clothes him—and you remain wan, hungry, in rags!"

"I would be willing to feed on the offal of swine, clothe myself in thorns that tear my skin to the veins—my happiness will be all the greater in paradise!"

"The Lord created the grain, the grapes, the honey, the fruits, the creamy milk, the soft fleece of the sheep—was all that done in order that any of His creatures should live on ordure and dress in thorns? Answer me, my poor brother."

"You are an impious fellow!"

"Alas! Almost all the slaves are, like this unhappy fellow, steeped in the abjectest besotment—the evil spreads by the day —it is done for old Gaul—"

"If so, let us sing the refrain of the Vagres:

"The Franks call us 'Wand'ring Men,' 'Wolves,' 'Wolves' Heads'-- Let us live like wolves! Let us live in joy! In summer under the green foliage, in winter in caverns warm!"

"Come, Simon, the bishop's miracle must be over by this time."

"Yes—I shall precede you alone, a little way in this underground passage; should I see light I shall return and notify you."

"But what about that slave, who is mumbling his prayers on his knees to the great St. Loup?"

"Lightning might strike at his very feet and he would not budge from the spot—he will go back as he came, on his knees. Follow me!"

And led by the ecclesiastical slave, the Vagres vanished in the subterranean passage which led from the former warm baths into the episcopal villa. As they proceeded in the dark, they sang in an undertone:

"The jolly Vagre has no wife. The poniard in one hand, the torch held in the other, he moves from burg to burg and villas kept by bishops; he carries off the wives and concubines of bishops and of counts, and takes the belles along into the thickest of the woods!"

CHAPTER IV.

THE DEMONS! THE DEMONS!

What were the prelate and the count engaged in while the Vagres were approaching the ecclesiastical villa through the underground gallery? What were they engaged in? They were emptying cup upon cup. The count's leude had returned to the burg in quest of the pretty blonde slave girl. While waiting for him, Bishop Cautin, hardly able to contain himself for the joy that he anticipated in the possession of the girl whom he coveted, had returned to his seat at the table. Neroweg had not yet recovered from his recent fright; ever and anon a shiver would run over him. Every time it occurred to him that hell had just yawned at his very feet and might be located under the very room in which he found himself, he would gladly have left the banquet hall. He dared not. He believed himself protected by the holy presence of the bishop against the attacks of the devils, who might elsewhere fall upon him. In vain did the man of God urge his guest to drain another cup; the count pushed the cup back with his hand while his gimlet eyes, resembling the eyes of a frightened bird of prey, rolled uneasily over the hall. Impassible in his seat, the hermit laborer remained sunk in meditation, or observed what took place around him.

"What ails you?" the bishop asked the count. "You look downcast and drink no more! A minute ago you were a fratricide, and now, thanks to the absolution that I gave you, you are white as snow. Is your conscience still uneasy? Can it be that you hid some other crime from me? If you did, you chose your time ill—as you saw, hell is not far away—"

"Keep still, father! Keep still! I feel so weak just now that I could not carry a lamb on my back—I who can otherwise raise a wild-boar. Do not leave your son in Christ alone! You are able to conjure the demons away—I shall not leave you till it is broad day—"

"You will nevertheless have to leave me the moment the pretty blonde slave arrives; I must take her to the women's section of the house near Fulvia."

"As truly as one of my ancestors was called the Terrible Eagle in Germany, I shall not quit you any more than your shadow."

"An ancestor of that Neroweg was called the Terrible Eagle in Germany—the meeting is odd," thought the hermit to himself. "It does seem that our two hostile families, the one Frank the other Gaul, having crossed each other's path in the past, must cross it again—and are to recross it, perhaps, again and again through the centuries to come—"

"Count, your terror proves to me that your soul is not at ease—I mistrust that your confession was not complete."

"Yes, yes; I confessed everything!"

"I hope to God it be so, for the salvation of your soul. But cheer up! Let us talk of the hunt. Oh! By the way of the hunt, I have a complaint against you and your forester slaves. The other day they pursued three stags into the very heart of the Church's forest—in that part of the wood that is separated from the rest of your domains by the river."

"If my forester slaves pursued any stag into your forest, I shall allow yours to pursue one into mine; our woods are separated only by a narrow road."

"A better boundary would be the river itself."

"In that case I would have to abandon to you fully a thousand acres of woodland, which lie on this side of the stream."

"Do you place much store by that little corner of your forest? The trees do not thrive very well at that spot."

"Not as poorly as you would make out. There are among them oak trees more than twenty feet around; besides, it is that portion of my domains that game seems to like best."

"You boast of the beauty of your trees; it is your right; but your domains would have a better and safer boundary if you took the river, and if you consented to yield to the Church that corner of a thousand acres."

"What makes you speak of my woods? I have no need of any further absolution from you—"

"No—you killed one of your wives, one of your concubines and your brother Ursio—you have expiated those crimes by endowing the Church—you have received absolution. Nevertheless, coming to think of it, there is one thing that both of us have overlooked—and it is of capital importance—"

"What is it, father?"

"Your fourth wife, Wisigarde, died a violent death at your hands. She did not receive priestly assistance at her death—her soul is in pain. She might come to torment you during the night in the shape of some frightful phantom until you will have drawn her poor soul from purgatory—"

"How can I do that?"

"Through the holy mass and through the prayers of a priest of the Lord."

"Well, father, I wish you to make those prayers for the soul of the departed."

"I shall grant your request. For twenty years prayers shall be recited at the altar for the repose of the soul of Wisigarde, but only under condition that you pass over to me the corner of your woods that is separated from your domains by the stream—"

"Give again to your Church! Ever give! Ever!"

"Would you prefer to be tormented by nocturnal phantoms?"

The Frank looked at the bishop with an angry and defiant eye:

"Rapacious Gaul! You are seeking to pluck piece by piece from me the share of the conquests that our kings have presented to my family as our hereditary possessions. Endow the Church still more! I will sooner endow the devil! Yes, by all the horns of Lucifer!"

"Do! Endow him! Here he is!" came from a rude loud voice that seemed to issue from the center of the earth.

At the sound of the voice the hermit started from his seat; the bishop threw himself back and quickly crossed himself, but a reassuring thought flashed through his mind, and he said to himself aloud in Latin:

"It must be my good assistant who remained below—the trick is good!"

The count, however, struck with terror and believing himself pursued by the archfiend in person, screamed aloud and fled from the banquet hall distracted. So precipitate was his flight and headlong his bewilderment that he nearly upset the leude who, back at that moment from his errand to the count's burg, entered the hall pushing before him the young blonde slave whom he was sent in quest of:

"Here is the slave girl, Odille," said the leude.

The bishop started to run towards the poor lass, but at the very moment when he dashed forward to seize her, a vigorous hand that rose from the opening of the now again removed mosaic slab held the prelate back by the fold of his robe, and a voice shouted:

"A profligate you shall no longer be, holy man of God! That pretty lass is not for you!"

When the startled bishop looked around, he saw with terror Ronan issuing from the underground recess at the head of his companions, all of whom were yelling at the top of their voices. In order to carry on the humor of the trick that the bishop played upon the count, the Vagres had all blackened their faces with the charred remains of the fagots that shortly before furnished the "flames of hell."

At the sight of those black men rising from under the ground, and yelling as if possessed, the leude who brought in the young slave also believed that they issued from hell, and rushed out close upon Neroweg's heels, crying:

"The demons! The demons!"

More and more frightened by these cries, the count ran to the stable, leaped upon his horse, and dashed full tilt away from the episcopal villa. His leudes followed his example; they, in turn, took to their mounts, and leaving their arms behind in the banquet hall, fled tumultuously, repeating in terror:

"The demons! The demons!"

CHAPTER V.

VAGRES IN JUDGMENT.

The episcopal villa has been invaded by the Vagres. They carried the place, and they did so without striking a blow.

Who is he who is celebrating night mass in the bishop's chapel? The wax candles are lighted on the altar with all the gorgeousness of an Easter Sunday. Their brilliant light illumines the near vault, while the rest of the chapel is thrown into the shade, down to the Gothic main entrance, that now and then a ruddy gleam flickers through like the reflection of an extinguishing bonfire. What bonfire was that? It was the bonfire of the episcopal villa in flames.

Was, then, the villa set on fire by the Vagres? Certes; for what other reason should they have brought along torches and straw?

In the center of the yard the riches of the bishop lie in a high heap—gold and silver vases, holy chalices, together with drinking goblets, Bible cases of precious wood, together with platters of the banquet table, patines, together with bowls used for cooling the bishop's wine; good sized and ripped-up bags, from which silver and gold sous roll out; costly cloth, purple and blue, that but awaited the tailor's scissors; warm and rare furs, some black as crows, others white as doves. In the way of trophies, the axes, bucklers and pikes of the leudes, who ran away out of fear for the devil, are stacked up at the four corners of the superb heap of booty. Gold, silver, steel, the brilliant colors of the cloths—they all scintillate and sparkle, each

with its own lustre, and all with the resplendence that is so
pleasing to the eye of the Vagre.

The Vagres are there! They are in the holy chapel of the
episcopal villa, where they do that which all Vagres do after
they have drunk their fill, ravaged and pillaged. Some are
snoring at the foot of the altar exhausted by their labors or
overcome by the fumes of wine; others balance themselves on
their unsteady limbs and cast loving glances at the wealth which
they are about to scatter on their route and that will make so
many poor people happy. The Vagres of Ronan are ever faithful to the sacred commandments of the Vagrery:

"Let us take from the rich and give to the poor. The Vagre
who preserves a sou for the morrow ceases to be a Vagre, a
'Wolf's-head,' a 'wand'ring man.' He ever divides the booty of
the previous evening among the poor, so that he be compelled
to pillage fresh renegade bishops, and Frankish oppressors of
old Gaul. Nor peace nor truce to the oppressors!"

And as to those other Vagres, who lean against the shafts
of the pillars, or are seated on the step of the altar near the
snorers—their eyes are as steady as their limbs; have they perchance, not also tasted the old wines of the episcopal villa?

Oh! They did drink, twice, ten times more than the others; but they are veterans at the trade, old Vagres, sturdy customers who drain a pouch at one gulp, and immediately after
are able to walk with steady step over a beam across the conflagration that they have lighted in the burg of a Frank, or the
villa of a bishop.

And these others—men with shaven heads, wan, clad in
rags; these women and these girls, some of whom are pretty—
who are they?

They are the slaves of the Church; they look happy at the
sight of their day of justice and vengeance. But other slaves
there are, not a few in number, who fled terrified into the woods.
They imagined they saw the fires of heaven roll down upon the

Vagres, who could be sacrilegious enough to put to the sack and fire the house of the vice-regent of God on earth, their holy bishop.

And what is Ronan doing? There he sits in full gala on the episcopal bench, decked in sacerdotal garb, and coiffed in the fur cap which count Neroweg left behind when he fled demented out of the banquet hall. Four Vagres assist Ronan. They are odd-looking clerks! Jolly deacons! Among them is Wolf's-Tooth, the giant whose waist a barrel's hoop would hardly encircle.

"Brother, are we all together?"

"Ronan, only the Master of the Hounds is missing. When the conflagration was at its height, he was seen by one of our men running towards the door of the bishopess; he leaped through the flames and re-issued at the garden door running with a fainting woman in his arms."

"He is doubtlessly engaged in making her regain consciousness. Well, while the bishopess is being revived, shall we try the bishop?"

"The holy man has tried people, whom he said were under his jurisdiction, as bishop of the city of Clermont. He is now under our jurisdiction. Let us try him!"

Louder than the Vagres themselves, the slaves of the prelate set up the cry:

"Let us judge the bishop!"

"Bring him forward, on the spot!"

Two Vagres went out in quest of the holy man of God, who had been kept locked up in a contiguous compartment. He was brought in pinioned. Pale and wrathful he was pushed before the tribunal of Ronan and his four Vagre clerks.

"Seigneur bishop," said Ronan to him, "thy 'charity,' thy 'piety,' thy 'exalted chastity' (thou seest I am giving thee all the honorary titles that thou and thine bestow upon one another,

holy men that ye are) thy 'exalted chastity' will be kind enough
to inform us of thy name?"

"Incendiary! Pillager! Sacrilegious wretch! Those are
your names! I damn and excommunicate you, you, together
with your whole band! You stand excommunicated in this
world and in the next, where you will suffer everlasting tortures!"

"Thy 'exalted chastity' answers my question with insults.
Seeing that thou refusest to state thy name, I shall answer for
thee. Thy name is Cautin—"

"May my name burn your tongue!"

"Slaves of the bishopric," proceeded Ronan addressing those
who surrounded him, "what charges have you to prefer against
your bishop?"

"He grinds us down with toil and with taxes. He oppresses
us from morning till night all the year long!"

"For food he lets us have a handful of beans, for clothes
rags, and for shelter rickety mud huts!"

"Our slightest oversights are visited with the whip!"

"He violates our daughters! What resistance can the female
slave offer when threatened? She submits with a shudder—
she weeps—"

"That a Frank should be ready to subjugate us and whelm
us with misery we can understand: he is a conqueror who abuses
his power. But that bishops, Gauls like ourselves, should join
the Frank in order to share with him the plunder that he levies
upon us—that we cannot understand; such action must draw
down the severest punishment upon the heads of the perpe-
trators. Oh! Our old priests, the venerated druids, never allied themselves with the Roman conquerors of Gaul. No! No!
With the sword in one hand, the mistletoe twig in the other,
they were ever the first to give the signal for war against the
foreigner; they roused the peoples to revolt with the words:
'The country and freedom!' The response came swift from the

masses; out of their midst arose the Chief of the Hundred Valleys, Sacrovir, Vindex, Marik, Civilis! And the Romans trembled in their very Capitol!"

"Bishop," Ronan proceeded, "has thy exalted truthfulness anything to answer to the accusations of thy slaves?"

"They are all damned criminals, sacrilegious wretches who will have to answer for their crimes when they appear before the throne of God, on the day of last judgment. Ever after they will gnash their teeth—"

"Bishop, has thy exalted purity nothing else to say than utter insults?"

"And may it please the Lord to turn these insults into so many tongues of fire to pierce your bodies, ye accursed men!"

"While waiting for the fulfillment of thy wishes, listen to the further indictment against thee: Thou didst covet the goods of one of thy priests named Anastasius; he declined to let thee have them; thou didst inveigle him to Clermont; thou didst there have him seized, bound hand and foot and thrown alive into a grave with a decomposing corpse. Wilt thou dare deny that thou art guilty of that felony?"

"A wonderful council this is, made up of beggars, sacrilegious wretches and slaves, to interrogate a bishop!"

"We shall proceed. Thy exalted poverty, in its rage to augment its wealth, conceived this evening, under guise of a miracle, a veritable bandit's trick: thou didst plunder Count Neroweg under pressure of the fear of the devil. Under the code of the Vagrery, to plunder a Frank is a pious act. But if the Vagres delight in pillaging our conquerors, it is only in order to administer to the wants of the poor by making them sharers in the plunder. On the other hand, to plunder a thief for self-gain is a sin according to the code of the Vagrery. Moreover, thou didst absolve the count of a crime in order that thou mightst possess a young slave, a girl of barely fifteen years. Now, then, under the code of the Vagrery, such episcopal profligacy also is a damnable sin that demands punishment."

And addressing himself to the Vagres, Ronan added:

"Bring in the young slave!"

Ronan was right. To impute fifteen years to the girl was to add to her actual age. Her blonde hair that was parted in two long and thick braids, reached almost down to her feet, which were bare, like her arms and shoulders. In fetching her from the burg, the brutal leude had barely given her time to dress before lifting her on the crupper of his horse. Accordingly, now that she faced the Vagres what suppliant fear was not readable in the large blue eyes of the poor child, who still trembled visibly! Her nocturnal ride on the crupper of the Frankish warrior's horse, the burning of the episcopal villa, the strange aspect of the Vagres—how many subjects of alarm to her young heart! The young girl's cheeks must once have been full and rosy; they now were hollow and pale. The infantine figure, bearing the stamp of suffering, was painful to behold. As the young slave stepped into the chapel a feeling of sadness came over Ronan; his very voice betrayed his emotion when he addressed her:

"What is your name, my child?"

"I am called Odille."

"Where were you born?"

"Far from here—in one of the uplands of the Mont-Dore."

"How old are you, little Odille?"

"My mother said to me this spring: 'Odille, it is to-day fourteen years that you have been the joy of my life.'"

"How did you become the slave of the Frankish count? Tell us your history."

"My father died young. I lived in the mountain with my grandfather, my brother and my mother. We lived off the yield of our herd, and we spun wool. No sorrow had ever befallen us except my father's death. One day the Franks scaled the mountain in arms. They took our herd and said to us: 'We shall carry you to the burg of our count to restock his domain with slaves and cattle.' My brother attempted to defend us. The Franks killed him. They tied my mother and me to one rope, and drove us together with our herd of sheep before them. My grandfather begged them on his knees to allow him to follow us. But the Franks said to him: 'You are too old to gain your bread as a slave.' 'But if I am left alone, I shall die of hunger on the mountain!' 'Die, then!' was their answer, and they made us move on before them. My grandfather followed us, weeping, at a distance. The Franks stoned him to death. On their way they captured other slaves, took in other droves of cattle, and killed other people of the mountain when they refused to follow. They descended into the valley; there they made some further captures of people and cattle. There were about fifty of us, men, women and girls. The Franks slaughtered all the children as being worthless. The first night we slept in a wood. On that night the Franks violated the women despite all their entreaties. I heard the sobs of my mother. They separated me from her in the evening and did me no harm. The chief of the band kept me, he said, for the count. The next morning we resumed our march, with me separated from my mother. More people were killed who did not wish to march on—more slaves and cattle were taken. After that the troop marched to the burg. Before arriving there a second night was spent in the woods. The chief who reserved me for the count made me sleep beside his horse. Early the next morning we proceeded on our route. I tried to discover my mother in the crowd—the Frank said to me: 'She died; two warriors contended for her last night; in the tussle she was killed.' I wished to lie down and die, but the chief raised me on his horse, and we arrived on the count's domain—"

"Dost thou hear, bishop?" broke in Ronan. "Dost thou hear, renegade Gaul? It is thy allies, the Franks, who in this

as well as in the other provinces, put old men and babes to
death as useless mouths, and carry away the men and women of
our race to restock the lands of Gaul which the kings have par-
celed out among their warriors after plundering us of our patri-
mony. It is thy allies, thy friends, thy brothers in Christ and
in God who commit these execrable deeds. And yet thou or-
derest these poor people, under the penalty of hell, to obey those
plunderers, those thieves, those ravishers, those murderers, who
violate and kill mothers under the very eyes of their daughters!
Didst thou hear that story, Gallic bishop?"

"The Franks respect the property of the Church and the
servants of the Lord—while you, accursed pack, you dare to lift
impious hands against both the property and the priests of the
Church!"

"Proceed," said Ronan to Odille.

"We arrived at the burg. The count had me taken to his
chamber. He threw himself upon me; I tried to resist; he
struck me in the face with his fist; my face was bathed in blood;
pain and fright rendered me senseless, and the seigneur count
violated me. I was afterwards locked up with other female
slaves in the apartment of his wife Godegisele, a very gentle
woman for so wicked a man. To-night, one of the leudes came
for me and brought me hither on his horse. He said to me that
I was to be the bishop's slave."

"And does that frighten you, poor child, to be a slave of the
seigneur bishop?"

"My mother and relatives were killed; I am a slave and
disgraced besides. I tried to strangle myself with my hair; but
I was afraid—and yet I wish I could die."

"And she is only fourteen, bishop! Didst thou hear?"

"Sit down on the steps of the altar, little Odille. Here you
have only friends; you are still young, do not despair."

The child contemplated the Vagre with wondering eyes; he
spoke to her in a gentle voice. She stepped towards the altar

and sat down; she looked at Ronan only; she listened only to his words.

"O! Master of the Hounds! Master of the Hounds!" cried one of the lusty Vagres, who stood near one of the small doors of the chapel opening into the garden. "Whither are you bound with the bishopess on your arm? Would she not like to come and see her darling husband, the holy Bishop Cautin, before we hang him?"

"My good seigneurs Vagres," said the bishopess, whose comely shape was hardly distinguishable in the shadow of the vaulted door of the chapel, "long have I cursed yonder man who is my husband. I now no longer curse him. Happiness renders one indulgent. Be merciful to him, as I pardon him. For the rest, I no longer was his wife—our carnal bonds were sundered. Let him go in peace. I at last enjoy my day of freedom and of love. Long live the Vagrery!"

"Shameless and sacrilegious woman! Accursed burgess! You shall burn for this in the everlasting flames of hell!"·

But Cautin's vituperation and threats were idle. The bishopess stepped out under the tall trees of the garden of the villa and continued her promenade, while Ronan again addressed the holy man:

"Sentence shall be passed upon thee by those whom thou hast oppressed. Ye poor ecclesiastical slaves, what shall be done to this wicked and profligate religious humbug who buries the living with the dead?"

"Let him be hanged! Death to the bishop!"

"Yes! Yes! Let him be hanged!"   ·

"He will die but one death, the infamous scoundrel! And our lives have been one prolonged agony!"

"What dost thou think of that?" said Ronan to the bishop. "Dost thou fancy the views of these poor people?"

"Brothers, in the name of Jesus of Nazareth, the friend of

the sorrowful, pardon this guilty man if you find his repentance sincere."

Who was it that spoke thus? The hermit-laborer, who had until then kept himself concealed in the shadow under one of the vaults of the chapel. As he spoke he stepped into the light and stood before the Vagres and the slaves who were venting their rage.

"The hermit-laborer!" cried the slaves with touching respect. "The friend of the poor, of the meek and the oppressed!"

"The consoler of those who weep!"

"How often has he not taken in the field the hoe of one of our exhausted companions, and himself finished the task of the slave in order to save him from the keeper's whip!"

"One day, as I was pasturing the sheep that I had in charge, two lambs went astray. The hermit-laborer looked for them until he found them and was able to bring them back to me. Blessed be he for his charity."

"Our little children always have a smile for the hermit-laborer."

"Oh! From the moment they see him they run to him and take hold of his robe."

"As poor as any of ourselves, he loves to make little presents to the children. He always has some fruit for them that he gathered in the woods, a piece of wild honey-comb, or some little bird that has fallen out of its nest."

"Love one another! Love one another like brothers, poor disinherited people! he always says to us.—Love renders toil less arduous."

"Hope! he also says to us.—Hope! The rule of the oppressors will pass away; and then the first will be the last, and the last will be the first."

"Jesus, the friend of the sorrowful, said the iron of the slave will be broken. Hope!"

"Unite! Love one another! Help one another, children of

one God, sons of one country! Disunited, you can do nothing; united you will be stronger than your oppressors. The day of deliverance may be nigh! Love, unity, patience!"

"Aye! Aye! These are the precepts that the hermit-laborer teaches us!"

"And these precepts, brothers, you must remember and act upon at this hour," replied the monk-laborer. "Jesus said: 'Woe to the hardened hearts! Mercy to those who repent!'"

"Insolent monk, dare you accuse me!"

"Hermit, good friend, you hear the 'holy' man—you perceive his repentance—what shall be done, my Vagres?"

"Brothers, if you love me, grant me the bishop's life!"

"The bishop made us suffer. An eye for an eye, a tooth for a tooth!"

"Will vengeance wipe out your past sufferings? Your ancestors astonished the world by their generous bravery—and would you slay a defenseless man?"

Vagres and slaves remained silent for a moment. After a short consultation with Ronan they directed him to stipulate the conditions for Cautin's life.

"Bishop, choose! Either be our cook or hang!"

"Sacrilegious bandits! After pillaging and setting my episcopal villa on fire, to demand that I be their cook! Monk, you hear them! Alas! Alas! And you have neither curse nor anathema for them! Is it thus that you defend me? What did you save my life for but in order to rejoice at my humiliation?"

"Hold your tongue! Jesus of Nazareth, whose life was as pure as yours is sullied; Jesus, when in the Roman pretorium, amidst the soldiers who whelmed him with mockery and physical outrage said: 'My God, pardon them, they know not what they do—"

"But these scamps do know what they are doing when they

make a cook of me! And would you have me pardon them their sacrilege!"

"Consider your past life—"

"Come, my Vagres," said Ronan; "come, day is dawning. Let us pack our booty on the bishop's wagons, and on the march! What a fine day will this be for the folks of this neighborhood!"

And stepping towards the little slave girl, who, seated on the steps of the altar Had quietly watched and listened to all 'hat took place:

"Poor child, you are without father or mother, will you come with us? The Vagrery is the world topsy-turvy. The slave and the poor are sacred to us; our hatred is for the wicked rich. If our life of adventure and dangers should frighten you, our friend the hermit will take you to some charitable person in a neighboring village, where you may be safe."

"I shall follow you, Ronan. I am a slave and an orphan," answered Odille weeping. "What can I do? Where would you have me go, if not with you who speak to me with so much kindness?"

"Well, then, come with me, and dry your tears, little Odille. No tears are shed among the Vagres. You shall ride on one of the wagons of the villa in which our companions will carry the booty. Come, take my arm, and let us walk out, poor little child. We shall go whithersoever chance may take us!"

And seeing that the hermit was stepping towards him:

"Adieu, friend!"

"Ronan, I shall accompany you."

"Will you join us in running the Vagrery? You, a hermit? You among us, 'Wand'ring men,' 'Wolves,' 'Heads of Wolves,' Vagres that we are? A saint in the company of demons?"

"They that be whole need not the physician, but they that are sick."

"Monk, you are right!" said Cautin to him in a low voice.

"You will not leave me alone in their hands? You will protect me against the Philistines?"

"It is my duty to render these people better than they are."

"Better! The sacrilegious scoundrels, who pillaged my villa, stole my beautiful goblets, my vases and all my money—"

"The homicidal sword will be turned into a pruning hook to prune the flowering vine; the peaceful and teeming earth will yield its fruit for all men; the lion will lie down beside the sheep, the wolf beside the lamb, and a little child will lead them! Do not blaspheme, bishop! The Creator made His children after his own image; He made them good in order that they may be happy; blind, wretched or ignorant are the wicked. Let us heal their ignorance, their wretchedness and their blindness—and good they will become!"

"Lies!" cried the bishop excitedly. "Behold yonder the woman who was my wife, with her orange skirt and gold embroidered red stockings—behold her on the arm of that bandit with the black hair. The infamous woman—they are in each other's arms."

"Jesus had only words of mercy for Magdalen the courtesan and for the adulterous woman; will you dare to throw the first stone at the woman who once was your wife? Come—come along—I pity you—lean upon my arm—you are about to faint—"

"Alas! Where do these accursed Vagres propose to take me?"

"That does not concern you—mend your ways—repent!"

"My God! My God! And there is no hope of being delivered on the road! Oh! We live in frightful days!"

"And who is it that made these days what they are, if not you, princes of the Church? Oh! For centuries did our fathers see Gaul peaceful and flourishing. She then was free!" replied the hermit with bitterness. "To-day she is again enslaved."

"Our fathers were miserable heathens! At this very hour they are gnashing their teeth in all eternity!" cried Cautin.

"We, on the contrary, have the true faith—and the Lord has terrible punishment in store for the wretches who dare insult His priests and plunder the goods of His Church. Look yonder, monk, is not that a sight to make one's heart break? Abomination and desolation!"

CHAPTER VI.

TO THE FASTNESS OF ALLANGE.

The sight that excited the wrath of the holy man filled the hearts of the Vagres with joy. It was broad day. Four large wagons of the villa, each hitched to teams of oxen, were slowly rolling away from the smoldering ruins of the late episcopal mansion. The wagons were loaded with all manner of booty: gold and silver vases, curtains and beddings, feather mattresses and bags of wheat, boxes filled with linen, hams, venison, smoked fish, preserved fruits, and all sorts of eatables, heavy rolls of cloth that had been woven by weaver-slaves, soft cushions, warm coverlets, shoes, cloaks, iron pots, copper basins, tin cans—all of them dear to the heart of a housekeeper. The Vagres followed the train, singing like larks at the rise of the beautiful June sun. On the front wagon, and seated on one of the cushions, little Odille—whom the bishopess in loving tenderness thoughtfully clad in one of her own beautiful, although rather too long robes for the child—no longer timorous but still laboring under the effect of her wonderment, opened her beautiful blue eyes, and, for the first time since many a long day, breathed in freedom the fresh and invigorating morning air that reminded her often of that of her own mountains from which she was torn, poor child, and cast into the burg of the count. Ever and anon Ronan approached the wagon:

"Take courage, Odille; you will get accustomed to us. The Vagres are not as wolfish as evil tongues pretend."

On another wagon, gorgeous in her gold necklaces and her most beautiful dress which her loving Vagre saved for her from the conflagration, the bishopess whiled away the time, either combed her long black hair with the aid of a little pocket mirror, or adjusted her scarf, or hopped about, crazy with joy, like a hen-linnet that had escaped from her cage. At last she enjoyed that day of freedom and love that she had so ardently dreamed about after having lived more than ten years almost a prisoner. The morning journey across the beautiful mountains of Auvergne, where at frequent intervals cascades of bubbling water were encountered, seemed to charm her. She chatted, laughed, sang, sang again, and threw sidelong glances at her Vagre every time that, with his light step and triumphant mien, he passed by her wagon. Suddenly, as her eyes happened to fall upon a distant object, she seemed moved with pity. She seized a straw-covered amphora that the Master of the Hounds had thoughtfully placed within her reach, and turning towards the rear of the car, where several women and girls, the bishop's slaves, having gladly resolved to run the Vagrery together with their quondam mistress, were huddled, she said to one of them:

"Carry this bottle of spiced wine to my brother, the bishop; the poor man loves to take what he calls his morning cup; but do not let him know that I sent you."

The young girl to whom the bishopess gave the flask answered with a nod of intelligence, leaped down from the cart, and looked for Cautin. Most of the ecclesiastical slaves fled into the mountains when the bishop's house was set on fire; they feared the wrath of heaven if they joined the Vagres; the others, however, being of a less timorous turn, resolutely accompanied the troop of the lusty men. They should have been seen—alert, frisk as if they had just risen from a restful night spent under the foliage of the wood, they marched with elastic step, despite the orgy of the previous night, and went and came, and skipped and chatted, and exchanged kisses with the women who were willing or with the pouches of wine that they carried along, and bit lustily into the hams, the chunks of venison and the episcopal cakes.

"How good it is to live a Vagre's life!"

On the last wagon, under the special watch of Wolf's Tooth and a few companions who brought up the rear, Cautin, bishop and Vagre's cook, accustomed to strut on his traveling mule, or to ride through the forest on his vigorous hunting steed, found the road rough, dusty and unpleasant. He perspired, panted, tossed himself about, moaned, grumbled, grunted under the weight of his heavy paunch and invoked to his aid all the saints of paradise.

"Seigneur bishop," said the young girl whom the bishopess charged with the amphora of wine, "here is some good spiced wine; drink it; it will give you strength to support the fatigue of the journey."

"Give it to me! Give it to me, my daughter! God will reward you for your attachment to your father in Christ, who finds himself obliged to drink by stealth the wine of his own cellar—"

And clapping the amphora to his lips, he drained it at one draught. When the flask was empty he dashed it against the floor, and looking at the young girl cried:

"And so you propose to run the Vagrery, little she-devil, confounded wench?"

"Yes, seigneur bishop; I am now twenty years of age, and this is the first day of my life that I have been able to say: 'I belong to myself—I can go and come, jump, sing, dance, just as I please'—"

"You belong to yourself, do you, brazen minx? You belong to me! But with the aid of God you will yet be re-captured either by the Church, or by some Frankish seigneur—and I hope you may fall into even worse slavery, God-forsaken wench!"

"I will then, at least, have tasted freedom—"

And the young woman dashed off, jumping and singing, in pursuit of a butterfly that fluttered in the bush.

The troop of Vagres arrived at the hovels of some slaves that belonged to the domain of the Church, and that lay scattered along the road. Little wan, sickly looking children, absolutely bare by reason of their parents' pinching poverty, were wallowing in the dust. Their fathers were off on the fields since dawn; their mothers, as wan-looking and thin as the children, sat at the entrance of their hovels upon bunches of decaying straw; they were clad in rags and busily plied their distaffs for the benefit of the bishop; their long and unkempt hair tumbled over their foreheads upon their bony shoulders; their eyes were hollow, their cheeks sunburnt and sunken; the aspect that they presented was at once so repulsive and painful that the hermit-laborer could not refrain from pointing them out to the bishop, saying:

"Look at those unhappy creatures!"

"Resignation, misery and sorrow here below, everlasting reward above—otherwise as everlasting and frightful tortures!" cried Cautin. "The Church so decrees; it is the law of God!"

"Blasphemer! Your words are like those of the imposter physicians who pretend that man was born for fevers, the pest and ulcers, and not for health!"

At the sight of the approaching and well-armed troop, the women and children were first afraid and ran to hide in their hovels; but stepping forward, Ronan called out to them:

"Poor women! Poor children! Be not afraid—we are your good friends the Vagres!"

The Vagrery caused the Franks and the bishops to tremble, but it was often blessed by the poor. Women and children, all of whom had at first fled with fear into their hovels, now emerged again, and one of the mothers said to Ronan:

"Do you want to know the road? I shall show it to you."

"Are you running away from the leudes of the seigneurs?"

said another. "None has passed this way; you can march on in safety."

"Women," answered Ronan, "your children are naked, you and your husbands toil from dawn to dusk; you are barely covered in rags; you lie down to sleep upon poorer straw than the swine; you live upon decayed beans; often you munch grass like cattle!"

"Alas! It is the truth! Our lives are wretched, indeed!"

"Here we have for you linen, cloth, dresses, covers, mattresses, bags of grain, full pouches, provisions of all sorts. Give, my Vagres! Give, Odille, to these poor people! Give, bishopess of the Vagrery! Give and give again!"

"Take—take, sisters!" said the bishopess with eyes moist with compassionate tears, as she helped the Vagres to distribute the booty taken at her house. "Take, sisters! Yesterday I was a slave as yourselves, to-day I am free! Take, sisters!"

"Take and make merry, dear women; and may your little ones never be torn from you!" said Odille as she also gave a hand in the distribution of the booty. And she wiped her eyes as she exclaimed: "How good Ronan, the Vagre, is to the poor!"

"Blessings upon you!" cried the poor mothers, weeping for joy. "It is better to meet a Vagre than a count or a bishop."

It was a pleasure to see with what ardor the Vagres, perched upon the carts, distributed what they had taken from the wicked bishop; it was a pleasure to see how the poor mothers' faces brightened with happiness at the unlooked-for alms. Amazed and enraptured they contemplated the heap of all manner of articles that they had never yet made acquaintance with. The children, more impatient than their elders, merrily hitched themselves by twos, threes and fours to a mattress in order to transport it into one of the huts, or they put their thin arms around a bundle of linen and sought to lift it in. Suddenly, however, a wrathful and threatening voice, a veritable mar-plot, froze the marrow of the poor folks with terror.

"Woe unto you! Damnation upon your families! if you dare to touch with sacrilegious hands the goods of the Church! Tremble! Tremble! It is a mortal sin! You, your husbands, your children, you will all be thrown into the flames of hell for all time!"

It was Bishop Cautin. Despite the remonstrances of the hermit-laborer, he dashed in among the startled slaves, and fulminated his anathemas.

"Oh! We shall touch nothing of all that is offered us, holy bishop!" answered the mothers with a shudder. "We shall not touch any of the goods of the Church."

"My Vagres!" cried Ronan, "Hang the bishop on the nearest tree! We shall not lack for a cook."

Already they were seizing the holy man, who now grew paler and trembled in greater terror than the most awe-struck of the mothers who had just been running over with joy, when the monk again interposed to save Cautin from the noose.

"The hermit!" cried the mothers and their children. "The hermit-laborer!"

"Blessed be you, the friend of the sorrowful!—"

"Blessed be you, the friend of little children!—"

And the hands of all the little ones took hold of the robe of the hermit, who said in his sweet and clear voice:

"Dear women, dear little ones; take what is given you; take without fear; Jesus said: 'Woe unto the rich who share not their bread with those who hunger, and their cloak with those who are cold.' Your bishop gives you all these good things. Take all that is offered to you!"

"Blessings upon you, holy bishop!" exclaimed the mothers, raising their arms in thankfulness to Cautin. "Blessed be you, good father, for your generous gifts!"

"I give nothing!" cried Cautin. "You shall burn eternally in hell, if you listen to that apostate hermit!"

The larger number of the women looked undecided from

Ronan to the bishop and the hermit. They put their hands forward and withdrew them again from the articles that were offered them. But two of the oldest of them resolutely drew away from the goods of the Church, and throwing themselves down upon their knees murmured affrighted:

"Holy Bishop Cautin! Pardon us for having even for a moment harbored the thought of committing so great a crime. Mercy! Mercy!"

"Fear not, my sisters!" resumed the hermit. "Your bishop gives you all these good things. He knows that the Lord has equal love for all his children, and does not wish that some should be naked and freeze, while others perspire under the useless weight of twenty gowns; that some should suffer hunger, while others are filled to repletion. Fear not that your bishop will either hunger or suffer cold; he has new and warm clothing on; he knows not what to do with so many robes; he can not drink all those pouches of wine; he can not eat up all these provisions! Take, take—the goods of a bishop are the property of the poor."

Most of the unhappy mothers, convinced by the words of the hermit, and also driven by the lash of their needs, began busily to transport the proffered goods of the Church into their huts, aided by their children. Only three elderly ones dared not to join; they remained on their knees and smote their breasts.

"Dear daughters in Christ! Persevere in your holy horror for sacrilege!" the bishop cried to the three kneeling women. "You will enter paradise and will hear the seraphim play on the harp before the Lord, while they sing His praises!"

"My Vagres!" again Ronan called out. "A rope! Let the hypocritical babbler be strung up high and dry! It is evident that he has made up his mind to hang!"

With a gesture the hermit arrested the anger of the Vagres and said:

"Bishop, do you recognize the words of Jesus of Nazareth as divine? 'Him that taketh away thy cloak forbid not to take away thy coat also.' What thought did Jesus mean to convey by these words, but that only too often theft has want for its cause, and that charity should be exercised and pity had for such want. Relinquish voluntarily these superfluous goods, you who have taken the vow of poverty, charity and chastity!"

"Keep still, tempting hermit, who dare contradict our bishop! We may not lay our fingers on the goods of the Church!" cried one of the three kneeling women. "We would be damned for all time!"

"Yes, yes," shouted the other two. "Keep still, hermit!"

"Poor creatures! Steeped in ignorance and blindness!" exclaimed Ronan. "Do you care for the life of your bishop?"

"We would undergo a thousand deaths for his sake!"

"Oh! Pious women!" cried Cautin ecstatically. "What a superb part of paradise will not be yours! And now, until the day of eternal life come, I give you absolution for all your past sins, and all the future ones that you may commit."

"Oh, beloved bishop!" cried the kneeling mothers smiting their chests. "A saint among saints! Thanks—thanks to you!"

"Listen to me, ye poor sheep who mistake the butcher for the shepherd," said Ronan to them. "If you do not forthwith profit by our offer, we shall hang the bishop before your very eyes."

"Here is a rope," said Wolf's-Tooth, and he put the noose around Cautin's neck.

"Dear daughters, take everything!" cried the prelate acting under a new inspiration. "Your father in Christ requests you, adjures you, orders you to accept the booty—accept it quick!" he added as he felt the noose tighten.

One of the three kneeling women rose and obeyed with alacrity; the other two remained on their knees and said:

"You are only trying us, holy bishop!"

"But these heathens are going to hang me——"

"A holy man like you does not fear martyrdom."

"No, my daughters, I do not fear martyrdom—but I think I am indispensable for the salvation of my flock. I pray you, carry that booty away! If you do not, I shall damn you! I shall excommunicate you! Confounded old hags! Miserable wretches, you will have to answer for my death on the day of judgment!"

"Holy bishop, you seek to try us to the last. You just said to us that to touch the goods of the Church is mortal sin. Would you order us to commit a mortal sin?"

"No! No!" screamed the other of the two mothers who had remained on their knees; she smote her breast and added: "Holy man, you could never think of ordering us to commit mortal sin! You are to receive martyrdom!——"

"And from the heavens above you will throw your blessings upon us, great and good St. Cautin!"

"Bishop, do you hear these poor old women? You sowed, now you are harvesting. Come, my Vagres, draw the rope!"

Once more the hermit interposed in order to protect the prelate. At that moment the Vagres who were on the carts were heard crying:

"The leudes! The Frankish warriors!"

"There are seven of them! They are on horseback! They are leading a gang of chained men! Up, my Vagres! Death to the leudes! Freedom to the slaves!"

"Death to the leudes! Freedom to the slaves!" shouted the Vagres and ran to their arms.

"The Franks have come to capture me and take me back to the burg of the count!" cried little Odille. "Oh, Ronan, protect me!"

"There will not be one of them left alive to carry you back!"

"Ronan, no imprudence!" said the hermit. "These horsemen may be only a scouting party riding ahead of a numerous troop. Send out scouters against scouters; keep the bulk of your men in reserve and have them entrench themselves behind the wagons."

"Monk, you are right. You talk like an experienced soldier. You must have made war?"

"A little—occasionally—whenever it was necessary to protect the weak against the strong."

"Frankish warriors!" cried Cautin clasping his hands with a triumphant air. "Friends! Allies! I am saved! Help, dear brothers in Christ! This way, my beloved sons in God! Fall upon this rabble. Deliver me from the hands of the Philistines! This way, my—"

Giving a jerk to the rope around the neck of the holy man, Ronan suddenly checked his flow of speech by drawing the noose tight.

"Bishop, no useless cries!" said the hermit; "and you, Ronan, no violence; drop that rope!"

"Very well; but I shall bind his arms; and if he again breaks in upon my ears I shall run my sword through him—"

"The Frankish riders have reined in their horses the moment they caught sight of the wagons," cried one of the Vagres; "they seem to be deliberating what to do."

"Our deliberation will not be long. There are seven of the mounted Franks; let six Vagres follow me, and by the faith of Ronan, it will not be long before there will be seven conquerors less in Gaul!"

"Here are the six of us—let us forward!"

The Master of the Hounds was among the six Vagres. Seeing him examine the handle of his axe, the bishopess leaped down from her wagon, and, her eyes sparkling, her nostrils inflated and her cheeks on fire, she rolled up the right sleeve of her silk robe, and thus baring her white, beautiful and strong arm up to the shoulder, she cried:

"Give me a sword! A sword!"

"Here is one! What will you do with it, beautiful bishopess in Vagrery?"

"I shall fight beside my Vagre!" Saying this the bishopess seized the proffered weapon like a Gallic woman of ancient days, and dashed forward upon the foe.

"Little Odille, you wait here for me. When the Franks are slain I shall return to you," said Ronan to the young girl, who, pale with fear, sought to hold him back with both hands and rested upon him her beautiful blue eyes now moist with tears. "Do not tremble, poor child!"

"Ronan," she murmured convulsively seizing the arm of the Vagre, "I have neither father nor mother left; you delivered me from the count and the bishop; you have a good heart; you are full of pity for the poor; you have treated me with the tenderness of a brother; it was only last night that I saw you for the first time, and yet it seems to me that I have known you long, long—"

And the girl took both the Vagre's hands, kissed them, and added with tremulous lips:

"If those Franks should kill you!—"

"If they should kill me, little Odille?"

Saying this the Vagre turned his head towards the hermit, and pointing to him with his eyes added:

"Should the Franks kill me, yonder good hermit-laborer will protect you."

"I promise you, my child, should misfortune befall your friend, I shall protect you."

"Little Odille," Ronan now said with almost embarrassed mien, "one kiss on your forehead—it will be first, and may be the last."

The child was weeping silently; she reached her girlish forehead to Ronan; he touched it with his lips, and raising his sword dashed off on a run. Hardly had Ronan left when the cry of the Vagres was heard attacking the leudes. At the cries, Odille threw herself distracted into the arms of the hermit, hid her face on his breast and sobbed aloud:

"They will kill him! They will kill him!"

"Courage, Franks! Courage, my sons in God!" shouted Cautin from the cart-wheel to which he was bound fast. "Exterminate those Moabites! Above all cut to pieces that she-devil wife of mine, that brazen woman with the orange dress with the blue sash and silver embroidered stockings. No mercy for the Jezebel! the shameless wench! the slattern! Hack her to pieces!—"

"Bishop! Bishop! Your words are inhuman. Remember the mercifulness of Jesus towards Magdalen and the adulteress!" exclaimed the hermit, while Odille, with her head resting on the breast of that true disciple of the young man of Nazareth murmured:

"They will kill Ronan! They will kill him!"

"Here I am back to you, little Odille! The Franks did not kill me. The people whom they brought in chains are all set free!"

Who said this? It was Ronan. What? Back so soon? Yes! The Vagres do their work quickly. With one bound Odille was in the arms of her friend.

"I killed one of them—he was just about to run my Vagre through with his sword!" cried the bishopess returning from the encounter. And throwing down her blood-stained sword, her eyes sparkling, her bosom half covered by her long black tresses that, together with her robe, were thrown into disorder by the heat of the combat, she said to the Master of the Hounds: "Are you satisfied with your wife?"

"Strong in the embrace of love, and strong in battle are your arms!" answered the young man delighted. "And now, a full cup of wine!"

"To drink in my very face wine that was mine! To court and caress before my own eyes that impure woman who was my wife!" murmured the bishop. "Oh, monstrous! These are the signs that foretell frightful calamities about to afflict the earth."

Three of the Vagres were wounded. The hermit attended them with so much skill that he might have been taken for a physician. He was about to proceed to another of the wounded men when his eyes fell upon the people whom the leudes had brought with them and who were now set free by the men of Ronan. These unhappy folks who only a few minutes before were prisoners, were covered with rags; nevertheless the joy of deliverance shone upon their faces. Invited by their liberators to eat and drink-in order to recruit their strength, they were eagerly acquitting themselves of their task. While they drained the pouches of wine and caused the loaves of bread and the hams to vanish, the monk said to one of them, a robust man despite his grey hair:

"Brother, who are you? Whence do you come?"

"We are colonists and slaves. We formerly owned and cultivated the parcels of land that the son of Clovis newly joined as benefices to the salic and military domains that the Frankish count Neroweg previously held from his father by the right of conquest."

"Did the count, accordingly, strip you of your fields and houses?"

"Would to heaven, dear hermit, that he had done so!"

"Your answer is strange!"

"The count, on the contrary, left the fields to us, and he even added two hundred acres to them, the accursed man! The two hundred acres belonged to my friend and neighbor Fereol, who fled out of fear for the Franks."

"Your property is doubled, friend, and yet you complain!"

"Indeed I complain! Is it that you do not know what is going on in Gaul? This is what the count said to me: 'My glorious King has made me count of this country, and, besides,

he has given me as a benefice, which I hope will become hereditary as my military lands, all these domains, including the cattle, houses and people upon them. You will cultivate for me
the fields that belong to you; I shall join several new parcels
to them; you will be my colonist and your laborers my slaves;
all of you will work for me and my leudes; you will furnish
them as well as myself with all that we shall need. You shall
help my mason and carpenter slaves in the building of a new
burg that I shall have erected after the Germanic fashion. It
is to be large, commodious and properly fortified, and it is to
be located in the center of an old Roman camp that I discovered nearby. Your horses and cattle having become mine will
haul the stones and logs of wood that are too heavy for men to
carry. Besides that you shall pay me a hundred gold sous annually, ten of which I shall give to the King when I annually
render him homage for the lands that I hold.' 'A hundred gold
sous!' I cried. 'My lands, jointly with those of my neighbor
Fereol, will not yield such a sum year in and year out! How
do you expect me to pay you a hundred gold sous, besides feed-
ing you, your leudes and your retinues, and keeping myself, my
family and my laborers, now your slaves, alive?' Threatening
me with his club, the count answered me saying: 'I shall have
my hundred gold sous every year—if you fail, I shall have my
leudes cut off your feet and hands—' "

"Poor man!" observed the hermit sadly. "And like so many
others you consented to the servitude? You accepted the hard
conditions?"

"What else was I to do? How could I resist the count and
his leudes? I only had a few laborers, and to them the priests
preached submission to the conquerors, who, sword in hand,
say to us: 'The fields of your fathers, fructified by their labors
and yours, are now ours—you shall cultivate them for us.' What
were we to do? Resist? It was impossible! Flee? That would
be to rush into slavery in some other region, seeing that all the

provinces are equally invaded by the Franks. I had a young wife—both servitude and a wandering life frightened me more for her sake than for mine—moreover, I was attached to the region and the fields on which I was born. The thought was unbearable to me of having to cultivate those very fields for another, and yet I preferred not to leave them. Myself and my laborers resigned ourselves to shocking misery, to incessant toil! Such was the life we led for many a year. By dint of hard work and privations I succeeded in supplying the wants of Neroweg and his leudes, and of making my lands yield from seventy to eighty gold sous a year. Twice did the count put me to the torture in order to force me to give him the hundred gold sous that he demanded of me. I did not own one denier outside of the moneys that I paid him. My torture and subsequent long physical pain was all the comfort that he had for his cruelty."

"And did the thought never occur to you," asked Ronan, "of choosing some fine dark night to set the burg on fire?"

"Alas! The priests persuade the slaves that the harder their lot is on earth, all the happier will they be in paradise. I could not rely upon my companions in slavery, besotted as they were with the fear of the devil and unnerved by misery. Besides, I had little children; and their mother, consumed with grief, was ailing; finally, this year, the poor creature fortunately died. My sons had grown up to be men, and they and I, together with a few other slaves who were all tired of unrequited and continuous toil for the benefit of the count and his leudes, finally took to flight. We took refuge on the domain of the Bishop of Issoire. It was but an exchange of masters, still we hoped to find the prelate a less cruel master than the count. The count was set upon recapturing me who had managed for so many years to extract from my lands so much wealth for him and his leudes. Having learned of our asylum, he ordered some of his leudes to take horse and reclaim us from the Bishop of Issoire. The bishop surrendered us. His men bound our hands, and the leudes were taking us back to the count when these good Vagres killed our captors and set us free. By my faith! Vagres we shall now be—all of us—I, my sons and the other slaves whom you see yonder. Will you have us, ye bold runners of the night?"

"Yes, yes!" cried the companions of the colonist. "It is better far to run the Vagrery than to cultivate our fathers' lands under the club of a count and his leudes!"

"Bishop! Bishop!" remarked Ronan to the prelate. "Behold what your allies have turned our old Gaul into! But, I swear by torch and fire, by blood and massacre, I swear, the hour shall come when neither prelates nor seigneurs will have aught but smoldering ruins and bleaching bones to rule over! Up! new brothers in Vagrery! Be like ourselves 'Wand'ring men,' 'Wolves,' 'Wolves-Heads!' Like ourselves you will live like wolves and happy—in summer under the leafy green, in winter in caverns warm. Up, my Vagres! Up! The sun is high! We have in these carts still much booty left to be distributed on our way. Let us proceed, little Odille and beautiful bishopess! Let us pillage the seigneurs, and give freely to the poor! Let us keep only just enough to feast upon to-night in the fastness of Allange under the dome of the stately old oak trees. On the march! And to-morrow, when the last pouch will have been emptied, then on the hunt again, my Vagres, so long as there shall be a single burg left standing in Gaul, or a single epis-copal residence! Let us burn down all the dens of tyranny! Death to the seigneurs and their bishops!"

And the troop resumed its march to the sound of the Vagres' song. When, at sunset, they arrived at the fastness of Allange, which was one of their haunts, all the booty that was taken at the episcopal villa had been distributed along the route among the poor. Only a few mattresses for the women, the gold and silver goblets out of which to drink the bishop's wine, and the neces-sary provisions for the night's festival were left. The eight teams of oxen were to furnish the roast for the gigantic feast, because gigantic it was to be seeing that the troop of Vagres had gathered many recruits on the route—slaves, artisans, laborers and colonists, all of whom were enraged with misery, without counting a number of young women, all of whom were eager to run the Vagrery.

CHAPTER VII.

VAGRES AT FEAST.

What delightful feasts are those held in Vagrery! Does, stags, wild-boars, killed by the Vagres the day before in the thickets of the forest that shade the fastness of Allange—all, together with the oxen from the wagons, have been dispatched and grilled over a roaring oven. What! An oven in a forest? An oven large enough to embrace oxen, does, stags and wild-boars? Yes; the good God has dug for the good Vagres a number of large pits in the secluded fastnesses of Allange. They are spacious craters, now extinct like other volcanic apertures in Auvergne. Is not one of these deep semi-circular grottoes, in which a man can stand upright, a veritable bake-house? Fill up the grotto with dry wood; one or two dead oaks will suffice; set the pyre on fire; it burns up high and becomes a brasier: the bottom, the walls, the lava vault—all are soon red hot, and into the chasm, ablaze like the mouth of hell, stags, does, whole wild-boars and oxen are rolled in to broil. That done, the opening of the grotto is closed with lava rocks, a huge oven of glowing embers. Four or five hours later, oxen and game, grilled to the point, are served steaming and toothsome upon the table. What! Tables also in Vagrery! Certes, and covered with the finest of green carpet. What table? What carpet? The lawn of a forest clearing. And for seats? Again that lawn. For tent the lofty oaks; for ornaments the arms suspended from the branches. For dome the starry sky. For chandelier the moon at her fullest. For perfumery the night odor of wild flowers. For musicians the nightingales and all the other songsters of the woods.

Several Vagres, placed on watch at the outskirt of the forest and near the approaches of the fastnesses of Allange, guarded the troop against a surprise in case that, the sack and burning of the villa becoming known, the Frankish counts and dukes of the region should fear an attack upon their own burgs, and start with their leudes in the pursuit of the Vagres.

Despite his ire, Bishop Cautin excelled himself as a cook. Long before had a certain sauce known to be a favorite with the bishop been the subject of talk in Vagrery. The holy man was ordered to produce it. He did. He filled with it a large caldron into which each one dipped his roast, whether of game or beef—it was a toothsome sauce, made of old wine and oil, aromated with wild thyme. It was pronounced delectable. Biting into her Vagre's roast with her white teeth the bishopess remarked:

"I now no longer wonder that he who was my husband always showed himself so implacable towards his kitchen slaves, and that he had them whipped for their slightest negligence— the seigneur bishop was a better cook than any of them. No wonder he was hard to please!"

Only two of the guests did not join in the spirit of the feast —the hermit-laborer and the young female slave who sat near Ronan. As to Ronan, he did ample justice to the repast; but the monk seemed to be absorbed in contemplation as he looked up at the starry vault overhead, and little Odille also dreamed—

as she contemplated Ronan. The gold and silver vases, whatever their previous destination, circulated from hand to hand; the wine pouches collapsed in even measure as the stomachs of the drinkers became inflated; merry jokes, loud outbursts of laughter, kisses stolen and given from and by Vagres and Vagresses;—it was a mirthful and giddy festivity. Ever and anon, nevertheless, and generally on the subject of some pretty face, a dispute would break out between two Vagres, just as used to happen during the ancient banquets of the Gauls. Then swords would be taken down from the trees and crossed by the combatants, but never in hatred, ever in the exuberance of spirit:

"That thrust is for you—mine shall the pretty girl be!"

"And this other thrust is for you—the damsel shall be mine!"

"Hit! That is for her roguish eyes!"

"Parried! Mine remains the daisy!"

"I'm wounded! Help, my belle!"

"I die! Good bye to my love!"

The wounded Vagre was attended to; the dead one was covered with leaves. Honor to the brave who will be born anew in yonder worlds, and long live the feasts of the Vagrery! And the exchange of repartees continued—some were mirthful, others strange, and not a few sad. The repartees reflected the state of affairs in Gaul, her people, and the miseries of the nation as she lay debased and demoralized at the feet of the conquerors; the repartees produced a picture better than chroniclers or historians could ever reproduce it, even if ever this country of iron should find its historian.

"Ah! What happy days these are!" exclaimed Wolf's-Tooth as he gnawed on the ivory of his second shoulder of doe. "Ah! what jolly days do we owe to these times of disorder, of pillage, of combats on the highways, of sieges of burgs and episcopal villas and of their smoldering embers that we leave behind! Ah!

What rollicking times do not these Frankish Kings furnish us with !"

"Ronan said it—old Gaul is on fire—let us dance and drink upon the ruins—let us make love on the ashes of the palaces and upon the extinguished coals of the episcopal villas that we turned into bonfires !"

"Oh, great bishop ! Oh, great St. Remi ! Blessings upon you, who, at the basilica of Reims, in the midst of incense and flowers, now over fifty years ago baptized Clovis as a submissive son of the Roman Church ! Blessings upon you, St. Remi, the patron of highwaymen and bandits !"

"Where is she ? Aye, where is she, the proud and powerful Gaul of the days of the Chief of the Hundred Valleys, of the Sacrovirs, the Vindexes, the Civiles, the Victorias ?"

"Who is the present inheritor of Gaul's one-time valor ? The Vagres, the 'Wolves-Heads,' the 'Wolves !' It is they alone who still carry on the struggle against the barbarians !"

"And yet we are hunted like wild beasts, put to the rack and hanged if taken !"

"But our nails are sharp and our teeth trenchant to tear to pieces and devour our enemies !"

"And yet they call us robbers !"

"And murderers !"

"And sacrilegious wretches !"

"Brothers, we but follow the example of our glorious new masters—the Frankish kings, dukes and counts; they kill, we massacre; they pillage, we steal; they lay waste, we burn down. Death to the seigniory !"

"Sad are the times in which we live !" said the bishopess as she unloosened her long black tresses to the wind. "These are days of sanguinary fury ! days of unbridled debauchery ! days of vertigo, in which one rushes into evil paths with wild ecstasy. Oh, holy virtue of our mothers ! tender chastity ! noble and undefiled love ! Where shall we look for you in these days ?

Shall we look for you in the hut of the female slave whom her masters outrage? Shall we look for you in the house of the free woman, whose very hearth is turned under her own eyes into a brothel? Oh! Let us shut our eyes, and die young! Will you die, my Vagre? To-morrow, at the first rays of the sun; to-morrow, at the hour when the birds awake; to-morrow put your hand in mine, and let us depart together for those unknown worlds, whither our ancestors bravely and willingly took their departure in order to live together!"

"Let love reign until to-morrow! And until then, a sweet kiss, my Vagress!"

The Master of the Hounds received the kiss, while his neighbor, grave like a man half-seas over, said in a magisterial voice:

"Brothers, I have an idea—"

"Your idea, Symphorien, seems to be to drain that amphora to the very bottom."

"Yes, to begin with—and then to prove to you—*logice* and *a priori*—"

"To the devil with your Roman tongue!"

"Brothers, not because one is a Vagre does it follow that he can not be versed in letters and philosophy. I used to teach rhetoric to the young clerks of the Bishop of Limoges. I received a call from the Bishop of Tulle for the same office. As I was crossing the Jargeaux mountains on the way from the one town to the other, I was captured in the woods by a band of bad Vagres—there are good and bad Vagres. And those Vagres sold me to a slave merchant, and he sold me again to the bishop of—"

"The devil take this rhetorician! Look at him traveling up hills and down dales."

"Such is frequently the effect of rhetoric. It carries one across the plains of imagination. But let me return to what I wanted to prove to you *logice*—it is this: We need not worry ourselves over the leudes nor any other armed bands that might be in pursuit of us, because, *logice*—the Lord God will perform a miracle in our favor to disengage us of our enemies."

"A miracle in favor of us, Vagres? Are we, perchance, on such good terms with heaven?"

"We are on all the better terms with heaven for living like wolves, like true wolves. Therefore, *logice,* the Lord will deliver us from our enemies by miracles. And that I shall now proceed to prove to you."

"To the proof, learned Symphorien—to the proof! We are waiting for your arguments."

CHAPTER VIII.

THE MIRACLE OF ST. MARTIN.

The rhetorician straightened himself up and proceeded to the proof.

"I'm at it," he said. "But first of all, brothers, answer me this question: Under whose royal claws did this beautiful land of Auvergne fall?"

"Under the claws of Clotaire, the last and worthy son of King Clovis. Having married the widow of his second nephew Theobald, Clotaire now owns Auvergne by double right. He is now in this year 558 the sole king of all conquered Gaul. Glory to the Saints in heaven! Now, then, that Clotaire is the wedder of the whole human race. The bishops have married him as many times as it has pleased him to celebrate fresh weddings; they remarried him even during the lives of most of his wives. They married him to Gundiogue, the wife of his own brother; they married him to Radegonde, to Ingonde and, a fortnight later to the latter's sister, called Aregonde; they married him to Chemesne, to several others, and finally to Waltrade, the widow of his second nephew Theobald. But all these are only peccadillos—"

"Learned, very learned Symphorien, you promised to prove to us *logice* that heaven would rain miracles in our favor; but your rhetoric tends to prove just one thing—that Clotaire is an eternal wedder—"

"My rhetoric first establishes the premises, you will presently see what conclusions flow from them—*ergo,* I shall establish one more prefigurement, which I shall also need for my argument. It is this: Among other crimes, this Clotaire committed one before which even Clovis might have recoiled. The affair happened in Paris in the year 533, in the old Roman palace inhabited by the Frankish kings. Now listen—"

"We are listening, learned Symphorien. It is pleasant to the ear to hear the praises of kings."

"Accordingly, it was about twenty-five years ago. Clovis had long before gone to paradise upon the recommendation of the bishops and after having partitioned Gaul between his four sons—Thierri, Childebert, Clodomir and this Clotaire, who is to-day the sole king of all these conquered provinces. Clodomir died shortly after and left two children. These were taken in charge by their grandmother, the widow of Clovis, old Queen Clotilde. She had her two little grandsons brought up beside her, until they should be of age to assure the inheritance of their father's kingdom. One day, when she was in Paris, Childebert, who lived in that city, sent secretly one of his confidential servants to the kind-hearted Clotaire with the message: 'Our mother Clotilde keeps the children of our brother near her, and she wishes them to enter into possession of his kingdom; come quickly to Paris in order that we may consider what is to be done with them, whether we shall have their hair cut short like the rest of the people, and have them locked up in a monastery, or whether we shall kill them and thus share among ourselves the kingdom of their father, our brother'—"

"The story begins to be affectionate."

"It is the fraternity in vogue among the Franks."

"What Vagre would ever think of killing his own brother's children in order to seize their property?"

"None! None would think of such a thing."

"We are wolves, and wolves do not devour one another—my brothers—"

"And were those children whom they sought to slay still young, learned Symphorien?"

"One was ten, the other seven—"

"Poor little creatures—"

"I pursue my narrative. Clotaire arrived in Paris, deliberated with his brother, and the two acting in concert visited old Queen Clotilde and said to her: 'Send us your grandchildren that we may embrace them, and forthwith announce them to the people as the heirs of their father's kingdom.' "

"Oh! These Frankish kings are ever as wily as they are bloodthirsty! It was a lure, was it not, learned Symphorien?"

"You will soon see what their project was. Clovis' widow was happy, and sent the little children to their uncles, saying to the little ones: 'I shall forget that I lost your father when I see you succeed him in his kingdom.' The moment the children arrived at their uncles' they were separated from their slaves and governors, and kept in close confinement. Clotaire and Childebert then sent an emissary to the children's grandmother. In one hand he carried a pair of shears, in the other a naked sword. He said to old Queen Clotilde: 'Glorious Queen, our lords, your sons, desire to know your preference with regard to your grandsons—do you wish them to be shorn, that is, locked up in a convent, or would you prefer to have them slain?' 'If they are to renounce their father's throne,' cried the old Queen indignant, 'I would prefer to see them dead rather than shorn.' The emissary returned and said to the two kings: 'You have the Queen's wishes to finish the work that you began.' Immediately thereupon King Clotaire takes the eldest by the arm, throws him on the ground, and plunges his knife under the boy's arm-pit."

"Poor, dear little one!" murmured Odille weeping. "He must have died calling to his mother for help—"

"The royal butcher knew the right spot to plunge his knife in the child's body," observed Ronan; "that is the proper way to kill lambkins. Proceed, learned Symphorien."

"At the cries of the child, his younger brother rushes in and throws himself at Childebert's feet, and clinging to his legs with all his strength, cries out to him: 'Uncle! Good uncle!

Come to my help! Do not let me be killed like my brother!' "

"Touched to the heart for an instant, Childebert says to Clotaire: 'Grant me the life of this child.' But Clotaire answers enraged: 'Either push the child off your knees, or you will die in his stead! It is you who led me into this affair, and now your heart seems to fail you!' "

"The good Clotaire was right," put in Ronan. "First to scheme the assassination of the children, and then to recoil before the deed was to insult the stock of the glorious King Clovis. But Childebert thought better, in honor of his royal family, did he not, learned Symphorien?"

"What else could he? Childebert pushed the child off from his knees 'and threw him towards Clotaire, who plunged his knife under the boy's arm-pit as he had done with the other, and killed him. The two kings forthwith put all the slaves and governors of the two children to death, and divided their kingdom among them."

"That is the manner in which monarchies are founded," observed Ronan. "Oh, by Rita-Gaur, the inspired Gaul of olden days who had a blouse woven of the beard of the kings! All these monsters deserve to be exterminated, do you not think so, friend?" he added, addressing the hermit laborer, who had silently listened to the narrative. "Is it not the duty of all sons of Gaul to take the field in permanence against these wild beasts who have invaded our country, reduced us to vile slavery?"

"It is better to prevent the evil than to kill the criminal," answered the hermit.

"Hermit, could you prevent a Frankish king from being born a rapacious thief?"

"He must be prevented from being born king, duke, count or seigneur, and taught that he is not the master of the life and goods of other human beings. Jesus of Nazareth said it: we are all equal. From the equality of men their fraternity will one day be born. To each his part in the common heritage.

Propagate that doctrine among your brothers, and the end will be reached without the spilling of blood."

Saying this the hermit-laborer relapsed into his previous silent revery.

"Twice have I camped on the trail of that last king of Auvergne—king by the grace of pillage and massacre," said Ronan, "and both times I failed to catch him. But, by Rita-Gaur, if ever Clotaire falls into my hands, I shall shave him—and so close to his shoulders that his head will never more grow again—"

"Ronan, you reckon without the demonstration of rhetoric. I have established the premises, let us now draw the conclusions. Therefore, *logice,* I shall prove to you that naught will avail you against Clotaire. The Lord protects him. Yes, the Lord has performed a miracle in favor of Clotaire, the butcher of children. Consequently, I was right when I said that I shall prove *logice* that the Lord will surely perform some miracle in our own favor, in favor of the good Vagres—"

"We were decidedly wrong in not hanging the bishop!"

"It will always be time to draw the Lord's attention upon us by some such pious deed. But tell us the miracle, learned Symphorien."

"It was in the year 537, about four years after Childebert and Clotaire stabbed their little nephews to death. Our two worthy sons of the stock of Clovis had no thought but of how to plunder and despatch each other. Accordingly, although united for a moment like loving brothers in the assassination of the two boys, Clotaire and Childebert declared war against each other. Theudebert, one of Clovis' grandchildren, joined Childebert; the two placed themselves at the head of their eudes, and, as was their wont, pillaged and laid waste the countries that they crossed, and marched against Clotaire. The good uncle did not consider his own forces strong enough to make head against the joint troops of his brother and his nephew; he declined battle and withdrew to the forest of Brotonne, between

Rouen and the sea. Theudebert and Childebert girdled the forest, and quietly awaited the night, confident of catching the beloved brother and uncle in the net. In pursuit of their plan, Childebert and Theudebert advanced noiselessly at the head of their troops. The sun was rising. They had arrived to within two or three hundred paces from the spot where Clotaire was encamped with his leudes, when suddenly a frightful hailstorm of stones and fire dropped down from the sky. The troops of Childebert and Theudebert were crushed by the stones and consumed by the heavenly fire."

"And what became of Clotaire?"

"Oh! Clotaire, the favorite of the Lord, as the miracle proved, saw the troops of his brother and nephew annihilated only a few paces from him by the stones and fire that rained down from the sky, while over his own head, the sky, as pure, limpid and serene as his own conscience, was of a smiling blue. Not even a breath of wind agitated the tops of the trees in the forest, while all around there was a cataract of fire. And thereupon a further shower of stones dropped down from the bosom of the clouds, and buried all the enemies of Clotaire."

Symphorien stopped for a moment to contemplate the effect of the miracle on his audience and then proceeded:

"And above all, you must not fail to observe that the account of the miracle expressly states that it was the great St. Martin himself, who, in paradise, prayed to the Lord that he give such a token of friendship for Clotaire. Now, then, St. Martin did not intercede with the Lord on behalf of the felonious Clotaire, but at the fervent prayer of Queen Clotilde."

"What! The grandmother of the two poor little victims of that monster of a Clotaire?" exclaimed little Odille clasping her hands. "She prayed for a miracle in favor of the murderer of her two grandsons?"

"My Vagre," put in at this juncture the bishopess passing her slender fingers through the waivy hair of the young man,

and placing her lips upon her lover's mouth, "is it not better
to proceed to yonder worlds than to remain and live in this
world of horrors?"

"Aye, horrible—horrible is this world," cried the hermit-
laborer with profound grief and indignation. "Oh! To see
the name of that God of mercy, of love and of justice thus pro-
faned and daily soiled! Oh! To see these crimes, that cause
nature to shudder, placed under divine protection! Oh, Jesus!
Jesus of Nazareth! You the divinest of all sages, you did foresee that your Church would be ill-understood, when, with your
spirit, afflicted unto death, you did, in your last and supreme
watch, weep over the approaching future of the world! Jesus!
Jesus! Centuries must elapse before your day shall arrive!"

"Be careful, friend!" said Ronan, "speak not so loud. Yonder holy man of a bishop, who sleeps not far from you, gorged
with wine and meat, might excommunicate you if he heard
you! But to the devil with sadness! We live in damnable
days—let us live like the damned! Up, my Vagres, up! You
are thrice holy! Let our Saturnalia cover all Gaul—let this
land of our fathers be the grave of the Franks, even if it has
to be the grave of ourselves. The ruins of our deserted cities
will tell future centuries: 'Here lies a great people! Free, it
was the pride of the world; enslaved by conquering kings, it
one day knew how to vanish from the world as it dragged its
tyrants with it into the abyss!' So, then, let us die rejoicing.
Up, my Vagres and Vagresses—let us dance and make love
until dawn! Let the Franks tremble in their burgs at our
daring songs! Let bishops flee for refuge in their basilicas!
Let them all whisper affrighted to one another: 'Woe is us!
Woe is us to-morrow! They are feeling very happy to-night in
Vagrery!'"

And the Vagres and Vagresses screamed, and sang, and
shouted. Wildly they tumbled about, and started a giddy reel
upon the sward by the pale illumination of the moon.

CHAPTER IX.

LOYSIK AND RONAN.

Wrapped in silence the hermit-laborer had listened to the conversation of the Vagres. Seated beside little Odille, he seemed to shield her with a paternal protection. The child seemed a stranger to what happened around her. When at the close of the repast Ronan gave his companions the signal for the songs and dance, they ran away tumultuously from the place of the recent banquet to give a loose to their bacchic gayety and indulge in a giddy dance on the sward of another and nearby clearing.

Approaching the hermit-laborer and the little girl, both of whom had kept their places as they gazed up at the sky, Ronan said to her in a merry voice:

"Will you dance, little Odille? The reel is started; it will last until dawn."

The young girl shook her head melancholically, made no answer, and continued to gaze at the sky.

"Odille, what is it you are dreaming about as you gaze at the moon? Whither do your thoughts fly, my child?"

"Sleep is overpowering me, and my thoughts are running over an old druid chant that my mother used to sing to me, to rock me asleep when I was little."

"What chant was that?"

"Oh! It is old, very, very old—my mother used to tell me. It has been sung in Gaul for over five or six hundred years."

"And what is its name?"

"The chant of Hena, the Virgin of the Isle of Sen."

"The chant of Hena!" cried the Vagre and the hermit simultaneously with a tremor of delight.

Both grew immediately silent, while Odille, astonished at their visible emotion, looked from the one to the other, and asked:

"You also seem to know the chant of Hena?"

"Sing it, my child," answered Ronan in a tremulous voice.

More and more astonished, little Odille was hardly able to recognize her friend. The dare-devil and merry Vagre had become pensive and grave.

"Yes, yes, my child! Recite that chant to us with your sweet voice of fifteen years," put in the hermit. "But not here —the dance and yonder wild carousal, although far enough away, would drown your voice—"

"The hermit is right. Come with us, little Odille, to yonder large oak. It will be far enough away from the dancers. It is surrounded by a soft moss carpet. You will be able to sleep there. I shall cover you up with my cloak to protect you from the damp."

From the foot of the oak tree where the girl took her seat between Ronan and the hermit, only the dim noise was heard of the giddy dance and songs of Ronan's companions, the Vagres and Vagresses. The moon, now on her decline, shed her silvery rays under the somber verdure of the leaves and lighted the hermit, Ronan and the young slave as if the sun shone through the trees. The child-like voice of Odille was soon heard striking up the first couplet of the chant:

"She was young, she was fair, and holy was she; Hena her name, Hena the maid of the Island of Sen."

At these words both the hermit and the Vagre lowered their heads, and without noticing the tears that the other was shedding, both wept. Odille sang the second couplet, but broken with the fatigue of the last twenty-four hours, and yielding to the influence of the chant's melancholy rhythm, that so often had lulled and rocked her to sleep on her mother's knees, the little slave's voice became fainter and fainter, while, at the distance the Vagres suddenly struck up in chorus and with resonant voices the refrain of another ancient chant of Gaul. These latter accents sent a new thrill through the frames of Ronan and the hermit. Without wholly drowning Odille's voice, the words reached their ears:

"Flow, flow, thou blood of the captive! Drop, drop, thou dew of gore! Germinate, sprout up, thou avenging harvest!"

The two men seemed struck with the singular coincidence: at a distance, the chant of revolt, of war and blood; close to them, the girl's angelic voice, singing the praises of Hena, one of the sweetest glories of Armorican Gaul. Presently, however, as Odille yielded more and more to the gentle pressure of slumber, her voice was heard ever fainter until from a murmur, it became hardly audible. The girl's head drooped on her breast, and with her back sustained by the trunk of the tree she fell into profound sleep.

"Poor child!" said Ronan as he covered her with his cloak. "She is overcome with fatigue. May her sleep give her rest and strength!"

"Ronan," observed the hermit fastening a penetrating look upon the Vagre, "the chant of Hena made you weep—"

"It is true, good hermit."

"What is the reason of such emotion?"

"A family remembrance—if a Vagre, a 'Wand'ring Man,' a 'Wolf,' a 'Wolf's Head' can be at all said to have a family—"

"And what is that family remembrance?"

"The sweet Hena, to whom the chant refers, was one of my ancestresses."

"How do you know that?"

"My father often told me so; in my childhood he used to relate to me the histories of olden days, of centuries ago."

"Where is your father now?"

"I do not know. He used to run the Bagaudy, perhaps he now runs the Vagrery, unless he has died the brave death of a brave man. I do not expect to be enlightened upon that until he and I meet again elsewhere—"

"Where?"

"In those mysterious worlds that none knows and that we shall all know—seeing that we shall all continue to live there—"

"You have, then, preserved the faith of our ancestors?"

"My father taught me that to die was to change vestments, because we leave this world to be re-born in yonder ones. Death is but a transformation."

"Is it long since you were separated from your father?"

"Let us drop that subject—it is a sad one. I prefer to keep up a cheerful mood. And yet, I feel drawn towards you, although you are not cheerful—"

"We live in days when, in order to be cheerful, one's soul must be either very weak or very strong."

"Do you think me weak?"

"I think you are both strong and weak. But as to your father—what has become of him?"

"Well, my father was a Bagauder in his youth; later, after the Franks christened us 'Vagres,' he became a Vagre. The name was changed, the pursuit remained the same."

"And your mother?"

"In Vagrery one knows but little of his mother. I never knew mine. The furthest back that I can carry my memory, I must have been seven or eight years old. I then accompanied my father in his raids, now in Provence, and now here in Auvergne. If I was tired of foot, either my father or one of his companions carried me on his back. It is thus that I grew up. We often had days of enforced rest. Sometimes the Frankish counts were so exasperated at us that they gathered their leudes and hunted us. Informed of their movements by the poor folks of the fields who loved us dearly, we would then retire to our inaccessible fastnesses, and there lie low for several days while the Franks beat the field without encountering even the shadow of a Vagre. At such intervals of rest in the seclusion of some solitary retreat, my father used to narrate to me, as I told you, the histories of olden days. Thus I learned that our family originated in Britanny, where the main stock lived and perhaps still lives to this very hour, free and in peace, seeing that the Franks have never yet been able to place their yoke upon that rugged province—its granite rocks are too hard, and its Bretons are like the granite of its rocks."

"I know the saying: 'He is intractable as an Armorican.'"

"My father often used the saying."

"But what induced him to leave that peaceful province, that still enjoys the boon of freedom, thanks to the indomitable bravery that continues to uphold the druid faith, which the evangelical morality of the young master of Nazareth has regenerated?"

"My father was about seventeen years of age when one day his family extended hospitality to a peddler during a stormy night. The peddler's trade took him all over Gaul; he knew and he told them of the country's trials; he also spoke of the life of adventure led by the Bagauders. My father was tired of the life of the fields; his heart was warm, and from his cradle he had drunk in the hatred for the Franks. Struck by the peddler's account, he considered the opportunity good for waging war upon the barbarians by joining the Bagauders. He left the paternal roof and joined the peddler by appointment about a league away. After a few days' march the two reached Anjou and met a troop of Bagauders. Young, robust and daring, my father was an acceptable recruit. He joined the band, and—long live the Bagaudy! Raiding from province to province, he came as far as Auvergne, which he never left. The country was favorable for his pursuit—forests, mountains, rocks, caverns, torrents, extinct volcanos! It is the paradise of the Bagaudy, the promised land of the Vagrery!"

"How came you to be separated from your father?"

"It was about three years ago—agents of the king, they were called *antrustions,* collected the revenues of the royal domain. They were numerous, well armed, and traveled only by day. We were waiting for the end of their reaping to gather in our harvest. One night they halted at Sifour, a little unprotected village. The opportunity tempted my father. We sallied forth believing that we would take the Franks by surprise. They were on their guard. After a bloody encounter we had to flee before the Frankish lances that followed us in hot pursuit. I was separated from my father during that midnight affray. Was he killed or was he merely wounded and taken prisoner I do not know. All my efforts to ascertain his fate have been vain. Since then my companions elected me their chief. You wanted to know my history—I have told it to you. You now know it."

"You have told me more than you think for. Your father's name was Karadeucq."

"How do you know that?"

"The name of your father's father was Jocelyn. If he still lives in Britanny with his elder son Kervan and his daughter Roselyk, he must be inhabiting a house near the sacred stones of Karnak—"

"Who told you—"

"One of your ancestors was named Joel; he was the brenn of the tribe of Karnak. Hena, the saint sung about in the druid chant, was the daughter of Joel, whose family traces its origin back to the Gallic brenn, whom the Romans called Brennus, and who, nearly eight hundred years ago, made them pay ransom for Rome."

"Who are you that you know the history of my family so accurately?"

"That chant of the slaves in revolt against the Romans—

'Flow, flow, thou blood of the captive! Drop, drop, thou dew of gore!'—was sung by one of your ancestors named Sylvest, who was cast to the wild beasts in the circus of Orange. And I imagine that your father taught you another thrilling chant, one sung two hundred and odd years ago, on the occasion of one of the great battles fought on the Rhine against the Franks, and won by Victorin, the son of Victoria, the Mother of the Camps—"

"You are right—often did my father sing that chant to me. It began this wise:

" 'This morning we said: How many are there of these barbarous hordes? How many are there of these Franks?' "

"And it closed this wise," replied the monk:

" 'This evening we say: How many were there of these barbarous hordes? This evening we say: How many were there of these Franks?' "

"Schanvoch, another of your ancestors, a brave soldier and foster-brother of Victoria the Great, sang that song—"

"Yes, Gaul, on that day proud, free and triumphant, had just driven the barbarians from both banks of the Rhine, while, to-day—but let us drop that topic, monk; if those days were glorious, the present ones seem to me all the more horrible. Oh! blameworthy was the credulity of our fathers, martyrs to this new religion—"

"Our fathers could not choose but place faith in the words of the first apostles, who preached to them love for their fellow men, the pardon of sins, the deliverance of the slaves, in the name of the young master of Nazareth, whom your ancestress Genevieve saw crucified in Jerusalem—"

"My ancestress Genevieve? You seem to be informed on every particular detail concerning my family. Only my father could have instructed you on such matters—you must have known him! Answer me!"

"Yes, I knew your father. Did you never notice, after you

entered the heart of Auvergne, that from time to time your
father absented himself for several days?"

"Yes, he did—I never knew the reason."

"Your father, each such time, went to visit a poor female
slave near Tulle. She was bound to the glebe of the bishop of
that city. That female slave, it is now at least thirty years ago,
one day found your father Karadeucq, who was then the chief
of the Bagauders, wounded and in a dying condition in a hedge
along the road. She took pity upon him; she helped him to
drag himself to the hut which she inhabited with her mother.
Your father was then about twenty years of age—the young
female slave was of about the age of that child who is asleep
near us. The two loved each other. Shortly after he was well
again, your father was one day discovered in the slave's hut by
the bishop's superintendent. The man considered Karadeucq a
good prize and sought to take him as a slave to Tulle. Your
father resisted, beat the agent, and fled and rejoined the Bagauders. The young slave became a mother—she gave birth to
a son—"

"I then have a brother!"

"The son of a female slave is born a slave and belongs to
his mother's master. When the boy, whom your father named
Lòysik in remembrance of his Breton extraction, was four or
five years old, the bishop of Tulle, who had noticed in the child
certain precocious qualities, had him taken to the episcopal
college, where he was brought up with several other young
slaves who were all to become clerks of the Church. From time
to time Karadeucq went at night to visit the mother of his son
at Tulle. The boy being always notified in advance by his
mother, always found some means of repairing to his mother's
hut on such occasions. There the father and the son held long
conversations concerning the men and things of the olden days
of Gaul when the country was glorious and free. Your father
preserved as a family tradition an ardent and sacred love for

Gaul. He strove to cause his son's heart to beat proudly at the
grand recollections of the past, to exasperate him against the
Franks, and some day to take him along to run the Vagrery
with him. But Loysik, who was of a quiet and rather retiring
disposition, feared such an adventurous life. Years passed. Had
your brother so desired, he could have won honors and riches,
as so many others did, by consecrating himself to the Church.
But shortly before being ordained a priest, he had the opportunity of gaining so close a view of the clerical hypocrisy, cupidity and profligacy, that he declined to enter priesthood and
he cursed the sacrilegious alliance of the Gallic clergy with the
conquerors. He left the episcopal house and went to the frontier of Provence, where he joined the hermit-laborers. He was
previously acquainted with one of their set, who had stopped
for several weeks at the episcopal alms-house for his cure."

"Did the hermit-laborers establish a colony?"

"Several of them gathered in a secluded spot to cultivate the
lands that had been laid waste and were abandoned since the
conquest. They were plain and good men, faithful to the recollections of old Gaul and to the precepts of the gospels. Those
monks lived in celibacy, but took no vows. They remained lay,
and had no clerical character. It is only since recent years that
most of those monks have begun entering the Church. But
having become priests, they are daily losing the popular esteem
that they once enjoyed, and the independence of character that
rendered them so redoubtable to the bishops. At the time that
I am speaking of, the life of those hermit-laborers was peaceful
and industrious. They lived like brothers, obedient to the precepts of Jesus; they cultivated their lands in common; and they
jointly and forcibly defended them whenever some band of
Franks, on the way from some burg to another, took it into
their heads, out of sheer wantonness, to injure the fields or crops
of the monks—"

"I must say that I love those hermits, who are at once husbandmen and soldiers, who are faithful to the precepts of Jesus, to the love for old Gaul, and to horror for the Franks. You say that those monks fought well—were they armed?"

"They had arms—and better than arms. See here," said the hermit drawing from under his robe a species of short sword or long poniard with an iron hilt; "observe this weapon carefully. Its strength does not lie in its blade but in the words engraven on the hilt."

"I see," said Ronan, "on one of the sides of the guard, the word *ghilde,* and on the other side two Gallic words—*friendship —community.* I suppose these are the device of the hermit-laborers? But what does the word *ghilde* mean? That is not a Gallic word. It is unknown to me."

"It is a Saxon word."

"Oh! It is a word from the language of the pirates who come down from the seas of the North, skirt the coasts, and often ascend the Loire in order to plunder the bordering lands. They are fearful marauders, but intrepid seamen! Think of their coming over sea from distant shores, in mere canoes, that are so frail and light that, at a pinch, they are carried on their backs. It is said that they have ascended the Loire more than once as far as Tours."

"And it is true. And thus Gaul is to-day the prey of barbarians from within and from without. She is at the mercy of the Franks and the Saxons!"

"But how can that Saxon word *ghilde,* engraven on the iron impart strength to the weapon, as you tell me?"

"I shall explain the secret to you. One of the monk laborers lived on the border of the Loire before he joined us. Being carried away by the pirates at one of their raids in Touraine, when he was still in his early infancy, he was brought up in their country. During his sojourn among them, he noticed that those men of the North drew immense strength from certain associations in which each owed solidarity to all, and all to each—solidarity in fraternity, in assistance, in goods, in arms and in life. These associations are generally believed to have sprung up from Christian fraternity; the fact is that they were in practice in those Northern regions many a century before the birth of Jesus, and they were called *ghildes*. Later the prisoner of the pirates succeeded in making his escape, re-entered Gaul, joined us hermit laborers—"

"Why do you break off?"

"An oath that I have taken forbids me to say more—"

"I shall respect your secret. But the confidence, with which I seem to inspire you, you also inspire in me. My brother, you said to me, was of the number of the hermit-laborers with whom you are associated. You must have known him intimately. Only he could have furnished you with the details concerning the family of Joel which he doubtlessly received from his own father. Why do you look at me so fixedly? Your silence disconcerts and moves me—your eyes are filling with tears—"

"Ronan, your brother was born thirty years ago—that is my age. Your brother's name is Loysik—that is my name."

"Loysik! My brother!"

"It is I. Did you not surmise as much?"

"Joy of heavens! You are my brother!"

Long did the hermit and the Vagre remain in close embrace. After the first ebullition of their tender joy, Ronan said to Loysik:

"And whatever became of our father?"

"I know not his fate—but let us trust in the goodness of God—let us not despair of some day finding him again—"

"And was it your brother's instinct that led you to accompany us?"

"I did not suspect you of being my brother until I noticed the degree to which you were moved by the chant of Hena. When you told me she was one of your ancestresses, I no longer entertained any doubt but that we were either brothers or close relatives. The account of your life proved to me that we were brothers."

"But why, then, did you follow us in Vagrery?"

"Did you not hear my answer to Bishop Cautin: 'It is not the well but the sick who stand in need of the physician?'"

"Would you blame me for being a Vagre, and would you blame our father for having been a Bagauder?"

"No less than you, Ronan, do I hold slavery and conquest in horror, seeing that Gaul, formerly powerful and teeming with happiness, is covered with ruins and brambles since the Frankish invasion. Proprietors, colonists, husbandmen have all fled before the barbarians who reduce them to slavery, or cause them to die of hunger by reason of the frightful floods of famine that have followed in the wake of the invading army. Driven by despair large numbers of those unhappy people run the Vagrery like yourself. Only slaves are seen here and there cultivating the lands of the Church and of the seigneurs, and the poor wretches bend under the weight of toil; not infrequently die of hunger or of maltreatment. The cities, once so rich, so flourishing by their commerce, are to-day ruined, almost depopulated, but being at least defended by their walls, they offer some measure of security to their inhabitants; and yet, the ceaseless civil wars between the sons of Clovis at times deliver even these places to the torch of the incendiary, to pillage and to massacre. During the fitful lulls of these feuds, the inhabitants hardly dare to leave their walls; the roads, infested with armed bands, render communication and traffic impossible. But too often the horrors of famine have decimated the population of whole cities. Alas! Such is the sad plight of our country."

"Aye, that is what the Frankish conquest has done for Gaul. She can no longer be free—let her disappear from the world burying the conquerors and the conquered alike under her ruins!"

"Brother, is not this Gaul that you lay waste with as much

inveterateness as the conquerors themselves, is she not our dearly
beloved country, our mother? Is it for us, her children, to
join hands with the barbarians in whelming her with sorrows
and trials? Like yourself, I wish to labor for the overthrow of
barbarism; like yourself I wish to put an end to the craven be-
sottedness of the oppressed; but I wish to destroy barbarism
with civilization, ignorance with enlightenment, poverty with
labor, slavery with the sense of national worth—a sense, alas!
now almost wholly uprooted, and yet once so powerful, in the days
of our fathers, when our venerated druids aroused the peoples
to arms against the Romans. Holy insurrections!"

"Tracked by the bishops, our last druids have died upon the
scaffold!"

"But the druid faith is not dead! No—no! The forms of
religions pass, but their divine principle remains for all time.
Revived, stimulated and regenerated by the gentle morality of
Jesus, the druid faith is born anew in our breasts. It has preserved its belief in the immortality of the soul of men, in their
successive re-incarnation in the starry world, to the end that
by fresh trials and sufferings the wicked may become good, and
the just still more perfect. Aye, humanity, whether visible or
invisible, must rise from sphere to sphere in its eternal effort,
in its continuous progress, towards infinite perfection. Such is
our faith, the faith of us Christian druids, who practice the
evangelical doctrine in all that it contains of tenderness, mercifulness, and the love of freedom—"

At this point Loysik was suddenly interrupted by a voice
that proceeded from a bush near the oak tree, shouting:

"Relapsed! Sacrilegious wretch! Worshiper of Mammon!
Hermit of the devil! Prop of Beelzebub! You shall be burned
for a heretic!"

It was the voice of Bishop Cautin. And almost at the same
instant, from afar, from the side where the Vagres were finish-

ing their night of wassail, these other cries were heard through the stillness of the approaching dawn:

"On guard! On guard! The leudes of Count Neroweg are approaching! The count himself is at their head!"

"On guard! The leudes of Count Neroweg are approaching! To arms! To arms!"

Awakened from her restful sleep by the tumult and hearing the cries of the Vagres, little Odille screamed with terror as she threw herself on the neck of Ronan:

"Count Neroweg! Save me!"

"Fear not, poor child!"

And addressing Loysik, Ronan added:

"Brother, fate sends to us a descendant of that family of Neroweg, whom our ancestor Schanvoch fought two centuries ago on the borders of the Rhine. I wish to kill that barbarian, rid Gaul of him, and protect our own family from the peril of his descendants—"

"Kill me!" murmured Odille, falling on her knees before the Vagre and clasping her hands. "I prefer to die at your hands rather than to fall back into the hands of the count—"

Touched by the girl's despair and of course unable to foresee the issue of the pending combat, Ronan remained pensive for a moment. He looked around. His eyes fell upon a spreading branch of the oak tree near which they stood. He leaped up, seized it, and bending it down said to his brother:

"Loysik, sit Odille on this branch; when it straightens up again it will carry the poor child up; she will then be able to reach the thicker foliage, and keep herself concealed until the end of the combat. I shall forthwith assemble the Vagres. Courage, little Odille, I shall return after the battle—"

And he ran towards his companions, while the slave, whom Loysik had placed upon the branch, disappeared in the midst of the thick foliage waving her hands at Ronan.

Dawn was lighting the forest. The tops of the trees were

crimsoned with the first fires of the orb of day. The Vagres, who just announced the approach of Count Neroweg and his leudes, had taken a path across the thicket that was impracticable for the horses of the Franks, a good deal shorter than the road that these were obliged to take in order to arrive at the clearing where the Vagres had halted for the night. The larger number of the Vagres being in their cups and exhausted with singing and dancing, were asleep on the lawn. Awakened with a start by the cries of the outposts, they rushed to their arms. The slaves, the colonists, the women, the ruined proprietors, who joined the Vagres on the previous day were differently affected at the tidings of the approach of the leudes. Some trembled from head to foot; others fled into the thickest of the forest; still others, a goodly number, preserved their courage, and hastily sought for means of the defense. In default of better weapons they supplied themselves with heavy knotted staves that they cut from the trees. The Vagres themselves numbered about a dozen excellent archers, others were armed with axes, iron maces, pikes, swords and scythes with the blades turned outward. At the first cry of alarm, the brave fellows gathered around Ronan and the hermit. Should battle be engaged with the leudes? Was it better to flee before them and await a better opportunity for an offensive stroke? Only few were for flight; the majority favored immediate battle.

While the council of war was being held two other pickets rushed to the clearing. They had concealed themselves in the underwood, and had been able to count with approximate accuracy the number of leudes whom the count led. There were barely a score on horseback; they were well armed; but fully a hundred foot soldiers followed these and were armed with pikes and clubs. Some were Franks, others were from the city of Clermont, whom the count requisitioned in the name of the King for the pursuit of the Vagres. Several of Bishop Cautin's slaves, who, out of fear of hell fire, did not wish to run the

Vagrery after the burning of the episcopal villa, swelled the foot soldiers of Count Neroweg. Ronan's troop numbered at most a score of men.

The council of war decided to engage in a general battle.

CHAPTER X.

THE MIRACLE OF ST. CAUTIN.

It is half an hour since the approach of Count Neroweg and his leudes was announced by the pickets. The Vagres have disappeared. There remains in the clearing where they feasted during the night naught but the remains and evidences of their sumptuous banquet on the lawn—empty wine pouches, gold and silver goblets strewn over the grassy and trampled ground; not far away stand the wagons that were brought from the episcopal villa, and further off the carcasses of the oxen lying near the still smouldering bake-oven. The silence in the forest is profound. Presently, one of the slaves of the villa, one of the pious guides of the leudes, emerges from the thicket that surrounds the clearing. He steps forward diffidently, listens and looks around as if apprehensive of an ambuscade. At the sight of the evidences of the feast that lie strewn about, he seems astonished and quickly turns around. Doubtlessly his first impulse is to return to the troop which he precedes, but as his eyes fall that instant upon the gold and silver vases that lie upon the grass, he stops, turns back, runs to the booty, snatches up a gold chalice and as quickly hides it under his rags. He thereupon lifts up his voice and calls to the leudes.

A distant and steadily approaching noise is heard in the woods. The bushes break down before the chests and under the iron hoofs of the horses. Voices call and answer. Finally Count Neroweg breaks through the thicket. He is on horseback and closely followed by several leudes. Most of his troop, as well as the footmen, being less impetuous than himself, follow at safer distance through the hedges on the way to join their master. Neroweg had expected to fall unperceived upon the Vagres. There was, however, not a soul in sight except the slave who now ran towards him crying:

"Seigneur, the impious Vagres who sacked the villa of our holy bishop have fled into the forest."

Neroweg raised his long sword and with one blow cut off the slave's head:

"Dog! You deceived me! You were in conspiracy with the Vagres!"

The slave's lifeless body sank to the ground, and the hidden gold chalice rolled over the grass.

"That gold vase is mine!" cried the count pointing at the chalice with his sword to one of his men who followed him on foot. "Karl, put that into your bag—"

These thieves always had close to their heels several men with bags ready for booty. But just as Karl was about to follow his master's orders, the latter's eyes fell upon the other articles of gold and silver that were taken from the episcopal villa and which now glistened attractively in the filtering rays of the rising sun. Neroweg put the spurs to his horse, and bounding forward cried:

"Those treasures are mine! Fill up your bag, Karl. Call Rigomer and have him fill his bag with all that it can contain!"

"The booty is not all for you alone, we have our share!" cried the leudes who now entered upon the clearing. "All these treasures must be divided alike—we are your equals!"

"We are equals in battle—equals also in the dividing of the booty—it is but fair—"

"Do you forget that at the pillage of Soissons even the great Clovis himself did not dare to dispute a gold vase with one of his warriors?"

"These treasures are ours as much as yours—we shall divide on the spot—"

The count did not dare resist the demands of his leudes. Although these warriors ever recognized him as their chief, they likewise ever treated him as their equal. Several of the plunderers now alighted from their horses and cast covetous glances at the chalices, their covers and other articles of the Church, together with the goblets, dishes, bowls and many other gold and silver utensils. Carried away by their greed, the leudes precipitated themselves upon the treasures, pushing and shoving one another, and were in the act of reaching out their hands to snatch up the precious goods, when a loud voice, that seemed to descend from the heavens above, thundered down upon them:

"Hands off, sacrilegious men! God hears you! God sees you! If you dare to reach out impious hands at the goods of the Church you will be damned forever!"

At the sound of the voice that seemed to come from heaven Neroweg grew pale, trembled at every limb, dropped from his horse and fell upon his knees. Several of the leudes followed his example and humbly prostrated themselves. They were terror-stricken!

"All on your knees, pagans that you are!" proceeded the voice in still more threatening accents. "All down on your knees! Accursed pillagers of the Church!"

The last of the leudes who still remained on their feet dropped distractedly on their knees, and with them the rest of the troop that followed on foot and were now upon the scene. The affrighted crowd bowed their heads to earth and smote their chests murmuring:

"A miracle! A miracle! It is the voice of the Lord!"

"And now, ye miserable sinners," the voice from above proceeded to thunder in tones increasingly wrathful, "now that you have bowed down to earth before the eye of the Lord and have attested your fear of His wrath, rise and hasten to help His servant who—"

The voice suddenly stopped short; the branches of a tall oak, near which Neroweg and his leudes lay upon their knees, bent and cracked under the weight of a heavy body that was rolling down, and thus broke its fall as it landed upon the ground, but so near to the count that the latter narrowly escaped being crushed by it. This additional phenomenon added to the terror of Neroweg and his leudes; the whole troop threw themselves down flat upon their faces and murmured in their fright:

"Oh Lord! Oh Lord! Have mercy upon us! Oh Lord, turn Your wrath from us!"

And what was it that actually tumbled down from the tree? It was Bishop Cautin, and his was the voice that had sounded from on high. Just before the arrival of the Franks, Ronan had pricked the holy man with the point of his sword, and forced him to clamber up the tree before him and keep himself there like a fat dormouse. Ronan accompanied the holy man up the tree, and with the point of his sword drove him to speak in the name of the Lord. Ronan's purpose was served so long as the holy man limited himself to throwing Neroweg and his leudes into consternation, but as soon as the bishop evinced an inclination to call them to his aid, the Vagre seized him. The sudden move choked off Cautin's sentence before he finished, the rotund and heavy bishop slipped, and tumbling down from branch to branch fell almost upon the back of the count. But the man of God was a wily customer. Although dazed for a moment by his fall, he quickly profited by the terror in which the Franks and the slaves were thrown as they lay face down, flat upon

the earth. He steadied himself upon his legs, and rubbed his
sore limbs, and puffing his cheeks he shouted:

"Miserable sinners! Adore your holy bishop who rede-
scends from heaven upon the wings of the Lord's archangels!"

"A miracle!" again cried the crowd with even intenser unction, and smiting their chests with redoubled fervor. "A miracle!"

"Holy Bishop Cautin, who descend from heaven—protect
us!"

"Is it your voice I hear, holy father?" queried Neroweg in a
subdued voice without daring to raise his face from the ground
or looking up. "Is it your own voice, holy bishop, or is it a
snare that Satan spreads for us?"

"It is myself—your bishop—to doubt it is sacrilege!"

"Whence come you, good father?"

"I descend from heaven. After the sack of the episcopal
villa, and seeing me carried away a captive by the Vagres—be
they forever accursed!—the Lord sent His exterminating angels
to my aid. They were clad in armor of hyacinthe, and armed
with flaming swords. They snatched me from the hands of
the Philistines, took me on their azure wings, and carried me
to heaven—"

"A miracle!" cried the entranced crowd in chorus. "A miracle!"

"Our holy bishop has seen the face of the Lord! Hosanna!"

"St. Cautin," cried up Neroweg, "you will protect me, dear
patron saint, my dear father in Christ! Will you not bless your
son?"

"Yes, I will bless you—provided always you prostrate yourself before the bishop of the Lord, and you enrich the Church!"

"I shall have a chapel built in your honor on this very spot,
holy bishop, in order to glorify this miracle—"

"That is far from enough—no, that is not enough. Listen,
count, listen attentively:

"Neroweg and his leudes fled like cowards from the episcopal villa when it was attacked by the Vagres.

"I order that the count relinquish one quarter of his goods
to me, the bishop of Clermont; I order that he rebuild the episcopal villa, which he allowed the Vagres to set on fire, and that
he richly ornament it.

"I furthermore order that Count Neroweg pursue the Vagres
without let, that he capture and put them to death—all of them,
but especially their chief and a relapsed hermit, a renegade, an
idolater who accompanies the accursed men.

"Finally, I order that the count burn to death, over a slow
fire, a certain Moabite woman, a witch, an infernal wench, who
once was bound to me by the bonds of holy matrimony.

"Let Count Neroweg carry out these, my orders; only at
that price shall his sins be remitted, and on the day of his death
I shall admit him into paradise.

"That is the message that the Lord entrusted me to bear to
you. Amen!"

Neroweg and a few of the leudes rose upon their knees open-
mouthed. As they did so they perceived two bearded Vagres
with their bows between their teeth crawling like serpents along
a large branch in order to reach a spot from which, skilful
archers that they were they could take deliberate aim at their
foes and nail them to the sod.

"Treason!" cried the count jumping to his feet and pointing to the tree. "Treason! The Vagres are there, hidden in
the tree branches!"

Hardly had the count said these words when a volley of arrows flew from the tree-top and riddled his troop. Finding
themselves discovered, the daring Vagres hesitated not one instant to engage in battle. So accurate was the aim of the
archers that every arrow found its quiver in the flesh of a foe.

"This is for you, Neroweg!" cried Ronan from the branch

on which he was perched. "This is for you, the descendant of the Terrible Eagle! There goes the Vagre's arrow!"

Unfortunately the arrow's head was flattened out against the iron casque of the count. The other Vagres who, until now had remained hidden in the bushes, rushed forward with loud yells and intrepidly attacked the troop of Neroweg. The combat became general.

Who were the vanquishers in that combat? The Vagres or the Franks?

Malediction! After a stubborn struggle, almost all the Vagres were slain. A few who escaped the sword and others who were too severely wounded to flee remained prisoners in the hands of Neroweg. Ronan, the Vagre, was among the latter. The superiority of arms prevailed over mere courage.

And Loysik? And little Odille? And the bishopess?

All prisoners—yes, they were all taken to the burg of the Frankish count, while Bishop Cautin, carrying with him his gold and silver vases, regained Clermont followed by a pious crowd of slaves who cried on his passage:

"Glory to our holy bishop! Glory to the blessed Cautin! Hosanna!"

PART III

THE BURG OF NEROWEG

CHAPTER I.

LEUDES AT HOME.

The burg of Count Neroweg is situated in the center of a space once occupied by a fortified Roman camp. The structure is reared on a highland plateau that dominates a vast forest at its feet. Between the forest and the burg lies a wide expanse of meadow lands, watered by a swift-running river. Beyond the forest, far away, the horizon is bounded by the volcanic mountain peaks of Auvergne. The seigniorial residence that shelters the count and his leudes is built after the Germanic fashion: in lieu of walls stout beams carefully planed and fastened together, rest upon a broad stone foundation. At intervals, and with the view of steadying the one-foot thick beams, buttresses of masonry rise from the stone foundation up to the roof, which, in turn, is constructed of oaken shingles and boards, one foot square, laid over each other. The roofing is both light and proof against the rain. The building is a long square, a wide wooden portico ornaments its front entrance, and it is supported on either wing by other structures similarly put together. These are thatched and are devoted to the purposes of kitchen, storerooms, washhouses, weaving and spinning, shoe-making, tailoring, and all the other needs of a household. In these wings are also situated the kennels, the stables, the perches for the falcons, the pig-sty, the cattle-sheds, the wine-presses, the brewery, and large outhouses filled with fodder for horses and cattle. In the main, or seigniorial building are also the women's apartments reserved for Godegisele, the fifth wife of the count, whose second and third wives still live. There Gode-

gisele spends her days in sadness; she rarely leaves her apartments and plies her distaff in the midst of her female slaves, who
attend to the several duties of the needle and the spindle or
loom. A frame chapel, in which a clerk, a messmate at the burg,
officiates, is connected with the women's apartment, the latter
being essentially a lupanar, to which no man save the count
himself is admitted. There, under the very eyes of his wife,
every evening after drinking, the count picks out his bed-fellow
for the night. The leudes distribute themselves promiscuously
among the outside female slaves.

These vast structures, together with a garden and a spacious tree-girt yard intended for the military exercises of the
leudes and of the foot soldiers, all of whom were freemen and
Franks, are surrounded by a fosse and earthworks, the ancient
vestiges of the Roman camp which dates from the conquest of
Julius Caesar. The parapets are considerably impaired by the
centuries, but they still present a good line of defense. Only one
of the four entrances of the fortified enclosure—facing, as was
the custom, north, south, east and west—has been preserved. It
is the one facing south. On that side, a draw-bridge built of
rough logs spans the fosse during the day, in order to afford a
passage to man, wagons and horses. But, as a means of precaution—the count is diffident and suspicious—the bridge is drawn
at night by its keeper. The deep fosse, boggy by reason of the
waters that it has drained from time immemorial and that stag-
nated in its bed, has so thick a layer of mud at its bottom, that
any one who should attempt to cross the slough would be completely engulfed. At a little distance from the yard and far
removed from the main building, but still within the fortified
space, stands an *ergastula,* built, like all Roman structures, of
imperishable bricks. The *ergastula* is a sort of deep cave, intended during the Roman conquest as a lock-up for the slaves
who were employed in field labor and in the building of roads.
Ronan, Loysik the hermit-laborer, the handsome bishopess, little

Odille and several other Vagres, all who had not died of their wounds since their capture, have for the last month been imprisoned in the *ergastula,* the jail of the burg, being thrown there immediately after the combat in the passage of Allange, where most of the Vagres lost their lives. The rest fled into the woods.

Certainly the position of the burg, the noble Frank's den, was well chosen. The old Roman fortifications place the residence above the danger of a sudden attack. On the other hand, is the seigneur count minded to hunt wild animals, the forest lies so near the burg that during the first nights of autumn the loving stags and does can be heard belling for one another's company; is he minded to hunt birds on the wing, the meadows that surround his home offer to the falcons any number of flocks of partridges, while further away large ponds serve as a retreat to the herons who, often in their aerial contests with the falcons, transfix the latter with their long sharp beaks; finally, is the seigneur count minded to fish, his numerous ponds teem with pike, carp and lampreys, while azure-backed trout and purple-finned perches furrow the limpid streams.

Oh, seigneur Count Neroweg! How sweet it is to you to thus enjoy the delights of this land that your kings conquered with their own and the swords of their leudes! You and your fellows, the new masters of this soil that our fathers' labors fecundated, live in idleness and sloth. To drink, eat, hunt, play at dice with your leudes, outrage our wives, sisters and daughters, and then attend church every week—such is the life of the Franks who now possess the vast domains that they plundered us of! Oh, Count Neroweg! How good it feels to inhabit that burg, built by Gallic slaves who were carried away from their own fields, homes and families, and who were made to carry on their backs, under the threat of the clubs of your warriors, the timber from the woods, the stones from the mountain, the sand from the river and the lime from the bowels of the earth—after which, streaming with sweat, broken with fatigue, dying with hunger, receiving for their only pittance a handful of beans, they lay down upon the damp ground, their heads barely sheltered with a roof of rushes! At early dawn the bites of dogs woke up the sluggards—aye, and those self-same keepers with sharp fangs, and trained for their office by the Franks, accompanied the slaves when they were led to their work, hastened their heavy steps when they returned at night bending under their heavy loads, and, if ever driven by despair, the Gaul assayed flight, the intelligent mastiff quickly drove him with its teeth back to the human flock, just as the butcher's dog drives back to the fold a recalcitrant ox or ram.

And did those slaves all belong, perchance, to the class of laborers and artisans, strong, rough men, broken from infancy to hard labor? No, no! Among those captives, more than one had been accustomed to comforts, often to wealth, and were carried away from their cities or fields with wives, daughters and sons, either at the time of the Frankish conquest, or later during the civil wars between the sons of Clovis; the women were consigned to the lodgings of the female slaves, there to attend to the female work of the household and furnish the Franks with subjects for debauchery; the men were assigned to hard out-of-door work, to the building of houses, making of roads or tending the fields. Other slaves, once teachers, merchants and even poets, were captured on the roads as they traveled in troops from one city to another in pursuit of their respective occupations, imagining themselves safe against any attack in these days of war, pillage and general devastation.

Aye, slavery thus rendered the rich Gaul, who was ever accustomed to comforts, the brother in misery and sorrow of the poor Gaul who previously knew what arduous work was. Aye, the woman of white hands and delicate complexion was thrown together with the woman whose hands toil had roughened and whose complexion the sun had tanned—both were rendered by slavery sisters in dishonor and shame, and were cast weeping, or, if they resisted, bleeding into the bed of the Frankish seigneur, whom, on the Sunday following a Gallic priest would regularly give remission for his sins!

Oh, our fathers! Oh, our mothers! By all the sorrows that you underwent! Oh, our brothers and our sisters, by all the sorrows that you now undergo! Oh, our sons! Oh, our daughters! By the dregs of the cup of humiliation and disgrace that you are made to drain! Oh, you all, by the tears that drop from your eyes, by the laceration of your bodies—you will be avenged! You will be avenged upon these abhorred Franks!

But let us step into the burg of the seigneur. By the faith of a Vagre! By the sweat and the blood of our fathers that have moistened and crimsoned every beam, every stone of this structure—it is a comfortable, spacious and handsome building, this burg of the seigneur count! Twelve well rounded oaken beams support the portico; it leads directly into the *mahl,* as these barbarous chiefs style the tribunal where they dispense their seigniorial justice—a vast, spacious hall, in the rear of which, and raised on a platform, is the seat of the count, and the benches of the leudes who assist him in the ceremony. There he holds his *mahl* and judges the crimes committed on his domains. In a corner of the room a stove, a rack and pincers are seen—no justice without torture and execution. In yonder opposite corner and even with the floor is a wide tank full of water and deep enough for a man to drown in. Near the tank lie nine plow-shares. These are all instruments for *judicial trials;* they are prescribed by the *Salic Law,* the law of the Franks, to which Gaul is now subject, seeing the land is in the power of Frankish conquerors.

And yonder door, made of solid oak, thick as a hand's palm, and covered with sheets of iron and enormous nails—that door is the door of the chamber in which the treasures of the noble seigneur are kept. Only he keeps the key. In that apartment are the large boxes, likewise ribbed with iron, where he locks up his gold and silver sous, his precious stones, his costly vases, both sacred and profane, his necklaces, his bracelets, his gold-hilted parade sword, his handsome bridle with its silver bit and his elaborately silver-ornamented saddle with stirrups of the same metal—all stolen from this noble land of Gaul.

Let us enter the banquet hall. It is night. By my faith! Those are curious candelabras. They are made of flesh and bone. Ten slaves—all burnt by the sun, worn and barely clad in rags—are ranked five on one side, five on the other of the table. They stand motionless as statues and hold aloft large flaming torches of wax that barely serve to light the place. A double row of rounded oak trunks, a sort of rustic colonnade, divides the spacious hall into three compartments along its full length, reaching at one end the door of the *mahl,* and at the other to the count's chamber, which, in turn communicates with the apartments of Godegisele and her women.

Between the two rows of pillars stands the table of the count and of the leudes, his peers. To the right and left, and on the other sides of the two rows of pillars, stand two other tables—one is reserved for the warriors of inferior rank, the other for the principal servants of the count: his seneschal, his equerry, his chamberlains, seeing that the seigneurs imitate closely the customs and style of the royal courts. In the four corners of the hall, the floor of which is, obedient to custom, strewn with green leaves in summer, and straw in winter, stand four large barrels, two of hydromel, one of beer, and one of herbed wine, Auvergne wine mixed with spices and absinthe—a beverage pressed by the slaves of the burg. Along the wainscoting hang the count's hunting trophies, together with his arms of war and the chase—heads of stags, does and wild goats, all garnished with their horns; wild boars' and wolves' heads with their fangs exposed. The flesh and skin have been removed from these trophies; nothing remains but the whitened bones. Boar-spears, pikes, hunting-knives and horns, fishing-nets, falcon coifs, implements of war, lances, francisques or double edged axes, swords, bucklers and shields painted in garish colors—all these are ranged along the walls. On the table lie spread sheep and wild boars roasted whole, mountains of ham and smoked venison, avalanches of cabbage in vinegar, the latter being a favorite dish with the Franks; chunks of beef, mutton and veal of the cattle fattened in the count's yards; small game, poultry, carps and pikes, the latter of which are of extraordinary size; vegetables, fruit and cheese raised and prepared on the fertile fields and farms of Auvergne; bowls and amphoras, incessantly replenished by butlers who run from the tables to the barrels and back again, are as speedily emptied by the Franks with the aid of wild bulls' horns that serve as their usual goblets. The horn used by Neroweg must have belonged to an animal of monstrous size. It is black and hooped from top to bottom in gold and silver. From time to time the seigneur makes a sign, whereupon several slaves standing at one end of the hall with drums and hunting horns, strike up an infernal music, which, however, is less discordant and deafening than the cries and laughter of the blockish Teutons, gorged gluttons, most of whom are at an advanced state of intoxication.

Who produced these wines, these mountains of venison, of fish, of beef, of pork, of mutton, of game, of poultry, of vegetables and fruit? Gaul! The country that is cultivated and rendered fruitful by a population of starvelings, whose representatives, wan with hunger and privation in the midst of such plenty, officiate as living torches to light the banquet. That heap of good things is produced by men and women who, huddled in mud and straw huts, are, at that very moment, and in utter exhaustion, partaking of a tasteless pittance.

Behold the Franks, gorged with food and wine; obscene jokes and challenges to drink and drink still more are bandied backward and forward; the hall is a roar of boisterous laughter; beyond all others the seigneur count is hilarious. At his side sits his clerk, who serves as his secretary and officiates in the oratory of the burg. According to the newly introduced custom that the Church authorized, the Frankish seigneurs are allowed to keep a priest and chapel in their houses. The clerk has been assigned to Neroweg by Cautin. When making the assignment, the wily prelate said to the stupid barbarian: "This clerk can neither grant you remission for the sins that you may commit, nor can he snatch you from the claws of Satan; only I have that power; but the constant presence of a priest at your side will render the attempts of the demon more difficult; that will afford you time, in urgent cases, to wait for my arrival without danger of your being carried off to hell."

The boisterous mirthfulness of the leudes is at its height. Neroweg wishes to speak. Three times he strikes on the table with the handle of his *scramasax,* the name given by the barbarians to the knife used at table, and habitually worn at the warrior's belt. Silence, or some degree of silence ensues. The count is to speak. With both his elbows leaning upon the table, he strokes and restrokes his long, reddish, greasy and wine-soaked moustache between his thumb and index. The posture and gesture always announces with him some scheme of vicious cruelty. The leudes are aware of this and greet his words in advance with gross and confident laughter. Without saying a word, Neroweg points out to his peers one of the slaves who, motionless, has been holding up a torch at the banquet. The fellow is a poor old man, wrinkled and haggard; his hair and beard are white and long; for only clothing he wears a tattered blouse and hose which expose his skin, yellow and tanned like parchment; his hose do not reach his bony knees; his bare and lank legs, scarred by the brambles among which he is forced to work, seem hardly able to support him. Compelled, like the rest of his torch-bearing companions, to hold up the light with out-stretched arm, and the whip of the Frankish overseer being ever ready to enforce the order with merciless cruelty, he felt his lean arm grow numb, weaken and tremble despite all he could do to prevent it.

After pointing at the slave, Neroweg turned to his leudes with cruel hilarity and said:

"Hi—hi—hi—we shall now have a good laugh. You old toothless dog, why do you not hold the candle straight?"

"Seigneur, I am very old—my arm grows tired despite myself."

"So, then, you are tired?"

"Alas! Yes, seigneur!"

"Yet you know that he who does not hold up his torch straight is regaled with fifty lashes!"

"Seigneur, my strength fails me!"

"Do you say so?"

"Yes, yes, seigneur—my fingers are numb—they can no longer hold the torch—it will soon fall down—"

"Poor old man—come, put out your torch."

"Thanks, thanks, seigneur!"

"Wait a moment. What are you doing?"

"I am going to blow out the torch—as you ordered me—"

"Oh, I did not mean it in that way."

And ever caressing his moustache, Neroweg cast ironical and cruel glances at his leudes.

"Seigneur, how will you have me extinguish my torch?"

"I wish you to put it out between your knees."

The Frankish leudes received the comical idea of the count with loud applause and wild yells and laughter. The old Gaul trembled from head to foot, looked imploringly at Neroweg, lowered his head and murmured:

"Seigneur, my knees are bare, the torch will burn me—"

"Ho! You old brute! Do you imagine I would order you to extinguish the torch between your knees if they were covered with oxhide or jambards of iron?"

"Seigneur, good seigneur, it will smart me terribly; for pity's sake, do not impose such a torment upon me."

"Bother! Your knees are bones!"

The bright sally on the part of the count redoubled the laughter and hilarity of the leudes.

"It is true I am only skin and bones," answered the old man seeking to soften his master's heart; "I am quite weak—please spare me the pain, my good seigneur."

"Listen—if you do not on the spot extinguish your torch between your knees, I shall have my men seize you and extinguish the torch in your throat—take your choice, quickly!"

A fresh explosion of hilarity proved to the old Gaul that he had no mercy to expect from the Franks. He looked down weeping upon his frail and tremulous legs, and yielding to one last ray of hope he addressed the clerk in suppliant accents:

"My good father in God—in the name of charity—do intercede in my behalf with my good seigneur count!"

"Seigneur, I ask grace for the poor old man."

"Clerk! Does the slave belong to me—yes or not? Am I his master—yes or not?"

"He belongs to you, noble seigneur."

"Can I dispose of my slave at my pleasure, and chastise him as I may choose?"

"My noble seigneur, it is your right."

"Very well, then! I want him to extinguish the torch between his knees; if not, by the great St. Martin! I shall extinguish it myself in his throat!"

"Oh, my good father in God—do intercede again for me! I beg you!"

"My good son," said the clerk with unction to the slave, "we must accept with resignation the trials that heaven sends us."

"Will you have done!" cried the count again smiting the table with the handle of his *scramasax*. "We have had words enough

—take your choice—either your knees or your throat for an extinguisher! Do you hesitate—"

"No, no, seigneur, I obey—"

And it was a very comical scene for the Franks. By the faith of a Vagre, there was truly cause for laughter. With tears rolling down his cheeks, the poor old Gaul first approached the burning torch to his trembling knees; the instant the flame touched him he quickly withdrew it again. But the count, who, with both his hands upon his paunch swollen with food and drink, was roaring with laughter and, like the rest of the leudes, shook with mirth, again smote the table violently with the handle of his *scramasax*. The slave understood the signal. With trembling hands he again drew the torch close to his icy knees, and assayed to put a quick end to the torture; he parted his legs a little and then brought them twice quickly and convulsively together so as to extinguish the flame between his knees. He succeeded in this, but not without emitting a piercing cry of pain; such was the pang he suffered that the old man fell over upon his back and lay on the floor deprived of consciousness.

"I smell grilled dog!" said the count dilating his nostrils like a beast of prey. The odor of burnt human flesh doubtlessly acted as an appetizer upon him, and he cried as if struck by a new idea: "My valiant leudes, the burg's prison is well stocked, I know. We have in the *ergastula,* loaded with chains, first of all, Ronan the Vagre and the hermit-laborer; they are now both nearly healed of their wounds; then we have the little blonde slave, she is not yet well, she still seems to be at death's door; besides that, we have the handsome bishopess—she is not wounded but is possessed of the devil—"

"But, count," spoke up one of the leudes, "what do you propose to do with those cursed Vagres, the little Vagress and the handsome witch whom we brought prisoners with us from the combat at the fastnesses of Allange? What manner of torture will you inflict upon them?"

"Oh! how I regret that they have not a thousand members to burn and hack to pieces in order to expiate the death of our companions in arms whom they killed in the fastness!"

"Will you have them tried here, count?"

"No—no—they shall be tried at Clermont. Bishop Cautin insists upon his jurisdiction over them. Oh! By the Terrible Eagle, my ancestor who skinned his prisoners alive, the Vagre, the hermit-laborer and the witch shall be submitted to frightful tortures. But they do not concern us this evening. When I mentioned to you the prisoners in the *ergastula,* my good leudes, what I meant to say was that we have there one of my domestic slaves who is charged with larceny by the cook slave. The latter asserts, the former denies the theft. Which of the two lies? In order to ascertain the truth, let us put the two cubs to the cold water and hot iron trials, according to the law of our Salic Franks."

CHAPTER II.

THE MAHL.

The tribunal assembles. The count presides over the *mahl* on his seat; seven leudes, ranked on benches on either side, assist him. The torch-bearing slaves stand behind the judges. The judgment seat is well lighted, while the rear of the hall, where the other leudes and warriors of the burg are grouped, remains in semi-obscurity, brightened, however, from time to time by the reflexion of the fire in the large stove which the blacksmith of the stables has lighted and blows into flame. The nine plowshares are being heated red in the stove. Before the stove, and even with the ground, is the wide and deep tank filled with water. The slave charged with larceny stands at the foot of the tribunal with his arms tied behind his back. He is a young man and looks frightened at the judges. The accuser, a man of ripe age, contemplates the tribunal confidently. Agreeable to the usage in such instances, six other slaves surround the two men. They are chosen by the accuser and the accused to affirm under oath what they believe to be the truth. They are called *conjurators.*

"To the trial! To the trial!" cries the count. "Mayor, inform the slave anew of the charge against him."

"Justin, a cook-slave of our seigneur, the count, happened to be alone in the kitchen; on the kitchen table lay a small silver dish used by dame Godegisele, the noble spouse of our master. Peter, this other slave, entered the kitchen bringing in some kindling wood. Immediately after his departure, Justin noticed that the silver dish had disappeared. He immediately announced the theft and accused Peter of having committed it. I told Justin that one of his ears would be cut off if the dish was not found. He answered me that he swore by the salvation of his soul that he told the truth and that the thief was this other slave."

"And I repeat it again, seigneur count. If the dish was stolen it could have been stolen only by Peter. I swear it upon my share of paradise. I am innocent. My *conjurators* are all ready to swear like myself upon the salvation of their souls."

"Yes, yes," answered the six slaves in chorus; "we swear that Justin is innocent of the theft—we swear upon the salvation of our souls, we swear upon our share of paradise."

"Do you hear, dog?" said Neroweg turning towards Peter. "What have you to say? What became of the silver dish, a precious article that I brought from the pillage of the town of Issoire? Will you answer, dog?"

"Seigneur, I did not steal the dish, I did not even see it on the table—my *conjurators* are ready to swear to it, like myself, upon my salvation—upon my share of paradise—"

"Yes, yes," put in the six in their turn, the *conjurators* of the accused slave. "Peter is innocent; we swear upon our salvation."

"My dear brother in Christ," said the clerk to the accused slave, "think of it. It is a grave sin, theft is, and falsehood is another grave sin. Take care—the Almighty sees and hears you—His hand lies heavy upon thieves and liars—"

"My good father, I stand in great fear of the Almighty; I follow His commandments as you teach them to us; I support my trials with resignation; I obey my master, the seigneur count, with the submission that you order us to the end that we may gain paradise; but I swear I did not steal the dish."

"Seigneur count," said Justin, "I swear by the eternal flames that I did not steal the dish, and only Peter can be the thief— I am innocent."

"Justin affirms and Peter denies; now I, Neroweg, order that, in order to ascertain the truth, they be both put to the trial— one to the trial of cold water, the other to the trial of burning irons—"

"Seigneur count," broke in the clerk, "you order that both the accuser and the accused be subjected to trial. But should the judgment of the Almighty prove that the accused is guilty, is not the accuser thereby declared innocent? Why should both be put to the trial at the same time?"

"If the accused and the accuser agreed between themselves to steal my dish," replied the count, "and if, in order to remove our suspicions, they mutually accuse each other, the trial will establish whether they are both guilty or innocent, or whether one is guilty and the other innocent."

"Yes, yes," cried the leudes enjoying by anticipation the spectacle of human suffering; "the double trial!"

"I am not afraid of the trial!" exclaimed Justin in a firm voice. "God will bear witness to my innocence—"

"And I am quite certain that I did not steal the dish," said Peter trembling, "and yet I am afraid of the trial!"

"Your companion, my dear son in Christ, sets you the example of a pious reliance upon divine justice, knowing the Eternal only condemns the guilty."

"Alas, good father!" said Peter to the clerk, "think of it, if the trial should turn out against me!"

"My son, it will be a proof that you did steal the dish."

"But no—no—I did not commit the theft."

"In that case, my son, you need have no fear of the judgment of God. His justice is infallible."

"Oh, good father, I hope you are right!"

"Speak not thus, my dear son. This law is holy, it is the Salic Law, the law of the Salian Franks, our conquerors. It is placed under protection by our Lord Jesus Christ. I shall read

to you the preamble of the law in the name of which you are to
be subjected to trial:

"'The illustrious nation of the Franks, founded by God,
strong in war, wise in council, of noble stature, of singular white-
ness and beauty, bold, agile and mighty in battle, has recently
been converted to the Catholic faith, which it practices pure and
free from the defilement of any heresy; the said illustrious nation has prepared and dictated the Salic Law through the me-
dium of the oldest members who then governed the nation. The
gast of Wiso, the *gast* of Bodo, the *gast* of Salo, the *gast* of
Wido, who inhabit the places called Salo-Heim, Bodo-Hei.n,
Wiso-Heim and Wido-Heim met during three *mahls,* carefully
discussed and adopted this law.

"'Long live he who loves the Franks! May Christ uphold
their empire! May Heaven enlighten their chiefs and fill them
with grace! May He protect the army, may He fortify the
faith, may He grant peace and happiness to those who govern
them under the auspices of our Lord Jesus Christ. Amen.'"

"Clerk, we have had words enough!" put in the count. "The
accused shall be put to the trial of the cold water—let his right
hand be bound to his left foot, and let him be thrown into the
tank head foremost. If he floats the judgment of God condemns
him; he will then be pronounced guilty and shall to-morrow
suffer punishment. If he sinks to the bottom, the judgment of
God will have absolved him."

At a sign of Neroweg several of his men seized the Gallic
slave, and despite the resistance that he offered and his supli-
cations, they tied his right hand to his left foot.

"Alas," moaned the wretched man, what a terrible law that
law is, good father! What a fate is mine! If I remain at the
bottom of the tank I shall drown, however innocent I may be!
And if I float, I shall be sentenced and executed as a thief!"

"The judgment of the Eternal, my dear son, can never go
wrong."

Already the Franks were raising the slave in their arms and were about to cast him into the tank when the clerk cried out: "And the consecration of the water!"

And stepping towards the slave who moaned aloud, the clerk placed upon the Gaul's lips a silver cross that he carried around his neck and said:

"Kiss this cross, my dear son."

The young slave devoutly kissed the symbol of the death of the Friend of the sorrowful, while the clerk pronounced aloud the formula adopted by the Church:

"Oh, thou who art about to undergo the trial of cold water, I adjure thee, in the name of our Lord Jesus Christ, in the name of the Father, the Son and the Holy Ghost, in the name of the indivisible Trinity, in the name of all the angels, archangels, principalities, powers and dominions, virtues, thrones, cherubim and seraphim, if thou art guilty, that this water may reject thee, without any sorcery preventing it from so doing; and Thou Lord Jesus Christ, give us such a sign of Thy majesty that if this man has committed the crime, he be rejected by this water to the praise and the glory of Thy holy name, and to the end that all may recognize that Thou art God. And you, water! Water created by the omnipotent Father for the needs of man, I adjure you, in the name of the indivisible Trinity which allowed the people of Israel to cross the Red Sea, dry-footed, I adjure you, water, to refuse to accept this body if he has eased his shoulders of the burden of good works. I so order you, water, confident in the virtue of God alone in whose name I demand obedience from you. Amen."

The consecration being finished by the clerk, the Franks raised over their heads the Gallic slave who screamed and struggled to free himself, and hurled him violently into the center of the tank amidst the loud guffaw of the count and the witnessing Franks.

"Never yet did otter, leaping from a willow tree after a

carp, make so beautiful a plunge," exclaimed the good seigneur
count holding his sides; he was laughing so heartily.   The witnessing Franks also laughed and roared, and crowded around
the tank saying to one another:

"He will float—the scamp!"

"He will not float—he is not guilty!"

"How he beats the water!"

"And that gurgling sound—glou—glou—glou!"

"Sounds like a bottle that is emptying itself—"

"There he comes to the surface!"

"No, he sinks again!"

Presently the slave rose and succeeded in keeping himself
for a moment on the surface. His face was livid and distorted, his
hair streaming, his eyes rolling back like the eyes of a man who
has escaped drowning by some desperate effort.   He beat the
water with the only arm that was free and cried:

"Help! I drown! Help!"

In his fright the innocent fellow forgot that the life which
he implored was reserved for the cruel punishment meted out
to thieves, seeing the *judgment of God* would have convicted
him as such.   The young man was pulled half dead out of the
tank; as he lay on the floor the Franks derived increased pleasure from his contortions, and the expression of his purplish
face, on which the stamp of terror was still visible.

"My son, my son, I warned you before," said the clerk in
threatening accents. "Theft is a grave crime! And falsehood
is another grave crime! Here you lie—guilty of both! The
sacred judgment of the Lord has, in His infallible and divine
truth, pronounced you guilty."

"Go to, miserable thief!" said to him one of his *conjurators*
who feared to share the punishment of Peter. "You assured us
of your innocence, we trusted your word, and you deceived us—
the judgment of God has condemned you! Go to, infamous
fellow—we shall gladly give a hand in your execution!"

"I am innocent! I am innocent!"

"And what about the judgment of God, blasphemer!" cried Justin, the accuser.

"Alas, I am nevertheless innocent—I did not steal the dish!"

"Hold your tongue, impious criminal! The trial that I shall now undergo with blind faith in the justice of the Lord will furnish further proof of your guilt!" retorted Justin.

"Good! Good, my dear son! Step aside from the miserable liar, thief and blasphemer! Your innocence will be quickly established; your piety will have its reward."

"Oh, I know it, good father! I long for the trial! May the holy name of God be glorified!"

"That dog, whom the judgment of our omnipotent Lord has pronounced guilty, shall receive condign punishment. Now let us pass to the trial of the red-hot irons. Although the first trial has proved to us the guilt of that slave, there is nothing as yet to prove that the other fellow is innocent. They may be both accomplices in the theft of my silver dish."

"Oh, my noble seigneur, I am in no fear!" cried the cook, his face beaming with celestial confidence. "I bless the name of God for His having reserved to me the opportunity to bear witness to my profound faith in our holy Roman Catholic and Apostolic religion, and to triumph a second time over the accusations of the wicked. I know, O Lord, that, faithful to your commandments, I shall triumph with humility."

With the believer impatiently awaiting the new triumph of his innocence, the clerk proceeded, agreeable to the usage, to consecrate and adjure the red-hot irons in the brasier, just as he had conjured the water in the tank. He ordered the red-hot irons with the same solemn invocations that they respect the soles of the slave's feet if he was innocent, and to burn him to the bone if he was guilty of having robbed his seigneur.

The conjuration being done, the stable blacksmiths drew

forth from the stove, with the aid of long tongs, the nine red-hot plow-shares that they held in readiness, and laid them down in a row flat upon the stone floor at a distance of two or three inches from one another. Ranged in that order, they presented a strange aspect—an enormous red-hot gridiron.

"Quick!" said the count. "The irons must not be allowed to cool off."

"What a jig will not the cub dance on that row of burning irons, if he was in the plot with the other thief to steal your dish!"

"And yet what a wondrous miracle is about to be accomplished if the cook is really innocent!" remarked another leude with impatient curiosity. "To walk over red-hot plow-shares without burning one's feet! It takes the God of the Christians to accomplish such a miracle!"

Such was the curiosity of the Franks that their cruel wish to see the slave dance upon the red-hot irons struggled strongly against the wish to witness a wonderful miracle. Hardly was the last plow-share ranged in its place upon the floor than Neroweg, fearing to have them cool off, called out impatiently to Justin:

"Quick! Quick! Walk over them!"

"Go, my dear son; fear naught!" added the clerk.

"Oh, I am not afraid, good father," answered the cook in a voice of inspired exaltation; and crossing his arms over his breast, he cried out fervently: "Lord God, Thou readest in the hearts of men; Thou hast already borne witness to my innocence—give in favor of Thy servant a new proof of Thy infallible justice—order the burning irons to be as soft under my feet as if I trod upon a carpet of moss and flowers!"

And, his face beaming with serenity, and his eyes raised heavenward, the Gallic slave moved with firm steps towards the gridiron of red-hot plow-shares. During the short interval that elapsed before the accused exposed himself to the *judgment of*

God, the count, his clerk and all the witnessing Franks seemed
impressed by the slave's imperturbable confidence; they looked
at one another; and Neroweg said in a low voice to the leudes
that sat beside him:

"The cook must be truly innocent of the theft."

"Proceed! March on, my son in God!" cried the clerk at
the moment when Justin was raising his foot over the first
plow-share. "The justice of the Eternal is infallible. You
said it—it is over a carpet of moss and flowers that your feet
are to walk."

But our fervent Catholic had barely touched the red-hot iron
with his feet when he emitted a frightful shriek. So intensely
unbearable was the pain that he tripped and fell down forward
on his knees and hands. As he thus tumbled over the red-hot
plow-shares he gave himself fresh and deep burns all over his
body, until, driven crazy, he made a desperate bound clean over
the implements of his torture, and, roaring with pain, rolled
down over the floor ten paces away, near where his companion
Peter lay, tied hand and foot.

"Glory to the judgment of the Lord!" cried the leudes in
chorus, struck with admiration. "Glory to Christ!"

"Did I not tell you so?" remarked the count complacently.
"The two thieves were both in the plot to steal my silver dish.
The ears of both shall be cropped to-morrow, and they shall be
both put on the rack until they reveal the place where they hid
the dish—"

"Hold your tongue, count!" cried Justin roaring with pain
and rage. "The only thieves and plunderers around are yourself
and your men. Had I stolen the dish, I would only have robbed
a thief—but I did not take it—as truly as I here renounce the
infamous religion that wrongly finds me guilty!"

"Wretch! Blasphemer of our holy religion! I order in the
name of God—"

"Hold your tongue, too, priest—you shall no longer dupe me.

Your alleged religion is but a lie and a fraud; it bears false witness against the innocent. Oh, how I suffer—how I suffer!"

"Your sufferings are but foretastes of the tortures that you will undergo in hell, where you will burn everlastingly, you sacrilegious thief! Oh, seigneur count, if this impious and audacious wretch continues to blaspheme, we shall not be able to conjure away the misfortunes that he will draw upon your house."

Terrified at the sacrilegious utterances of the Gallic slave; pale, trembling and shuddering at the thought that, attracted by the dreadful blasphemies of the condemned man, the devil might suddenly appear in person, take possession of the malefactor and carry him straight to hell, Neroweg thundered to the blacksmith at the stove:

"Are the tongs still in the brasier and red-hot?"

"Yes, seigneur, to command."

"The accursed fellow shall no longer blaspheme and place my burg in danger of being visited by the devil. Let the sacrilegious criminal be seized, and his tongue be burned out with the red-hot tongs. Tell me, clerk, do you believe the Lord will be pacified if I inflict that punishment upon the slave?"

"I believe, seigneur count, that there is no punishment too terrible for this accursed man who has renounced his religion, and called its holy priests impostors."

"Clerk, shall I have him quartered in order to be all the surer that the devils will be conjured away from my burg?"

"The first punishment that you mentioned will suffice—the accursed man will have been punished in the member that sinned—his criminal and blasphemous tongue; it will thereafter utter no more blasphemies."

The tongue of the Gallic slave was burned and pulled out with red-hot tongs. The count went back to the banquet hall with his leudes, and there proceeded to drink himself drunk before retiring to his wife in the women's apartment.

CHAPTER III.

THE SPECTRE OF WISIGARDE.

While her lord and master, Neroweg, together with his leudes, was drinking himself to the point of intoxication in the banquet hall, Godegisele, the count's fifth wife, sat in her chamber amidst her female slaves and diligently plied her distaff by the light of a copper lamp. Although still young, Godegisele was of delicate health and frail. Her complexion was waxen; her long pale-blonde hair was braided in two strands and fell from under her *obbon*—the name given by the Franks to a sort of skull-cap woven of gold and silver thread—over her shoulders, that were bare like her arms. The advanced stage of pregnancy in which she was imparted to her sweet sad features an expression of suffering. Godegisele wore the costume of the Frankish women of high condition—a long decolleté robe with open and flowing sleeves, and held by a scarf around her now unshapely waist. Her arms were ornamented with gold bracelets, studded with precious stones, while a sea-eel necklace that derived its name from the fish, which, when captured, twists itself around the arm in such a manner that its head touches the tip of its tail—wound its golden, ruby-dotted coil around her neck. One thing there was about Godegisele's robe that rendered it incongruous. Its wearer was frail, slender and short, but the rich robe seemed to have been made for a large and robust woman. About a score of young wretchedly clad female slaves sat around Godegisele upon the leaves that the floor was strewn with, while the count's wife occupied an armed stool over which a silver embroidered carpet was thrown. Several of the girl slaves were handsome. Some worked at their

distaffs like their mistress, others were engaged at their needles;
occasionally they exchanged a few words in a low voice and in
the Gallic tongue, which their mistress, being herself of Frankish extraction, understood poorly. One of them, named Morise,
a young and handsome girl with raven-black hair who was sold
to a noble Frank when ten years of age, spoke the language of
the conquerors fluently, on account of which Godegisele con-
versed with her in preference. At this moment the count's wife
dropped her distaff which she held across her knees and said
to the slave in a tremulous voice:

"And so, Morise, you saw her assassinated?"

"Yes, madam, I witnessed the sad scene. On that day she
wore that same green robe with silver flowers that you have on,
she also had on the handsome necklace and bracelets that I see
on your arms and neck."

Godegisele shuddered and could not withhold a fearful glance
from her bracelets and robe, the latter of which was twice too
large for her.

"And—for what reason did he kill her, Morise? What was
it that angered him?"

"He had drunk more than usual on that evening—he entered here, where we now are, unsteady of foot. It was winter—
there was a fire in the hearth. His wife Wisigarde sat at a
corner of the chimney. The seigneur count then had among us
a washerwoman, named Martine, for his favorite. He said to
Martine: 'Come, come, confounded wench—let's to bed—and
you, Wisigarde,' he added addressing his wife, 'take a lamp and
light us.'"

"That, certainly, was a great shame upon Wisigarde."

"All the more, madam, seeing she was of a proud temper
and impetuous nature. She often whipped and bit us, and she
quarrelled a good deal with the seigneur count."

"What, Morise! Did she dare quarrel with him?"

"Oh, she feared nothing—nothing! When she was in a rage, she roared and ground her teeth like a lioness."

"What a terrible woman!"

"Well, madam, that evening, instead of yielding to the whim of the seigneur count, and taking the lamp to light him to his bed, Wisigarde began scolding them both—the count and Martine."

"She certainly invited death! My blood freezes in my veins at the thought of it."

"Thereupon, madam, I saw, as clearly as I see you now, the count's eyes grow bloodshot and froth rise to his lips. He threw himself upon his wife, struck her in the face with his fist, and then, giving her a kick in the stomach, threw her to the ground. She was in as towering a rage as himself, and did not cease hurling invectives at him; she even tried to bite him, when, after he had thrown her upon the ground, he planted both his knees upon her chest. Finally, he held her throat so tight in both his large hands that her face became violet and she was strangled. After she lay dead, he went to bed with Martine."

"Morise, I fear me the same fate for myself, some day. That terrible count will yet kill me."

And shuddering over her whole frame, Godegisele dropped her head upon her bosom, and her distaff fell down at her feet.

"Oh, madam, you should not be so alarmed. As long, at any rate, as you will be pregnant, you will have nothing to fear—the seigneur count will not want to kill at one blow both his wife and child."

"But after I shall have given birth to that child—I shall then be killed like Wisigarde!"

"That will depend, madam, upon the humor of the seigneur count. He may prefer to cast you off and return you to your parents, as he did the other wives whom he did not kill."

"Oh, Morise! Would to heaven that monseigneur the count would return me to my family! What a misfortune to me it

was that Neroweg should have seen me when he visited Mayence! What a misfortune that the wisp of straw which he
threw at my breast when he took me to wife was not a sharp-
pointed dagger! I would have at least died amidst my own
family."

"What wisp of straw was that, madam?"

"Do you not know that it is the custom with us, that when
a Frank weds a free girl, he takes her right hand, and with his
left throws a wisp of straw into her bosom?"

"No, madam, I did not know that."

"It is the custom in Germany. Alas, Morise, I repeat it,
would that that wisp of straw had been a dagger! I would have
died without undergoing my present agony. And now that I
know about the murder of Wisigarde, my life will be but one
long and cruel agony."

"But, madam, you should have refused to wed the count,
seeing he inspired you with such horror."

"I dared not, Morise. Oh, he will surely kill me! Woe is
me! He will kill me!"

"Why think you, madam, that he will commit such a crime
again? You never as much as whisper a word, whatever he
may do or say. He abuses us, the female slaves, seeing he is
master, and you never complain; you never set foot outside of
the women's apartments, except for a short walk along the
fosse of the burg. Why, madam, I ask you, do you apprehend
that your husband will kill you?"

"When he is intoxicated he does not reason."

"That is true—there is always that danger."

"But that danger is continuous; he is every day intoxicated.
Oh, why did I come to this distant region of Gaul, where I feel
an utter stranger!"

And after a long interval of sad revery:

"Morise—my good Morise!"

"Madam, I am at your orders."

"You, all of you slaves, do not hate me, do you?"

"No, madam; you are not wicked like Wisigarde—you never whip and bite us."

"Morise, listen to me."

"Madam, I listen. But why are you silent? And your cheeks, otherwise so pale, growing incarnate—"

"It is because I dare not tell you. But listen, you are—you are—one of monseigneur the count's favorites."

"I have no choice—if not willingly, I must submit by force. Despite my repugnance for him, I prefer to share his bed whenever he orders me, than to be striped by his whip, or be sent out to turn the wheel of the mill; and by quietly submitting, I am employed in household work; that is easier than to be employed at the hard labor of the fields—it is a choice of evils—this is the lesser, and the food is not as poor."

"I know—I know. I do not blame you, Morise. But answer me without lying: when you are with the count, you do not, do you, seek to irritate him against me? Alas, we know of slaves who have in that way caused the death of their mistresses, and who thereupon became their seigneur's wife."

"I have such an aversion for him, madam, that I swear I never open my mouth but to say 'yes' or 'no' in answer to any question that he may put to me. Moreover, since he is always intoxicated at night when he calls me in, he hardly speaks. You see I have neither the chance nor the wish of speaking to him against you."

"Is that really true, Morise? Really?"

"Yes, yes, madam."

"I would like to make you some little present, but monseigneur never lets me have any money. He keeps all his money under lock and key in his coffers, and for only *morgen-gab,* the morning present that it is customary in our country for the husband to make to his wife, the count has given me the robes and jewels of his fourth wife, Wisigarde. Every day he de-

mands of me that I show them to him, and he counts them. I
have nothing to offer you, Morise, nothing but my friendship,
if you promise me not to irritate monseigneur against me."

"My heart would have to be very wicked, if I were to anger
monseigneur against you."

"Ah, Morise! How I would like to be in your place!"

"You, a count's wife—you would prefer to be a slave! Impossible!"

"He will not kill you."

"Bah! He would as soon kill me as any one else, if the
fancy took him—but you, madam, have in the meantime, beautiful dresses, rich jewels, slaves to serve you—and besides, you
are free."

"I do not step out of the burg."

"Because you do not wish to. Wisigarde rode on horseback
and hunted. You should have seen her on her black palfrey,
with her purple robe, and her falcon on her finger! At any
rate, though she be dead, she never wasted time grieving—while
you, madam, do nothing else than work at your distaff, or gaze
at the sky from your window, or weep—what a life! What a
sad existence!"

"Alas, it is because I am always thinking of my own country, of my parents, so far away—so far away from this country
of Gaul, where I am an utter stranger."

"Wisigarde did not trouble herself about such matters—she
drank deeply, and ate almost as much as the count."

"He always told me and my father that she died of an accident. And so you assure me, Morise, that it is there—on that
spot—that he killed her?"

"Yes, madam, he threw her down with a kick—she fell
near that beam—and then—"

"What ails you, Morise—why do you tremble?"

"Madam, madam, do you not hear?"

"What? Everything is quiet."

"There is someone walking in seigneur the count's room—I hear the seats pushed about."

"Oh, it is he—it is my husband!"

"Yes, madam, it is his step."

"Oh, I am afraid—remain near me!"

It was Neroweg. His latest libations had thrown him into a state of almost complete intoxication. He stepped into his wife's apartment with a drunken man's unsteady foot. At the sight of their master, all the slaves rose timidly. As to Godegisele, she was in such a tremor that she was hardly able to rise from her stool. The count stopped for a moment at the threshold, leaned one hand against the door-case, and, with his body swaying backward and forward, let his eyes travel over the scared slaves with a besotted and semi-libidinous look. After repeated hiccoughs he called out to his wife's confidant:

"Morise—come—come, confounded wench!"

And looking at Godegisele he added:

"You look pale—you seem troubled—my dove. Why so pale?"

The poor creature's mind doubtlessly ran upon the circumstances of the fateful night when her husband strangled his fourth wife, shortly after having used these very words towards his then favorite slave: 'Come, come, confounded wench!' Neroweg's words threw his wife into greater perturbation and frightened her to a degree that all she was able to say was:

"Monseigneur! Monseigneur! Mercy!"

"What! What ails you? Answer!" shouted the count brutally. "Do you, perchance, object that I told Morise to come? Dare you cross me?"

"No! Oh, no! Is not monseigneur master in this place? Are not his female slaves at his orders? And am not I, Godegisele, myself, his humble servant?"

And the unhappy woman, wholly losing her head in her terror, as she imagined herself on the point of being strangled

like Wisigarde, who owed her death to her refusal to light her
husband and his night's companion to the conjugal bed, hastened to stammer:

"On the contrary—if monseigneur wishes, I shall light him
to his bed with this lamp."

"Oh, madam!" Morise whispered to her mistress. "What
an unfortunate inspiration is that! It is to recall to the count's
memory the murder of his other wife."

Indeed, at the last words of Godegisele a shudder ran through
Neroweg; he brusquely stepped towards her; seized her threat-
eningly by the arm and bellowed in a maudlin voice:

"Why do you propose to light me to bed with a lamp?"

"Mercy, monseigneur! Do not kill me!"—and she dropped
upon her knees. "Oh, do not kill me, your servant, as you
killed Wisigarde."

The count suddenly grew as pale as his wife, and, stricken
with a terror that stimulated his inebriety, he cried:

"She knows that I strangled Wisigarde! She is uttering the
same words that Wisigarde uttered when I killed her! This is
the work of some evil spirit! Wisigarde herself or her spectre
will perhaps appear this night before my bed and torment me!
It is a warning from heaven—or from hell. The devil must be
conjured away!"

And turning to Morise:

"Run quick for the clerk! He shall pray at my side during
the night—he shall not leave me. The spectre of Wisigarde
will not dare to approach me with a priest at my side."

The count's terror increased amain while Morise ran out
for the clerk, and Godegisele, more dead than alive with fear,
clung on her knees to the beam as she felt her strength wholly
leaving her. The count noticed not her distress, but also dropping on his knees smote his chest and cried:

"Lord, God! Have mercy upon a miserable sinner! I paid
for my brother's death, I paid for the death of my wife Wisi-

garde, I shall pay still more to keep Wisigarde from haunting me! I shall to-morrow start the building of the chapel in the fastness of Allange; I shall have the villa of Bishop Cautin rebuilt! Lord! Good Lord God! Have mercy upon a miserable sinner! Deliver me from the devil and from the spectre of Wisigarde!"

And the fervent and devout believer, besotted with terror and intoxication, furiously smote his chest as, filled with frightful anxiety, he awaited the arrival of the clerk.

Such was the humanity, generousness, enlightenment of the race of the conquerors of old Gaul! What a tender attachment to their wives! What a respect for the sweet bonds of the family and for the sanctity of the domestic hearth! Oh, our mothers! Virile matrons, so venerated by our ancestors! Proud Gallic women of yore, who sat beside your husbands at the solemn councils of the state, where peace and war were decided upon! Wives beloved, valiant and strong in arms! Holy virgins! Women emperors! O, Margarid, Hena, Meroe, Loyse, Genevieve, Ellen, Sampso, Victoria the Great—rejoice! Rejoice that you have quitted this world for the mysterious worlds where we shall live forever! Rejoice at the strongness of your hearts! What indignation, what shame, what a grief to your souls at the sight of your sisters—although of a different race from your own and hostile—at the sight of women—the wives of kings, seigneurs and warriors—treated, the wicked and the good alike, with such contempt and ferocity by their barbarous husbands!

Such are those Franks whom the bishops invited to the quarry of Gaul! Such are the conquerors whom the priests of Christ fondle, caress, flatter and bless!

CHAPTER IV.

THE LION OF POITIERS.

Seigneur count! Seigneur count Néroweg! Wake up! Instead of having spent the night, as you expected, in the arms of one of your female slaves, out of fear for the devil you spent it on your knees, close to your clerk, and repeating in a maudlin and besotted voice the prayers that the holy man mumbled, half asleep, into your ears. After having eaten and drunk his fill he would have by far preferred his own bed to your company. Finally reassured by the first peep of day—a time that bars out the demons—you fell asleep on your couch, furnished with bearskins, the trophies of the chase. Seigneur count Neroweg, awake! One of the five sons of your good King Clotaire, to-day the sole master of Gaul—all the other sons and grandsons of the pious Clovis, who rests in consecrated ground in the basilica of the venerated apostles at Paris, having died—one of the five sons of that King Clotaire, Chram by name, a bastard son—but what does that matter!—and governor of Auvergne in his father's name, Chram is approaching! He comes, a signal favor, with his three favorites, a goodly number of leudes in the train of his *antrustions,* as the royal favorites proudly style themselves. Awake, Neroweg! Awake, seigneur count! There is Chram, coming to pay you a visit. Brilliant and numerous is the cavalcade of his suite. The three dear friends of Chram, still dearer friends of pillage, of murder and of rape, accompany the royal personage, do you not hear? Their names are Imnachair, Spatachair, and the "Lion of Poitiers," the renegade Gaul, who, like so many others of his stripe, rallied to the conquering Franks.

The "Lion of Poitiers" earned his name by reason of his carnivorous taste for rapine and flesh dripping blood.

Seigneur count! Seigneur count Neroweg! Will you not wake up? Wake up also your wife Godegisele, who spent the night dreaming of strangled wives. Be up and doing. Let Godegisele array herself in the most resplendent jewels of your fourth wife Wisigarde! Hurry, hurry, seigneur count! Let Godegisele don her most attractive raiment! She may be to the taste of Chram or of his favorites. He is a gracious king, an accommodating king. There is none more so. Is a woman, whether free or slave, pleasing to the eye of any friend of his, he forthwith equips his favorite with a *royal diploma,* by virtue of which he takes the woman that he covets.

Quick, quick, seigneur count! Order your leudes to take horse and your foot soldiers to put on their gala armors, and yourself, seigneur count, head your band, cased in your parade armor and carrying on your side the magnificent gold-hilted Spanish sword, which you stole on the occasion of the plundering of the land of the Visigoths, the "damned Arians" and "accursed heretics," upon whom the Catholic bishops let you loose with the fagot in one hand, the sword in the other, exactly as you let loose your pack of hounds upon the wild beasts of the forest! Be quick, be quick, leap upon your roan horse harnessed in its saddle and bridle of red leather, with bit and stirrups of silver! Quick! Ride out at a gallop to meet your glorious Prince Chram; ride out at the head of your horsemen and footmen! Already your royal guest and his suite, whose approach one of their forerunners has announced, are only at a little distance from your burg. Seigneur count, hasten to greet him and lead him into your seigniorial residence! You hardly expected to hear such auspicious tidings; moreover your good friend and protector, Bishop Cautin accompanies Prince Chram.

"A curse upon the arrival of this Chram," said Neroweg. "However short the stay of him and his men at my burg, they will drink up my wine, eat up all my provisions, and who knows but also pilfer some of my gold and silver vases. Neither I nor my companions have any love for these court leudes, who always have the air of looking down upon us because they quarter in palaces and cities."

Thus spoke count Neroweg as, followed by his warriors, he rode out to meet Prince Chram, whom he found, together with his suite, within two bows' shot of the fosse that girded the burg.

What a beautiful, noble, glorious, luminous sight is that of a longhaired prince, especially when his hair consists of a long tangled mop, that scissors have never touched, such being one of the distinctive attributes of the royal Frankish family. Unfortunately, although still young, Prince Chram, being worn by drunkenness and all manner of enervating excesses, was almost wholly bald. Only from his neck and temples did a few long and straggling locks of light hair tumble down upon his chest and arched back. His long dalmatica of purple fabric, slit on the side at the height of his knees, half hid the shoulders and crupper of his black horse. Bandelets of gilt leather criss-crossed his tight-fitting hose from his ankles up to his knees. His spurred shoes rested upon gilt stirrups; his long gold-hilted sword was sheathed in white cloth and hung from a superbly ornamented belt. In lieu of a whip, he carried a cane of precious wood with a head of chiseled gold, upon which, when the worn-out debauchee walked, he leaned heavily. Prince Chram's face was villainous. On his right Bishop Cautin rode as proudly as a man of war. From time to time the prelate cast an uneasy glance at Chram, because, though he sufficiently detested Chram, he was well aware that Chram detested him still more. At the Prince's right rode the "Lion of Poitiers," the hardened criminal who, together with Imnachair and Spatachair, both of whom rode close behind him in the second rank, constituted a trinity of perdition ample enough to damn Chram, had not Chram been damned in his very mother's womb, as the

priests express it. Insolence and profligacy, haughty disdain
and cruelty were so profoundly graven on the features of the
"Lion of Poitiers," the renegade Gaul, that even a hundred
years after his death it should not have been difficult still to
trace upon the bones of his face the words "profligacy, insolence and cruelty."

After the Frankish fashion these three seigneurs wore
rich short-sleeved tunics over their jackets, tight-fitting hose,
and gaiters of cured leather with the fleece on the outside.
Behind Chram and his three friends rode his seneschal, the
count of his stables, the mayor of his palace, his butler, and
other officers of the first rank, because the Prince kept a royal
establishment. A little distance behind these distinguished per-
sonages came his bodyguard which consisted of leudes and other
warriors armed cap-a-pie. Their tufted casques, their polished
and brilliant cuirasses and greaves glittered in the sun. Their
spirited horses pranced under their rich caparisons. The stream-
ers at the head of their lances fluttered on the breeze, while their
painted and gilded bucklers dangled from the pommels of their
saddles. As showy and imposing as was the appearance of the
princely suite, so miserably shabby and grotesque was the aspect
presented by the leudes of the count. A considerable number
of his suite wore incomplete and rough, dented armor; others,
the possessors of cuirasses, had their heads covered with woolen
caps; the swords, no less ill-kept than the cuirasses, were mostly
orphaned of their sheaths, and in several instances the imple-
ment of war was held to its rider's belt by cords, while the shaft
of more than one lance was crooked, and was still as rough as
when first taken from the brush. Most of the horses of the
count's leudes matched their riders in their appearance. It was
not yet the hour for the slaves to proceed to the fields, and a
goodly number of Neroweg's companions, in default of battle
steeds, sat astride of draft and plow horses bridled with ropes.
By the faith of a Vagre, it was a joyful sight to watch the wild

and envious looks that the leudes of the count cast at the suite of Chram, and the insolent and mocking looks that the princely retinue threw upon the count's ramshackle troop. Behind the Prince's men, came the pages, the servants and the slaves who were on foot and led the ox-teams and dray-horses that drew heavy laden carts which the inhabitants of the regions crossed by the Prince and his suite were honored with the privilege of filling up gratuitously.

Count Neroweg advanced alone on horseback towards his royal guest, who, reining in his mount, said to Neroweg:

"Count, on my way from Clermont to Poitiers, I thought I would stop at your burg."

"Your glory is welcome on my domain. It is partly made up of salic lands; these I hold of my father, who held them both of his sword and the bounty of your grandfather, Clovis. It is your right to lodge, when journeying, at the houses of the counts and beneficiaries of the King, and to them it is a pleasure to extend to you hospitality."

"Count," insolently put in the Lion of Poitiers, "is your wife young and handsome? Is she worth the trouble of courting?"

"My favorite," observed Chram, making a sign to the renegade Gaul that he moderate his language, "who asks to know whether your wife is young and handsome, my favorite, the Lion of Poitiers, loves to joke, by nature."

"I shall then answer the Lion of Poitiers that neither he nor you will be able to decide whether my wife is young and handsome or old and ugly; she is with child and unwell, and will not leave her apartments."

"If your wife is with child," replied the Lion of Poitiers, "who may the father be?"

"Count, do not mind his raillery. I told you, my friend is a joker by nature."

"Chram, I shall not take offence at the jokes of your favorite. Let us proceed to the burg."

"Lead the way, count, we shall follow."

The joint cavalcades started for the burg, and the conversation proceeded.

"Count, admit to our royal master Chram that, in concealing your wife, you keep your treasure under lock and key for fear of its being stolen from you."

"My favorite, Spatachair, who holds that language to you, Neroweg, is also of a humorous disposition."

"Prince, meseems you select very gay, and perhaps too bold a set of friends."

"Neroweg, you hide your wife from us—it is your right. We shall hunt her up in her nest—that is our right. There is no lock or key safe against a good thief. The hunt is up."

"Chram, this is another of your humorous friends, I suppose?"

"Yes, count, the most humorous of all—the boldest—his name is Imnachair."

"And my name is Neroweg; I shall ask seigneur Imnachair what will the thief do when he has found the nest and the dove?"

"Neroweg, your wife will tell you all about it, after we shall have discovered the belle—we shall put our hands on that treasure as surely as I am the Lion of Poitiers."

"And I," cried Neroweg, "as surely as I am the King's count in this country of Auvergne, shall kill like a dog or a prowling fox whomever would attempt the role of a lion in my house!"

"Oh, oh, count, you hold bold language! Is it the brilliant army which you lead at your heels that makes you so audacious?" queried the Prince's favorite, nodding towards Neroweg's ramshackle leudes. "If that band is up to its looks, we are lost!"

Two or three of the count's leudes who had been drawing

nearer, and heard the insolent jokes of Chram's favorite grumbled aloud in angry accents:

"We do not like to see Neroweg bantered!"

"A count's leudes are matches for royal leudes!"

"The polish of the steel does not make its temper."

One of Chram's men turned towards his companions, and laughing, pointed at the count's people with the tip of his lance while sarcastically alluding to their rustic appearance:

"Are these plow-slaves disguised as warriors, or warriors disguised as plow-slaves?"

The royal cortege answered the sally with a loud outburst of laughter. The two sides were beginning to cast defiant looks at each other when Bishop Cautin cried:

"My dear sons in Christ, I, your bishop and spiritual father, recommend to you coolness and good will. A truce with unseasonable jokes!"

"Count," said Chram to Neroweg flippantly, "mistrust this profligate and hypocritical bishop. Do not bestow upon him alone the privilege of singing your wife's praises—holy man though he be, he would as leave sing the praises of Venus, the goddess of the pagans!"

"Chram, I am the servant of the son of our glorious King Clotaire; but as bishop I am entitled to your respect."

"You are right; nowadays you bishops have become almost as powerful, and above all as rich as ourselves, the Kings."

"Chram, you mention the power and the wealth of the bishops of Gaul. You seem to forget that our power is of the Lord, and our riches are the goods of the poor!"

"By the slack skin of all the purses that you have rifled, you fat weasel who suck the yellow of the eggs and leave only the shell to the sots, for once you have told the truth. Aye, your riches are the goods of the poor, but you have bagged these goods for yourself."

"Glorious Prince, I have accompanied you to the burg of

my son in Christ, Count Neroweg, in order to fulfill the act of high justice that you know of, but not in order to allow our holy Catholic and apostolic religion to be impudently made sport of in my person!"

"And I maintain that your power and riches increase by the day. I have two daughters; who knows but they will yet see the royal power shrink in even measure as the grasping usurpations of the bishops, with whom we shared our conquest, gain ground—a parcel of bishops whom we enriched, to whom we have been the men at arms, and who are ungrateful towards their benefactors!"

"Men at arms to us, men of peace? You err, O, Prince! Our only arms are sermons and exhortations."

"And when the people laugh at your sermons, as the Visigoths did, the Arians of Provence and Languedoc, then you send us to extirpate their heresy with fire and sword! Those are your real arms!"

"Glory to God! In those wars against the heretics, the Frankish Kings took an immense booty, they caused the orthodox faith to triumph, and snatched the souls of men from the everlasting flames by leading them back to the bosom of the holy Church."

He who might have assisted at the recent supper at the episcopal villa, where the bishop had Neroweg for his guest, would not have recognized Cautin. The holy man, being then in *tete-a-tete* with the count, a stupid, brutal and blind believer, cared not to clothe himself in the dignity of language. But now, in the presence of Chram, a brazen jester whom he detested, he felt the need to impose, both with language and bearing, respect and fear, if not upon the Prince himself and his favorites, the latter of whom were as impudent as himself, then at least upon their suite, who were infinitely less intelligent and proportionally devout. There was another grave apprehension that weighed upon Cautin's mind. He was in great fear that

the audacious example of Chram and his friends might shake
the naïve and fruitful credulity of Neroweg, from which Cautin
drew much profit by the cultivation and exploitation of the devil.
From the corner of his eye the bishop saw the count give a sly
ear to the insolent jests of Chram, which seemed at once to
please and frighten him. The Prince doubtlessly **was** wondering whether Neroweg was blockish enough to believe in the
miraculous powers of the bishop, and to pay as dearly as he was
reputed to do for the absolutions of the prelate. Cautin, being a
man of extraordinary ability, saw his opportunity to strike a
master blow. Being in the habit of closely watching the weather
and of observing the premonitions of the storms that are so sudden and of frequent occurrence in mountainous countries, he, as
well as so many other priests, utilized his weather-wisdom to
frighten the simple-minded. The prelate had for some little
time noticed a black cloud, which, barely visible at first over the
crest of a peak in the distant horizon, was bound soon to spread
over the sky and darken the sun, which, at the moment, was
shining brilliantly. Accordingly, at the first fresh insolent jest
on the part of Chram at the impositions practiced by the clergy,
the prelate answered, measuring the length of his words with the
progress made by the spreading storm-cloud:

"It is not for an unworthy servant of God, for a humble
earth worm like me, to defend the Church of the Eternal; the
Lord has His own power and miracles with which to convince
the incredulous, His celestial punishments with which to chastise the impious. Woe, I say, unto the man who dares now, in
the face of that sun that shines at this moment with such vivid
luster over our heads," the bishop proceeded with ever louder
voice; "woe, I say, and malediction unto him who, in the face of
the Almighty, Who sees, hears, judges and punishes us; malediction upon him who dares insult His divinity in the sacred person of His bishops! Is there any present, Prince or seigneur,
who dares outrage divine majesty?"

"There is here the Lion of Poitiers, who makes you this answer: Cautin, bishop of Clermont, I shall break my switch
over your back if you do not quit speaking with such insolence."

By the faith of a Vagre! The Lion of Poitiers, the renegade
Gaul, had some occasional good quality. But his bold words
caused most of those who heard them to shudder; the royal suite
as well as the leudes of the count looked scandalized. To these
faithful it seemed a monstrous thing to break a switch over the
back of a bishop, even if, as in the instance of Cautin, he was
guilty of burying a human being alive in the sepulchre of a
corpse.* A profound stupor succeeded upon the threat made by
the Lion of Poitiers. Even Chram himself looked shocked at
the audacity of his favorite. Cautin took in the scene at a
glance. Simulating a saintly horror and turning full towards
the Lion of Poitiers, who defiantly swung his switch, the prelate
cried, raising his hands heavenward:

"Unhappy, impious man, have pity upon yourself! The
Lord has heard your blasphemy. Behold how the skies darken—
the sun hides its face—behold the precursors of celestial wrath!
Down on your knees, my dear sons! Down on your knees! Your
father in God bids you! Pray the Eternal to appease His
wrath, kindled by the frightful blasphemy!"

And Cautin precipitately descended from his horse. But he
did not kneel. Standing erect with his hands outstretched to
heaven, in the posture of a priest officiating at the altar, he
seemed to be communing with some invisible being as if conjuring away the celestial wrath.

At the bishop's voice, Chram's servants and slaves, all of
whom were terrified by the seemingly sudden storm, threw themselves upon their knees; most of the Prince's cortege likewise
leaped down from their horses and knelt, in no less consternation than the slaves and servants at the sight of the sun's face
suddenly darkened when the Lion of Poitiers threatened the

---

* Bishop Gregory of Tours. Histoire des Franks, IV. 12.

bishop with his switch. Neroweg, who was one of the first on his knees, unctuously smote his chest; Chram, however, together with his favorites and a few others of his familiars, kept their saddles, hesitating out of pride to follow the bishop's orders. With an imperious gesture and threatening accent the latter cried:

"Down on your knees, O King! The King is no more than the slave in the eye of the Almighty. Both King and slave must bow down to earth in order to appease the wrath of the Eternal. Down on your knees, O King! Down on your knees, both you and your favorites!"

"Dare you issue orders to me?" cried Chram pale with rage at the sight of the abject submission of his men to the bishop's orders. "Who is master here, you or I, insolent priest?"

A thunder clap that reverberated in the hollows of the mountain closed the mouth of Chram, and served the knavery of Cautin to perfection. Louder and more imperiously than before the prelate repeated:

"Down on your knees! Hear you not the thunder of heaven, the rumbling voice of the Almighty? Will you draw down a shower of fire upon the heads of us all? O, Lord, have pity upon us! Remove the cataracts of burning lava, that, in Your wrath at the impious, You are about to shower down upon them, and, perhaps, upon us also, miserable sinners that we all are! Even the purest of heart can not claim to be irreproachable before Your majesty, O, Lord!"

Several fresh claps of thunder, preceded by blinding flashes of lightning, carried the fright of Chram's suite to the highest pitch. The Prince himself did not remain wholly unaffected, despite his innate incredulity, audacity and superb insolence. His pride nevertheless still revolted at the idea of yielding to the bishop's orders, and murmurs, at first subdued, but speedily breaking out in open threats, rose from all parts of his suite, cortege and retinue.

"Down on your knees, our Prince—on your knees!"

"Insignificant as we are, we do not wish to burn in the fire of heaven for the sake of your and your favorite's impiousness!"

"Down on your knees, our Prince! Down on your knees! Obey the orders of the holy bishop—it is the Lord who speaks to us through his mouth!"

"Down on your knees, King! Down on your knees!"

Chram was forced to yield. He feared to irritate his followers beyond the point of safety; above all, he feared setting a public example of rebellion against the bishops, who were such useful props to the conquerors. Grumbling and blaspheming between his teeth, Chram finally and slowly alighted from his horse and motioned his two favorites Imnachair and Spatachair, both of whom took the hint, to do as he did, and drop down upon their knees.

Left alone on horseback, and looking down upon the prostrate crowd, the Lion of Poitiers braved the increasingly loud clatter of the thunder peals with intrepid front and a sardonic smile upon his lips.

"Down on your knees!" cried several voices in towering anger. "Down on your knees, Lion of Poitiers!"

"Our King Chram has knelt down, and the impious man, the cause of all the trouble through his sacrilegious threats, he alone refuses obedience!"

"The blasphemer will draw a deluge of fire upon our heads!"

"My sons, my dear sons!" cried Cautin, who was the only one on foot, as the Lion of Poitiers was the only one on horseback. "Let us prepare for death! A single grain of darnel will suffice to rot a muid of wheat—a single hardened sinner will, perhaps, cause the death of us all, however innocent we be. Let us resign ourselves to our fate, my dear sons—may the will of God be done—He will, perhaps, open to us the doors of paradise!"

The terrified crowd began to utter increasingly angry cries

at the Lion of Poitiers. Neroweg, in whose bosom still rankled
the insulting jests of the insolent royal favorite, half rose, drew
his sword and cried:

"Death to the impious wretch! His blood will appease the
wrath of the Eternal!"

"Yes! Yes! Death!" came from a crowd of furious voices,
so loud that the rattle of the thunder failed to drown the human
explosion.

Overhead the sky looked like one sheet of flame; the flashes
of lightning succeeded one another rapidly, vivid, blinding. The
bravest trembled; Prince Chram himself began to regret his jests
and sneers at the bishop. Seeing that the Lion of Poitiers remained unperturbed, and that he answered Neroweg's threats
and the furious outcries of the crowd with a look of disdain,
the Prince said to his favorite:

"Come down from your horse and kneel beside us—if you
refuse, I shall let them cut you to pieces—never have I witnessed such a storm. You were wrong in threatening the bishop
with your switch; I myself regret having used offensive language towards him—the fire of heaven may from one moment
to the other drop down upon us."

The Lion of Poitiers crimsoned with rage, but realizing the
fate that further resistance on his part would draw upon him, he
yielded. Grinding his teeth, he followed the orders of Chram,
alighted from his horse, and after a further instant of hesitation, dropped upon his knees and shook his fist at Cautin. The
bishop, who had remained erect, towering above the cowering
crowd at his feet, answered the gesture of the Lion of Poitiers
with a look of triumph that he cast upon Chram and his favorites; he regaled his eyes by letting them wander over the Prince,
his favorites, the assembled leudes, the servants and slaves—all
bowed down to the earth with fear and respect before him. Rel-
ishing his signal victory he said to himself:

"Yes, we triumph! Yes, royal stripling, the bishop is

mightier than you. There you are at my feet with your forehead in the dust."

The bishop then knelt down himself and cried out aloud in a penetrating voice:

"Glory to Thee, O Lord! Glory to Thee! The impious rebel, seized with holy terror bows down his haughty forehead. The devouring lion has become the most timid lamb before Thy divine majesty. Calm Thy just wrath, O Lord! Have mercy upon us all, here upon our knees before Thee! Dissipate the darkness that obscures the firmament! Remove the fiery clouds that the obduracy of a sinner drew over our heads! Deign, O Almighty Lord to give a public manifestation that the voice of Thy unworthy servant has reached Thy throne!"

The prelate said many more admirable things, now measuring and grading his utterances of grace and mercy according as the storm receded and subsided, just as, at its approach, he modulated his threatening words. The skilful man closed his conjuration to the roll of the receding thunder—"the last rumblings," he said "of the Eternal's angered voice," finally appeased by his prayers. Soon thereupon the sky cleared; the clouds dispersed, the sun shone anew in all its pristine splendor; and the royal cortege, now again as serene as the sky, resumed their tramp towards the burg of Neroweg singing at the top of their voices:

"Glory, eternal glory to the Lord!"

"Glory, glory, our blessed bishop!"

"Hosanna! *Gloria in excelsis Deo!*"

"The Lord miraculously turned from us the angry fire of heaven!"

"The impious man bowed down his rebellious head!"

"Glory! Glory to the Lord!"

CHAPTER V.

IN THE TREASURE CHAMBER.

While the slaves of Chram were busy leading the horses to the stables, and placing the loaded carts and the saddles under the shelter of a broad shed that served for cover to large stocks of hay, the royal leudes ate and drank with the appetite and thirst of men who were on the road since early morn. Having, together with his three favorites, done honor to the count's repast, Chram said to Neroweg:

"Take me to a place where we can talk privately. You surely have some secret chamber where you keep your treasure—let us closet ourselves there."

Neroweg seemed in no haste to comply. Doubtlessly he was not over-anxious to introduce the son of his King into the secret retreat. Noticing the count's hesitation, Chram proceeded to say:

"If there is another apartment in your burg that is more secluded than your treasure chamber, it will suit me better. Your wife's chamber, perhaps? Let us go there."

"No—no. Come to my treasure chamber. But first wait till I have issued the necessary orders so that your people may not want for anything and the horses be properly tended.

Saying this Neroweg took one of his leudes aside and whispered to him:

"Ansowald, you and Bertefred will arm yourselves well and remain near the door of the apartment into which I am to go with Chram. Hold yourselves in readiness to run in at my first call."

"What do you fear, seigneur count?"

"The family of Clovis has a strong liking for other people's goods. Although my coffers are under triple locks and ribbed with iron, I like to feel that you and Bertefred are ready at the door with your hands on your swords."

"We shall do as you bid us."

"Order Rigomer and Bertechram to hold themselves equally well armed at the door of the women's apartment. Let them strike without mercy whomsoever should attempt to introduce himself into Godegisele's chamber. Let them immediately give the alarm. I mistrust the Lion of Poitiers. Neither do I take the other two favorites of Chram to be less pagan or less dissolute than the wild lion himself. I hold them capable of anything—just as their royal master. Did you count the number of armed men in Chram's suite?"

"He brought in only one-half of his leudes—his *antrustions,* as the haughty crew style themselves. They look down with contempt upon us because they are pursuivants of a King."

"Shortly ago as they were at table," put in Bertechram, "they affected to eat with disgust and they examined the bottom of the pots as if to make sure that they were clean. They do not cease sneering at our earthen and tin wares—especially at our kitchen utensils."

"I know—I know—they want to drive me to exhibit my gold and silver wares, many a piece of which they will purloin. But I am on my guard."

"Neroweg, blood may yet flow before evening if the insolent fellows do not desist from their impertinencies. Our patience is near the end of its tether."

"Fortunately, however, we, your faithful leudes, together with the footmen and the slaves whom we can safely arm, are as numerous as the men who compose the escort of Chram."

"Come, come, my good companions; do not heat yourselves, my friends. If any quarrels should break out at table, dishes will be broken, and they will have to be replaced. We must bear that in mind."

"Neroweg, honor is before dishes—even if the dish be of gold or silver."

"Certainly, but it is unnecessary to provoke a quarrel. Keep yourselves on your guard, and see to it that watch is kept at the door of the women's apartment—hand on sword."

"It will be done as you order."

A moment later Prince Chram and the count found themselves alone in the latter's treasure room. They were engaged in an important and serious conference.

"Count, how much are the treasures worth that are locked in these coffers?"

"Oh, they do not contain much—they are large on the principle that it is always well to be provided with a large pot and a big coffer, as we say in Germany, but they are almost empty."

"So much the worse, count. I wished to double, triple and even quadruple the value of their contents."

"Are you jesting?"

"Count, I desire to increase your power and wealth beyond even your hopes. I swear as much by the indivisible Trinity."

"I then believe you. After this morning's miracle, you would not dare to risk drawing upon my house the fire of heaven, by taking so redoubtable an oath in vain. But what is your reason for wishing to add so greatly to my power and wealth?"

"Because I have a personal interest in so doing."

"You convince me."

"Would you like to have domains as vast as those of a King's son?"

"I surely would."

"Would you like to have, instead of those half empty coffers, a hundred others bursting with gold, precious stones, vases, goblets, bowls, armors and costly fabrics?"

"Certainly I would."

"Would you, instead of being count of a city in Auvergne, govern a whole province—in short, be as rich and powerful as you could wish?"

"By the indivisible Trinity, are you serious? Explain yourself; I drink in your words."

"I swear to you by the Almighty God."

"Do you also swear by the great St. Martin, my patron saint?"

"I swear it also by the great St. Martin that my tender is serious."

"Well, then, to the point. What is your project?"

"At this hour my father Clotaire is outside of Gaul warring against the Saxons. I propose to profit by his absence and make myself King in the place of my father. Several counts and dukes of the neighborhood have entered into the conspiracy. Will you be with or against me?"

"And what about your brothers, Charibert, Gontran, Chilperic and Sigebert? Will they leave your father's kingdom to you alone?"

"I shall have all my brothers killed."

"Clovis, your grandfather, as well as his sons, all rid themselves of their nearest relatives in the same fashion. You would be proceeding according to the traditions of your house."

"Answer, count; will you pledge yourself by a sacred oath to combat on my side at the head of your men? If you will, then, by an equal oath, I shall pledge myself to make you duke of whatever province you may choose, and to relinquish to you the goods, treasures, slaves and domains of the richest seigneurs who may have sided with my father against me."

"What you demand of me, if I understand you rightly, is that I pledge myself, in my own name and the name of my leudes and pursuivants, to *obey your mouth,* as we express it in Germany?"

"Yes, that is my demand."

"But what fate do you reserve for your father?"

"His own bodyguard came near cutting him to pieces just before the war with the Saxons. Are you aware of that?"

"Such a rumor did reach us."

"Well, then, my plan is to have my brothers killed; to declare that my father died in the war with the Saxons; and then to pronounce myself King of Gaul in his place."

"But when he returns from Saxony with his army, what will you do then?"

"I shall take the field against him at the head of my leudes, and I shall kill him—just as he killed his nephews."

"I am thinking of what may happen to me. If in the war with your father you go down, and I am found mixed up in the affair—it will go ill with me. I would then be stripped as a traitor of all the lands that I hold in *benefice,* only my salic lands would be left to me."

"Do you expect to win in a game without taking any risks?"

"I would much prefer that! But listen, Chram. Let the counts and dukes of Poitou, Limousin and Anjou take your side against your father, then I and my leudes will *obey your mouth.* But I shall not openly declare myself in your favor until the others shall have first taken up arms openly."

"You wish to play a safe game."

"Yes, I wish to risk little and gain much—I sincerely admit it."

"Very well—then let us exchange pledges."

"Wait a moment, King; we shall swear upon a sacred relic."

"What are you doing? Why open that coffer? Leave the lid up so that I may see your treasures. By my royal hair, I never in my life have seen a more magnificent Bible case than this!" exclaimed Chram as Neroweg lifted the precious Bible case from the coffer. "It is all gold, rubies, pearls and carbuncles. From what pillage did you get that?"

"In a city of Touraine. The gospels within are all written out in gold letters."

"The case is superb. I am dazzled by it."

"King, we shall take our pledge upon these gospels."

"I consent. Well, then, upon these holy Gospels, I, Chram, son of Clotaire, swear by the indivisible Trinity and by the great St. Martin, and according to the formula consecrated in Germany, that, 'if you, Neroweg, count of the city of Clermont in Auvergne, yourself and your leudes, who once stood on the side of the King, my father, will now come over to the side of me, Chram, who propose to constitute myself King over you, and that if I do so constitute myself, I shall make you duke of some great province of your own choice, and shall give you the domains, houses, slaves and treasures of the richest of the seigneurs who may have stood by my father and against me. Amen.' "

"And I, Neroweg, count of the city of Clermont in Auvergne, swear on these Gospels, by the indivisible Trinity and the great St. Martin, that if the counts and dukes of Poitou, Limousin and Anjou, instead of continuing as heretofore on the side of your father, openly go over to your side, and in arms, for the purpose of establishing you, Chram, as King over them, then I together with my men, will do likewise in order that you may be established King over us. And may I be consigned to the eternal fires if I fail in my oath! Amen."

"And may I, Chram, be consigned to the eternal fires if I fail in my oath! It is sworn before God."

"It is sworn before the great St. Martin."

"And now, count, allow me to examine this magnificent Bible case. Count, I have never seen anyone comparable with you for the quickness with which you open and close a coffer. Our oath now binds us together, and I can speak to you plainly. The first thing that I now have to do is to rid myself of my four brothers, Gontran, Sigebert, Chilperic and Charibert."

"The glorious Clovis, your grandfather, always proceeded in

that fashion when he thought proper to join some new kingdom or other heritage to his possessions. He always killed first and seized afterwards. He then had no adversary to combat."

"My father Clotaire has also been of that opinion. He began by killing the children of his brother Clodomir, whereupon he seized their heritage."

"Others, like your uncle Theodorik, on the contrary, seized first, and then sought to kill—that was unskilful. A corpse is more easily plundered than a live body."

"Count, you are endowed with the wisdom of a Solomon; but I can not kill my brothers myself. Two of them are very strong men, while I am rather feeble and worn out. Moreover, they will not willingly furnish me with the opportunity. They mistrust me. I have fixed upon three determined men to commit the murders; they are men that I can reckon with. I need a fourth."

"Where shall we find him?"

"Here—in the country of Auvergne."

"In my burg?"

"Yes; perhaps in your own house."

"What!"

"Do you know the reason why Bishop Cautin has been anxious to accompany me to this place?"

"I do not."

"It is that the bishop is in great hurry to try, sentence and witness the execution of the Vagres and their accomplices who are held prisoners in the *ergastula* of this burg—above all because he wishes to witness the execution of the bishopess."

"I still do not understand you, Chram. The two criminals, together with the women who are their accomplices, are to be taken to Clermont, so soon as they shall have recovered from their wounds, to be tried there by the *curia.*"

"According to the reliable rumors that have reached us, the bishop fears, and not without good reason, that the populace of

Clermont may rise in revolt in order to set the bandits free the moment they arrive in the city of Clermont. The names of the hermit laborer and Ronan the Vagre are dear to the race of slaves and vagabonds. It would be just like them to raise a riot and seek to set the bandits free—while here, at the burg, nothing of the sort need be feared."

"Such an uprising would be serious."

"I promised Bishop Cautin that, if you consent, then I, Chram, now King in Auvergne in my father's name, shall issue orders that the criminals be tried, sentenced and executed here at this burg, before your own justiciary *mahl.*"

"If my good father Cautin thinks so, I shall accept his opinion. I am as desirous as himself to witness the execution of those bandits, and I would sooner give twenty gold sous than see them escape death, a thing that, as you say, might happen if they are taken to Clermont and the vile population of the city should rise in their favor. But what has this to do with the murder of your brothers?"

"Is Ronan the Vagre healed of his wounds? I understand he is. He has the reputation of being a resolute bandit."

"He is a demon—a prop of hell."

"Suppose that after that demon shall have been sentenced to some frightful death he were told: 'You shall have grace, you shall be set free, but upon condition that you kill a certain person—after the murder is committed you will receive twenty gold sous for your reward'—do you think he would refuse such an offer?"

"Chram, that devil of a Ronan and his band killed nine of my bravest leudes; they pillaged and set fire to the episcopal villa and the place is to be rebuilt at my expense. As sure as the great St. Martin is in paradise, the cursed Vagre shall not be set free, he shall not escape the death that his crimes deserve!"

"Who says otherwise?"

"You speak of granting him grace."

"But after he shall have committed the murder, then, instead of counting out twenty gold sous to the Vagre, twenty blows with an iron bar will be counted out on his back, after which he can be quartered or otherwise disposed of in short order. Ah, that seems to amuse you."

"I laugh because it reminds me of the swindling baldrics and necklaces with which your grandfather Clovis one day rewarded his accomplices after they dispatched the two Ragnacaires. The Vagre will return in order to receive the twenty gold sous promised to him, instead of which a hundred blows will be bestowed upon him with an iron bar."

"Determined men are rare. If the Vagre carries his part of the affair to a successful issue, then my four brothers will be dead before the week is over—their death insures the success of my projects. It is to your interest as well as mine that we avail ourselves of the Vagre. So it is understood that you will spare his life."

"But what about the bishop, who has come to enjoy the sight of the bandit's death? He will not consent to let the fellow free."

"Cautin will console himself over the Vagre's escape by seeing the bishopess roast, and the hermit laborer hang."

"But suppose the Vagre promises to commit the murder but fails in carrying out his part of the bargain?"

"And the twenty gold sous that he will surely expect to receive after the murder is committed?"

"You are right—his cupidity will drive him to the deed and insure his return. But how is his flight to be connived at?"

"You can convene your *mahl* within two hours. The culprits can be tried and sentenced at one session."

"Yes, that can all be done."

"To-day the trial and sentence—to-morrow the execution. Between now and to-morrow we have the night left. You will have the Vagre led out of the *ergastula* after dark, and taken to

Spatachair, one of my favorites. Leave the rest to me. To-morrow we shall say to the bishop: 'The Vagre has fled'—why do you laugh, Count Neroweg?"

"At that Vagre who will be thinking that he is to gain twenty gold sous, and who will receive instead a hundred blows with an iron bar, and then be quartered."

"As you see, count, your vengeance will lose nothing by the arrangement, while it will insure the success of our plans. Un-less I could speedily find a fourth determined man, as the Vagre, there would always be a brother left who might lay claim to my father's kingdom. Answer, are we agreed upon the Vagre's flight?"

"Yes, yes—we are agreed."

"Accordingly your *mahl* is to be convened within two hours in order to proceed to the trial."

"Within two hours it will be in session."

"Adieu, Neroweg, count of the city of Clermont—but duke to be of Touraine, and one of the richest and most powerful seigneurs, made such by the friendship of Chram, King of all Gaul, after the death of his father and all his brothers! Adieu!"

CHAPTER VI.

THE BEAR OF MONT-DORE.

The sun is sinking behind the western mountain range. Night is approaching. A man, grey of hair and beard and of about fifty-eight to sixty years of age, but still as alert and vigorous as at the springtide of life, clad in a Gallic blouse, a wallet over his shoulder, a fur cap on his head, and travel-stained shoes, issues from the forest. He is on the road that leads to the burg of Count Neroweg. The appearance of the grey-bearded man suggests a mountebank, one of the class that travels from city to city and village to village exhibiting trained animals. On his back he carries a cage with a monkey and, held to a long iron chain, he leads a large-sized bear, that, however, seems to be a peaceful traveling companion. He follows his master with as much docility as a dog. The mountebank stops for a moment at an elevated part of the mountainous road from where the plain and the hill on which the burg is built can be seen. Two slaves with shaven heads, and bending under the weight of a heavy load which they carry suspended from an oar the ends of which rest on their shoulders, appear in view. They are proceeding along a path, which, a few paces ahead of him, runs into the road on which the mountebank is walking. He hastens his steps in order to fall in with the slaves, but these, frightened at the sight of the bear wabbling behind his master, suddenly stop short.

"Friends, you need not fear; my bear is not wicked; he is quite tame."

He thereupon called to his bear as he pulled in the animal's chain, and said:

"Come to me, Mont-Dore!"

The bear promptly obeyed the call, drew near and modestly sat down on his haunches; he then raised his head submissively up to his master, who, as he stood before the animal, half hid him from the slaves. Feeling reassured, the latter resumed their way and, out of prudence, walked a few paces ahead of the mountebank at what they considered a safe distance from the bear.

"Friends, what large residence is that which I see yonder, girt by a fosse?"

"It is the burg of our master, Count Neroweg."

"Is he at the burg to-day?"

"He is in royal company."

"In royal company?"

"Chram, the son of the King of the Franks, arrived there this morning with his bodyguard; we come from the pond where we caught this mess of fish for to-night's supper."

"As true as my beard is grey that is a good windfall for a poor man like me. I shall be able to amuse the noble seigneurs exhibiting my bear and monkey to them. Do you believe, my children, that I shall be allowed admission to the burg?"

"Oh, we do not know. Strangers are not usually allowed to cross the fosse of the burg, without special permission from the seigneur count. The drawbridge is guarded by day, and raised at night.

"Nevertheless, last winter, I know, another exhibitor of trained animals visited the burg, and the seigneur count was greatly entertained with their performances. He may not refuse to tender a similar entertainment to his royal guest."

"Perhaps not. If he does, then the evening's entertainment will help to while away the time of the seigneurs until to-morrow morning's spectacle."

"What spectacle is that to be, my friends?"

"The four people who were sentenced to-day will be executed—Ronan the Vagre, the hermit laborer, a renegade monk who joined the Vagrery; a little female slave, their accomplice; and the bishopess, an accursed witch; they say she once was the wife of our blessed bishop Cautin."

"Oh, have they been capturing Vagres in this region, my friends? And so they were all sentenced to-day?"

"The *mahl* assembled at noon. The King's son and our holy bishop were present. Ronan the Vagre and the hermit laborer were first put to the torture."

"Then they must have denied that they had run the Vagrery, did they?"

"No. Ronan, the accursed bandit, on the contrary, boasted that he was a Vagre."

"Why, then, the torture?"

"That is just what the son of the King said. He thought that the torture had no purpose with Ronan. He opposed it strongly."

"But our holy bishop," explained the other slave, "declared that a truth extracted by torture was doubly certain, it being in the nature of a judgment of God. Thereupon no one raised any further objection, and matters took their course."

"At the bishop's orders," resumed the first slave, "the feet of the Vagre and of the hermit laborer were dipped into boiling oil—they confessed a second time."

"And thereupon they were both carried back to the *ergastula,* because they could not walk."

"And to-morrow they will be taken out for execution. It is said that the manner of their death will be frightful—but it never could be frightful enough to atone for the crimes that Ronan the Vagre—"

"And what crimes did he commit, my friends?"

"Did not the sacrilegious wretch, at the head of his band, pillage and burn down the episcopal villa of our holy bishop?"

"How, my friends, do you mean to say that Ronan the Vagre,

the impious wretch, dared to commit such a crime? And what about the women, were they also put to the torture?"

"The little slave is still near death's door of a wound that she inflicted upon herself in an attempt to commit suicide. She made the attempt in a fit of despair when she saw that the Vagres were cut to pieces."

"As to the witch of a bishopess, they were preparing to apply the torture to her, when our holy bishop interposed, saying: 'We must be careful not to weaken the witch; she may succumb to the pain; it is better that she remain as strong as possible, in order that she escape not one of the torments of to-morrow's execution.'"

"Your bishop is wise, my friends. And where do the bandits await death?"

"In the underground prison of the burg."

"I hope that there is no chance of the accursed people escaping!"

"As to Ronan the Vagre and the hermit laborer, even if they were free, they could not walk a step, their feet are all blistered."

"Oh, I forgot that, my friends."

"Besides, the *ergastula* is made of bricks and Roman cement. The walls are as hard as rocks. Then, the cave is closed with a row of iron bars, each as thick as my arm, and it is always guarded by armed sentries."

"Thank God, it is not possible, my friends, for the accursed criminals to escape execution—they deserve all that they will get! I see that you are not of the wicked slaves, unfortunately but too numerous, who sympathize with the Vagres."

"The Vagres are demons. We would like to see them executed to the last one. They are implacable enemies of the Franks and the holy bishops!"

"I see from your speech that you have a kind master."

"He is all the better master, his clerk told us, for making us

suffer a good deal. Sufferings here on earth insure to us paradise after death. So we are resigned!"

"You can not escape salvation, my good friends, being ani-
mated with such sentiments. I hope that all your companions
at the burg are like you, good Christians, resigned to their lot."

"There are impious and unbelieving people everywhere. Many
of the slaves at the burg would gladly run the Vagrery if the
opportunity were to present itself. Some of them do not even
respect our holy bishops, sneer at the priests, hate our seigneurs,
the Franks, and object to being slaves. But we always denounce
them to the clerk of our count."

"You are truly good Christian companions! But are there
many such wicked slaves at the burg?"

"Oh, no! There may be fifteen or twenty of them among
the hundred that we are in the domestic service, and I suppose
there may be two or three hundred of them among the four
thousand and more colonists and field slaves whom the count
owns on his domains."

"My good friends, do you know it seems to me that it will
bring me good luck to spend a few hours in a house peopled with
such good slaves as you are? I wish you would announce me
to the count's steward. If the noble seigneur is willing to amuse
himself with the capers of my bear, he will issue orders to admit
me."

"We shall announce you. The steward will decide."

And the two slaves, who, streaming with sweat, had laid
down for a moment the net in which they carried a mess of
large fish, freshly taken from the pond, and some of which
were still seen wriggling, through the meshes, again lifted up
their heavy burden and resumed their way to the burg.

As soon as the two slaves disappeared from sight, the bear
raised himself on his legs, pulled off his head, dashed it on the
road, and cried:

"Blood and massacre! They are to burn my beautiful bishopess to-morrow! And Ronan, our brave Ronan, he also is to be executed! Shall we allow that, Karadeucq?"

"I shall avenge my sons—or shall die beside them! O Loysik! O, Ronan! Tortured! Tortured! And executed to-morrow!"

"As true as the remembrance of the bishopess sets my heart aflame, the torture of to-day, the executions of to-morrow, the arrival of that Chram with his armed men—all these events upset our plans. Instead of being taken to Clermont for trial, Ronan and the bishopess are to be executed at the burg to-morrow morning—instead of being healed of their wounds and able to use their legs, Ronan and his brother are rendered helpless. The leudes of Chram, together with those of the count and the foot soldiers, constitute a garrison of more than three hundred armed men; they occupy the burg—and who is there to set free Ronan and Loysik, neither of whom can walk, the little dying slave, and my beautiful bishopess. Only you and I! Karadeucq, if I can see how we are to come out of this fix, I shall be willing to become a bear in truth—not a trick bear, as now I am, but a real bear! Oh, if anyone had said to me, when, disguised like so many others in some animal form, I celebrated the saturnalia of January nights—if anyone had said to me: 'My gay lad, you will celebrate the calends of winter in mid-summer,' I would have answered: 'Go to, good man, it will be warm, then!' And I would have spoken the truth. I would be cooler in an oven than in this hide! Rage and heat make one swelter. You are silent, my old Vagre—what are you thinking about?"

"About my children. What is to be done—what is to be done?"

"I am better in action than in council, especially at this moment, when rage is making me crazy. Poor, brave woman! Burned to-morrow! Oh, how came I to be separated from her at the fastness of Allange during the combat engaged in by our

archers from the branches of the oak trees against the soldiers
of the count! Poor, poor woman! I thought she was killed!
our rout was complete, it was impossible for me to assure myself concerning the fate of my sweetheart! Too happy to be
able to escape the massacre with a few others of our band, and
to dive into the thickest of the woods, after giving ourselves one
of our haunts, the rocks on the peak of Mont-Dore, for *rendezvous*—I fled. Finally, after the lapse of a few days, about a
dozen of our band met at the appointed place; it was there that
we met you also in the company of two runaway slaves—you, our
old Vagre, whom we had given up for lost over two years ago.
It was from you that we learned of the fate of your two sons,
the little slave and the bishopess. Strange, what sentiments I
experience for that brave woman! The memory of her never
leaves me. My heart breaks with grief at the knowledge that
she is in the hands of the count and the bishop. In all Vagrery
there is no Vagre more Vagre than myself for a life of adventures; nevertheless, were some unforeseen accident to cast the
bishopess and myself in some solitary corner of the earth, I believe I would live there quietly with her ten, twenty, a hundred
years! You surely take me for a fool, old Karadeucq, or better
yet for a ninny, seeing that I weep and act stupidly! But, the
devil take grief! The hour calls for action!"

"O, my sons! my sons!"

"If my skin would save them and the bishopess—I do not
mean this bear-skin, but my own!—by the faith of a Vagre, I
would sacrifice it! You know that when you laid your plan
before us, and that a ready fellow was needed to impersonate a
bear, I promptly offered myself. I told you then how, at Be-
ziers, I was an all the more inveterate disguiser at the calends
because the priests forbade them; and that at those saturnalia I
especially impersonated bears, and so well as to be taken for one.
I was thereupon unanimously chosen bear in Vagrery, and—But
I suppose you think that I am talking too much. It is my only

refuge! It diverts me! If I remain silent and think, then my heart breaks and I am useless."

"Loysik! Ronan! executed to-morrow! No—no—heaven and earth!"

"Whatever may have to be done in order to save your sons, the bishopess and little Odille, I shall follow you to the end. When it was decided that you were to be the mountebank and I the bear, we had to find a good-sized bear, and kind enough to let us have his head, jacket and hose. I took my axe and my knife, and climbed up Mont Dore. Good hunter, good hunt. I almost immediately ran across a friend of my size. Probably taking me for his comrade, he ran at me, ready to hug me to his heart, with his arms—and also his jaws, wide open. Anxious not to injure his coat with too many blows of my axe, I stabbed him adroitly in the heart, after which I carefully undressed my accommodating friend. His jacket and hose seemed, by the faith of a Vagre! cut on purpose for me. I joined you at our haunt, and down we came to the plain, determined to do anything in order to save your two sons, the little slave and my bishopess. Let us resume, I am growing more collected—what shall we do? Our plan was to enter the city of Clermont on the night before the execution; we were certain that we could cause a portion of the slaves to revolt; the people would join and the Vagres were to be ready. That project must now be given up, also the idea of lying in ambush on the road and attacking the escort that was to take the prisoners to Clermont. Our purpose in entering the burg in our disguise was only to gather information concerning the time of their departure and the probable route that they would take, while ten of our companions were to wait hidden in the skirts of the forest. Our ten friends are ready, either to proceed with us to Clermont, or to join us on the road, or even to approach the fosse of the burg to-night. Shall we give our good Vagres the signal that we agreed upon? To-day's events, to-morrow's executions and the large number of troops

gathered in the burg, thwart all our plans. What is to be done?
You have been thinking long, old Vagre—have you decided upon
a plan?"

"Yes—come, my brave Master of the Hounds!"

"To the burg? But it is still daylight."

"It will be dark before we arrive."

"What is your plan?"

"I shall tell you on the way. Time presses. Come, come,
be quick!"

"Forward, march! Oh, I forgot—the jacket!"

"What jacket?"

"The one that I must put on for buffoonery—besides it is a
prudent measure; the turned-down hood will conceal whatever
defect there may be at the jointure of the fur between my neck
and my head. The hood will also partially cover my bear face—
mayhap the Franks have sharper eyes than those two blockheads
of slaves. Let us first complete the disguise."

While the lover of the bishopess spoke, Karadeucq pulled a
rolled-up jacket out of his wallet; the false bear put it on; it
reached back and down to his hind legs, and being pulled well
over his head, left only his nozzle exposed to view, while the
wide sleeves almost reached down to his clawy paws. The black
fur of the belly and thighs remained wholly uncovered. Nothing
could be imagined more grotesque than the bear in his costume.
By the faith of a Vagre! the animal could not choose but furnish subject for laughter to the guests of Neroweg, especially
after the copious libations of their supper.

"Now, Karadeucq, I shall conceal my poniard in one of the
folds of the jacket—by the way, it is the very Saxon knife that
I picked up as I fled from the defile of Allange. I picked it up
on the field of battle. You can see on the hilt of the arm the
two Gallic words—*'Friendship,' 'Community'*—graven in the
iron. 'Friendship'—that is a good omen. Friendship, as well

as Love, leads me to the burg. Blood and massacre! I shall
free at one blow both my friend and my sweetheart!"

"Come, come! O, Ronan! O, Loysik! I shall save you
both—or we shall die together! Come, forward, my brave companion."

CHAPTER VII.

IN THE ERGASTULA.

When, more than five hundred years ago, the Romans conquered and owned, though they could not subjugate, Gaul they
constructed their *ergastulas*—slave pens—of solid, lasting material. There they locked up their chained Gallic slaves at night.
Such a cave was an adjunct also to the old Roman camp on
which now stood the burg of Neroweg. The bricks and cement
were still so closely joined that they jointly constituted a body
more solid than marble itself. Hardly could men, equipped
with all the necessary implements for boring, and working from
dawn to dusk, succeed in effecting an opening through the wall
of this prison. The opening of the vault was barred by enormous
rods of iron. Without, a strong body of Franks, armed with
axes, were keeping ceaseless watch; some were lying on the
ground, others walked up and down. From time to time these
watchmen cast a wistful glance towards the burg, which lay
about five hundred paces from them. The principal building,
however, was hidden from their view by the gables of the barns
and stables that adjoined the seigniorial mansion from that side.

Why did these watchmen cast such wistful glances to the
side of the burg? Because, issuing through the open windows,
the cries of the wassailers, from time to time, also the rattle of

drums and blare of hunting horns, reached their ears. There
was a feast in Neroweg's hall. On that evening he was enter-
taining his royal guest Chram at his best.

An iron lamp, that swung under the vaulted entrance of the
antique *ergastula,* threw a dim light around the gate of the
underground cell and also partially lighted it within.

Steps were heard. A leude appeared followed by slaves bearing baskets and bowls.

"Boys! Here's some beer for you, also wine, venison, bread
and cheese. Eat, drink and be merry. The son of the King is
on a visit at the burg."

"Three cheers for Sigefrid, wine, beer and venison!"

"But keep a close watch on the prisoners—let not one of you
step aside—keep your eyes wide open."

"Oh, those dogs do not move any more down there than if
they had fallen asleep forever under the cold ground, where they
will be to-morrow. You need not fear, Sigefrid."

"Outside of the seigneur King, the bishop or Neroweg, whosoever should approach the iron railing to speak with the prisoners—"

"Will instantly fall under our axes, Sigefrid—they are sharp
and heavy."

"At the slightest event, let the horns blow the alarm—we
shall then immediately rush to your aid."

"Those are all wise precautions, Sigefrid, but superfluous.
The bridge is raised; besides, the slime in the fosse is so deep
that anyone trying to cross it would sink over his head in it.
Finally, there are no strangers at the burg. Including the King's
bodyguard we are more than three hundred armed men—who
would attempt to free the prisoners under such circumstances?
Moreover they are as incapable of walking as a rabbit whose
four paws have been cut off. So you see, Sigefrid, your precautions, however wise, are superfluous."

"All the same, keep close watch until to-morrow. It is only one night of watch to you."

"And we shall spend it merrily, drinking and singing."

"They seem to be merry in the banquet hall, Sigefrid. Tell us what is going on."

"The sun of May does not more greedily pump up the dew than our topers do the full kegs of wine and beer; mountains of victuals vanish in the abysses of their stomachs—they no longer talk, they yell; a little longer they will all be roaring! Chram's leudes at first affected daintiness and choice manners; but at this hour they guzzle, swallow and laugh like any of us. After all they are good and gay customers; some little jealousy on our part at first irritated us against them; the rivalry has been drowned in wine. Only shortly ago old Bertefred, hiccoughing and weeping like a calf, embraced one of the young warriors of the royal suite, and called him his darling little son."

"Ha! Ha! Ha! That was a droll scene!"

"Finally, in order to complete the scene, I just learn that a mountebank with a dancing bear and a monkey has been let into the burg. Neroweg proposed the amusement to King Chram, and the steward issued orders to admit the man and his animals in the banquet hall. They were sent for amid the shouts of glee of the whole convivial party. I want to go back quick and share the sport."

"Happy Sigefrid! He will see the gambols of the bear and the grimaces of the monkey."

"Now, boys, I promise you that after the King has enjoyed himself, I shall request the count to have the mountebank sent to this part of the house with his animals, so that you also may be amused by him."

"Sigefrid, you are a good companion!"

"But always keep your eyes upon the prisoners."

"Be easy! And now to the wine, beer and venison! While we wait for the man, his bear and monkey, let us empty the pots in honor of the good King Chram and of Neroweg! To the assault of the victuals!"

The iron lamp that swung under the vaulted entrance of the antique *ergastula* lighted up the group of Franks eating, laughing and drinking at the entrance. The lamp also threw its ruddy light across the iron railing and upon the Gallic prisoners who sat, gathered together, near the entrance of the prison, the rear of which remained in deepest darkness; nearest to the iron railing lay little Odille; the girl lay on her back with her arms crossed over her girlish bosom like a corpse about to be buried. Indeed the girl's pallor was that of a dying person. Near her and holding the child's head in her lap sat the bishopess, still handsome, although somewhat paler and reduced in flesh; she contemplated the girl with the loving eyes of a mother. A few steps away sat Ronan; his feet were wrapped in rags; his wrists were manacled; unable either to hold himself on his feet or on his knees he leaned his back against the underground wall. The Vagre looked at Odille with a tenderness equal to that of the bishopess. Manacled like his brother, whose torture he had shared, the hermit laborer was seated near Ronan and seemed deeply moved at the tender care that the bishopess bestowed upon the young slave girl.

"Die, little Odille," said Ronan, "die, my child. It is better far that you die of the wound which your brave hand inflicted upon yourself, when, a month ago, you thought I was dead. It is better far that you die now, than to be burned alive to-morrow."

"Poor little one, the strain of this day's experience has exhausted her strength! Look, Ronan, her face, alas! grows paler and paler."

"Let us bless this pallor of death, beautiful bishopess; it announces the approach of death—a death that will save the poor child the agony of the burning pyre. Did not her wound already protect her against the brutalities of the count and the torture of to-day? Die, die, little Odille, we shall live again in yonder world. Were I free I would have made you my wife for life in Vagrery, if you consented. I have loved you dearly for your sweetness, your beauty, and the misfortune of the shame that you were smitten with so young—an innocent girl even after your dishonor! Die, little Odille! As sure as I and my brother Loysik will be executed to-morrow I stand in less dread of the agony in store for me than of the thought that you are yourself to burn alive! Oh, if my feet were not in blisters I would drag myself to your side. Oh, if my hands were not manacled I would smother you with a loving hand, as our mothers, the Gallic women of yore, killed their children in order to snatch them from slavery. Beautiful bishopess, could not you, whose arms are free, gently strangle that poor child? The slender thread of life that hardly holds her, would be easily torn!"

"I have thought of that, Ronan, but I lack the courage."

"But should she unfortunately live till to-morrow, her fate will be yours. Keep in mind that you will be stripped naked by that band of Franks, and whipped by them with switches!"

"Keep still, Ronan, shame mantles my cheeks! To me, a woman, that part of the punishment—to be exposed naked before those men—is the worst!"

"Your husband, the bishop, knew that, just as he was aware that, if you were tortured to-day, you would lose some of the strength necessary to endure to-morrow's punishment to the end, on account of which he spared you.—You will both thereupon be impaled. Before impalement, poor dear victims, your nipples will be torn from you with burning tongs. Finally you will both be thrown upon the pyre with whatever little life may be still in you. As you see, the torture is finely graded, and will not you, you who have the power, snatch 'the dear girl from such torment? Oh, I see, you finally take the decision—your hands are creeping up to Odille's neck. Courage, no weakness! Remember that our mothers themselves put their beloved little ones to death. What! You hesitate—your hands drop down again! You weep!"

"I have not the courage—I cannot."

"Craven soul!"

"No, Ronan, I am no craven. No—were she my daughter I would kill her."

"I understand. Odille is a stranger to you—you cannot love her enough to decide to kill her. We must pardon the bishopess for her want of kindness, not so, Loysik?"

At that moment the young slave moved, gave a slight sigh, half raised her head, her eyes opened and looked around for Ronan. When they finally fell upon him she said, after a moment, in a weak voice:

"Ronan, is the night over, and is it now day?"

"This is not the light of day my child; it is the light from the lamp that burns outside our prison. Your strength seems exhausted, you were in a torpor."

"I dreamed a sweet and sad dream. My mother rocked me on her knees singing the chant of Hena, and then she said to me weeping: 'Odille, it is you they are going to burn!' I then woke up and believed it was day. Oh, Ronan, it is a long time till to-morrow! And the execution! The execution! How it will be prolonged—unless the pain be so intense that I die immediately."

"And will you not regret life?"

"Ronan, I tried to kill myself when I thought you were dead; you are sentenced to death like ourselves; I have neither father nor mother; what should I regret, all the less seeing that we are to live again in yonder worlds near those whom we have loved? We shall soon meet again."

"By the faith of a Vagre, what is death, beautiful bishopess? Only a change of vestments and lodging. As to the execution, two or three hours of suffering is the extreme, and the end is certain. Do you know, Loysik, what grieves me most at this hour? It is to quit this world, leaving our dearly beloved Gaul forever in the clutches of the Franks and bishops!"

"No, no, brother—centuries are centuries to man, they are hardly hours to mankind in its eternal progress! The world in which we live seems large to us—and yet, what is it, rolling and confounded among the myriads of the starry worlds who at this hour of the night glisten in our eyes from the vast expanse of the vault of heaven—mysterious worlds in which we are to re-live successively, in body and soul, but with bodies new and evermore repurified! Brother, at the time of the conquest of Caesar, our ancestors, then enslaved and loaded with chains centuries ago in the very *ergastula* where we now are, said, per-haps, as you just now in despair: 'Our dearly beloved Gaul is forever enslaved to the Roman conqueror'—and yet not two centuries and a half had passed before, by dint of heroic insur-rections against the Romans, Gaul again won back, step by step, although paying dearly for it with the blood of our fathers, the country's rights, liberties, and even final independence during the glorious era of Victoria the Great!"

"You are right, Loysik; you are right."

"And do you forget the prophetic vision of that august wo-man—the vision that our ancestor Schanvoch transmitted to us in the narrative of his days, and that our father so often told us of?"

"In that vision, Victoria saw Gaul enslaved, exhausted, bleeding, prostrate and crushed down under heavy burdens, dragging herself along the ground under the whip of the Frank-ish kings and the bishops! And then again she saw Gaul free, proud, radiant, trampling under foot the collar of slavery, the crown of kings and the tiara of Popes! Gaul then held in one hand a bundle of fruits and flowers, in the other a standard sur-mounted by the Gallic cock—the red flag."

"What, then, do you fear? Think of the past! First bent down under the Roman conquest, Gaul re-rises through the

courage of her sons and becomes again free and redoubtable!
Let the past give you faith in the future! Perchance that future
is still far away. What is time to us—to us, who at this supreme moment have but the last few hours of our life to count!
Oh, my brother, I have a profound faith, an invincible faith, in
the final rejuvenation and enfranchisement of Gaul!—centuries
are centuries to man; they are but instants in the eternal
progress of mankind!"

"Loysik, you reassure me, you confirm my confidence. Aye,
I shall leave this world with my eyes fixed upon the radiant
vision of renascent Gaul! Still one sorrow I carry with me—
our uncertainty regarding the fate of our father. What may
have become of him?"

"If he still lives, Ronan, may he never know of our end!
He loved us so tenderly—his was a large heart. At a season of
national insurrection and at the head of a province risen in
arms, he might have become a hero like the Chief of the Hundred Valleys, who was his idol! At the head of a band of men
in revolt, our father could be nothing but a chief of Bagauders
or Vagres.* You know my sentiments with regard to those terrible reprisals, which, however legitimate they may be, leave
only ruins and disaster behind them. But without approving
his conduct, I feel inclined to acquit him of blame, because his
vengeance never smote but the wicked."

"Brother," said Ronan, "they seem to be in high feather at
the burg! Do you hear the distant din of their merriment?
Oh, by the bones of our ancestor Sylvest, the young and brilliant Roman seigneurs, who, crowned with flowers laughed with
cruel laughter and careless of the future on the gilded balcony
of the circus, while their slaves, who were consigned to the wild

---

* "I do not know by what diabolical influences they accomplished it, but they seduced in this fashion an immense multitude of men, who set themselves to pillaging
and despoiling all whom they met on their way, and distributed their spoils among
those who had nothing."—Bishop Gregory of Tours. Histoire des Franks, IV., 10.

beasts, awaited death in the sombre vault of the amphitheatre, just as we to-night await it in this underground prison—they were also quite hilarious. Aye, those Roman seigneurs were indeed hilarious; and yet from the depths of their dungeons the Gallic slaves shook their chains in cadence and sang the prophetic words: 'Flow, flow, thou blood of the captive! Drop, drop, thou dew of gore! Germinate, sprout up, thou avenging harvest! Hasten, thou mower, hasten! It is ripe! Whet your scythe, whet it! Whet your scythe!'"

CHAPTER VIII.

IN THE BANQUET HALL.

Neroweg feasted his royal guest Chram at his best. At first he hesitated to take his gold and silver vessels, the fruit of his ravages, out of his coffers and exhibit them on his table. He feared to excite the cupidity of Chram and his favorites, apprehending that the latter would indulge their nature for pilfering, or that the former might make some covetous demand upon him. In the end, however, yielding to a barbarian's vanity, the count could not resist the desire to display his wealth before the eyes of his guests. Accordingly, he produced from his ample coffers the large amphoras, the goblets, the large bowls, the huge dishes —all of massive gold or silver, fashioned in the Greek, Roman or Gallic style and as varied as the plunderings from which these riches proceeded. Among these valuable articles were also several goblets of jasper, of porphyry and of onyx studded with precious stones; there were also strewn over the table several hand basins made of rare wood, hooped in gold and inlaid with carbuncles. But none of these precious articles was to be used by the count's guests; the valuables were heaped upon the table without order like piles of booty; they were intended merely to delight the sight or tickle the envy of the guests who could purloin none of the articles by reason of the distance at which they were heaped from them upon the vast table of the banquet hall. In front of Prince Chram and Bishop Cautin the count had ordered to be spread in the shape of a table cloth a bit of purple cloth embroidered in gold and silver and similar to that which covered their seats. Prince Chram and the bishop alone were allowed to use a jasper goblet studded with precious stones. They ate from a dish of solid gold in which the food destined for them was spread. The plates before the other guests were of wood, tin or clay. In order to do further honor to the King's son the count had donned over his greasy skin jacket and his leather hose an antique dalmatica of silver cloth with gold bees embroidered upon it, a present made to his father by King Clovis. Around his neck Neroweg wore two heavy gold chains, on several links of which he had ingeniously fastened a number of earrings intended for women and glistening with precious stones. A peacock would not have been prouder of its plumage than was that Frankish seigneur under his dalmatica and jewels, with his shaven chin, his long reddish moustache and his yellow hair drawn back and fastened at the top of his head by a gold bracelet studded with rubies, from which the coarse and unkempt hair fell back over his neck like the tail of a horse.

The aspect presented by the banquet hall matched that of the host. It was a mixture of luxury, barbarism, slovenliness and dirt. Around the table of rough wood, covered by rich cloth only in front of Chram and the bishop, and bearing in its center the heaped-up pile of costly vessels, ragged slaves moved about under orders of the seneschal, the steward, the cup-bearer or other head servants of the count, all clad in the skin jackets that they wore in all seasons, and which were as soiled as otherwise uncouth. The number of torch-bearing slaves intended to light the banquet table had been doubled, tripled and quadrupled; the number of barrels set up at the four corners of the hall was likewise increased; they were stood up one on top of the other, presenting the appearance of squatty pillars. In order to reach the higher kegs and fill up the pots of beer the cup-bearers were compelled to serve themselves with a ladder. By this time, however, the upper barrels had long been emptied. The old wine of Clermont that they once contained was cheering, warming and mounting to the heads of the convivial crowd.

Yielding to his natural inclination for carousal, and delighting in advance at the prospect of seeing Ronan the Vagre, the hermit laborer and the beautiful bishopess executed on the morrow, Bishop Cautin could hardly keep his seat. He drank, frolicked, bantered and even indulged in sallies of aggressive sarcasm. Despite his aversion for Chram the bishop dared not shoot his arrows at him; and he stood in even greater awe of the Lion of Poitiers. The Gallic renegade, rancorous as the devil himself, had said to the man of God, accompanying the word with the looks of an enraged lion: "You forced me to alight from my horse and kneel down before you; I shall have my revenge; I shall abide my time." The real butt of the bishop's sarcasm was Neroweg, habitually stupid and dumb.

"Count," Cautin said to him, "your hospitality comes from an overflowing heart; of that I am certain; but your food is execrable in its abundance; it is all meat and fish, boiled and grilled, served in profusion but without taste; it is a true barbarian's feast, who lives upon his flocks, hunting and fishing; there is not here a single appetite-provoking and delicate dish; we are filled and that is all! I take his glory, Prince Chram, for witness."

"Our host and friend does his best," said Chram, who, finding his projects already somewhat deranged by the torture of Ronan the Vagre, was anxious to keep the count in good humor.

"Before the cordial spirit of Neroweg's hospitality, I think little of the feast itself."

"But I do think of it, glorious Prince," rejoined the bishop. "I have told the count a hundred times that his cooks are detestable; they do not know how to prepare the food. Tell me, Neroweg, how much did you pay for the slave who is the chief of your kitchen?"

"I paid nothing for him. My leudes found him on the road to Clermont, they took him and brought him to me in bonds. Yesterday, however, he had his feet burned by the trial of the judgment of God, and his tongue was afterwards pulled out in punishment for his blasphemies. He must have been indisposed to-day and helped himself with other slaves who are less skilful than himself in the preparation of food."

"Oh, I understand! Of course having had his tongue cut out he was not able to taste the sauces; but he is nevertheless a wretched cook. And I am not surprised; what can one expect of a cook who is picked up accidentally on the high road! You do not seem to know, count, that bad cooks spoil the best of dishes. Here, for instance, are some cranes—think of it, cranes! a toothsome meat, more succulent than any if properly prepared. Now just see how that ass, that churl of a cook serves them up—boiled in water!"

"Come, father, be not angry, we shall have them roasted next time."

"Roasted! that would be still more criminal! roasted cranes! Come this way, steward, I will give you the recipe for the cook—if he is capable of carrying it out."

"Oh, holy bishop, with the help of the whip the cook could not choose but carry out the recipe."

"I must humbly declare that I am not the inventor of the way in which cranes must be prepared. I read it and learned it from the writings of Apicius, a celebrated Roman gourmand, who died, alas, many years ago, but his genius will live as long as cranes will fly."

"Let us have the recipe, father."

"Here it is: You wash and dress your crane, you then put it in an earthen pot, with water, salt and anise—"

"Well! that is just what my cook did; he washed the crane in water and salt—"

"But let me finish, barbarian, and you will soon enough see that the lazy ass stopped in the middle of the road instead of proceeding to the end. Now you must allow the water in which your crane is laid, to be boiled down one-half; thereupon you put it into a pan with olive oil broth flavored with wild marjoram and coriander; when your crane is done to the turn, pour in some wine mixed with honey and spices, a pinch of cumin, a taste of benzoin, a bit of rue and some caraway seed boiled in vinegar; pour in flour to give consistency to your sauce, which will then be of a handsome gold brown tint; you pour this over your crane after having placed the bird handsomely on a large platter with its round neck gently curled in a circle and holding in its long beak a spray of greens. And now I ask his glory, Prince Chram, I ask our illustrious friends here assembled—is there any comparison between a crane, prepared in such a style, and this shapeless, colorless thing that seems to be swimming in a bowl of greasy water?"

"If God, the Father, needed a cook, he would certainly choose you, sensuous bishop," said the Lion of Poitiers; "you would be no disgrace in paradise as the chief of the celestial kitchens."

At the impious jest the holy man made a grimace of rage, remembering only recently he had actually officiated as cook, but not in paradise—it was in Vagrery. He filled his cup and drained it at one draught, looking askance at the royal favorite.

"Come, Count Neroweg," said Spatachair, "there is mercy

for every sin; some other day you will treat us to a choicer feast —and you will promise your wife to preside at the banquet."

"And by the faith of the Lion of Poitiers, I promise not to chuckle her under the chin too freely."

"When you give that banquet, Neroweg," added Imnachair, despite the glances of Chram to check the insolence of his favorites, "when you give us that banquet, you will not make us eat and drink, as you do to-day, out of copper and tin vessels, while you spread out before our dazzled eyes your gold and silver utensils in the center of the table—far from our reach. It almost looks, you vainglorious rustic, as if you took us for thieves."

"Neroweg offers his hospitality in the way that suits him," put in Sigefrid, the count's leude, in a tone of muffled anger; "those who eat the meat and drink the wine of this house have no right to complain of the dishes—if these don't suit them, let them go and fill up elsewhere."

"Are we, the King's men, to be chaffed for what we eat and drink at this burg?"

"That would be the height of impudence! As to me, I was surfeited before I touched a mouthful of these mountains of cold provisions."

"Moreover, it is an insult," cried another of the guests. "We members of the royal bodyguard will brook no insult."

"Do you think yourselves above us, because we are leudes of a count? If you do, we may measure the distance between us, by measuring the length of our swords."

"It is not swords, but hearts that we should measure."

"Do you pretend to say that we, the faithful men of Neroweg, have smaller hearts than you?"

"A challenge let it be, thick-headed rustics!"

"The thick-headed rustic is more than a match for the effeminate court soldier. And you will find it out on the spot if you dare put your hands to your swords."

"Six against six, or more, if you prefer."

"Nothing will suit us better than to cross swords with you."

The altercation between the half tipsy Franks had started at one end of the table; at first it was conducted in a low voice, but it soon reached such a pitch of loudness and exasperation that Chram, the bishop and the count hastened to interpose and restore peace among the table companions. It was with an ill grace and exchanging wild looks of hatred that the intoxicated leudes subsided.

Karadeucq and his bear, both preceded by the steward, had reached the threshold of the banquet hall when the disturbance between the leudes was silenced. The steward approached his master and said:

"Seigneur, the mountebank with his bear and monkey are ready."

"What, count, have you bears in this place?"

"Chram, he is a strolling mountebank with his animals. I thought it would amuse you at the close of the banquet, and I ordered him to be brought in."

The news of the proposed entertainment was joyfully received by all the Franks, and made them forget their recent quarrel and hard feelings. Some stood up, others rose on their haunches in order to be the first to see the man, his monkey, and his bear. When Karadeucq appeared, loud roars of laughter shook the walls of the hall. It was not that the aspect of the old Vagre was amusing, but nothing could be imagined more grotesque than the appearance of the lover of the bishopess under the bear's skin. He stepped forward heavily, clad in the jacket with its hood thrown back and seemed dazed by the light of the torches, although all the thirty or forty of them cast but a flickering and subdued light over the vast hall. Thanks to this rather dim and unsteady light, and also to the wide jacket that half enveloped the Vagre, his ursine appearance was perfect. Moreover, in order to keep the curious at a distance,

Karadeucq pulled in the chain to which the animal was attached and cried:

"Seigneurs, do not come too near the teeth of the bear, he is often sullen and ferocious."

"Mountebank, keep close watch on your beast; should he unfortunately hurt anybody in this hall, I shall have him cut to pieces, and you will receive for your share fifty lashes on your back!"

"Seigneur count, have pity on me, poor old man that I am; I only have my animals to earn my bread with—I have requested your noble and very noble guests not to approach my bear too closely, in order to prevent any unfortunate accident."

"Step forward; I wish to have a closer view of your jolly companion; he will not, I presume, dare to paw me, the son of King Clotaire."

"Oh, very glorious Prince! these poor brutes are deprived of intelligence and cannot distinguish between the great seigneurs of the world and the humble slaves."

"Step forward, step forward—a little closer."

"Very glorious King, look out—it will be less dangerous to be close to the monkey—I can let him out of his cage."

"Oh, monkeys, I am not very curious to see those wicked animals. I have pages, plenty of them. Ha, ha, ha—look at the droll fellow with his jacket. Look, Imnachair, how clumsily he carries himself—how he grunts—for all the world he looks like the Lion of Poitiers in his morning gown, after spending a night with women and wine."

"What else should I do, Chram! I consider lost every night that I do not put to use in your style with wine and women."

"Lion, you are unjust—I have become temperate and chaste."

"Through exhaustion—O, chaste and sober Prince—did you renounce the pure girls and good wine!"

"If so, you should rather pity than blame me. Ho, there, mountebank, what tricks can your bear perform? Is he clever?"

"If you order it, glorious King, my bear will ride on horse-back on my cane, and myself holding him by the chain, he will gracefully gallop around the hall."

"Good; let us see him do it."

"Attention! Mont-Dore."

"How do you call him?"

"Mont-Dore, glorious King. I give him that name because I caught him when he was still but a cub on one of the peaks of Mont Dore."

"I am no longer surprised if your bear is ferocious. He was born in one of the most notorious lairs of the accursed Vagres, those wandering men, those wolves, those heads of wolves who haunt only rocks, forests and caverns. But as sure as this morning we put one of them to the torture, we shall end by wiping them all out, just as Count Neroweg did the other day with a band of them who took refuge in the defile of Allange."

"Oh, glorious King, may the Almighty deliver us from these pestilential Vagres! May He grant me the favor of never run-ning across any of them except as he hangs from the gibbet—the way I saw the first and last one whom I ever laid eyes upon—it was a terrible sight! The thought of it still makes me tremble."

"Where did you see that Vagre on the gibbet?"

"Near the frontier of Limousin; over the gallows was this inscription: 'This is Karadeucq the Vagre—so shall his likes be treated.'"

"Karadeucq! The old bandit who with his bedevilled band so long raided Limousin and Auvergne!"

"Pillaging burgs and episcopal mansions!"

"A worthy example, followed by the band of Ronan, the other dog that is to be executed to-morrow!"

"Well, I am glad to hear it, at last we are delivered from that Karadeucq! He was thought to be running the Vagrery in some other regions, but his return was always apprehended."

"Oh, glorious Prince, he will never be back again—unless the bandit descended from his gibbet, and that is unlikely. When I saw him dangling in the air his corpse was already half eaten up by the carrion crows, and both his hands and feet were chopped off."

"Are you quite certain you saw the name of Karadeucq on that gibbet? It would be truly a great deliverance for the country."

"Glorious King, his name is so uncommon in our country that it struck me the moment I saw it; hence I remember it well."

"It is a Breton name," said Bishop Cautin; "it is one of the names common in those heretical and cursed regions that to this hour stubbornly resist the authority and orders of our councils. Oh, Chram, will the Frankish Kings never have the power and the will to reduce to obedience that savage Armorica, that hot-bed of druid idolatry, the only province of Gaul that until now has been able to withstand the arms of King Clovis, your grandfather, and his worthy sons and grandsons?"

"Bishop, you have an easygoing way of talking about such matters. More than once did Clovis and the Frankish Kings, my ancestors, dispatch their best warriors to the conquest of that pestilential country, and our troops were every time cut to pieces in the marshes, the defiles and the forests of Armorica. No, those indomitable Bretons are not human—they are demons! Oh, if all the other regions of Gaul had been peopled with that infernal race, ever rebellious to the Catholic church, we would still be struggling to maintain our power. But, old mountebank, you seem greatly affected; I noticed a tear roll down your grey beard; why so?"

"If only one tear did run down my grey beard, it is because old men's eyes are stingy of tears."

"And why would you have shed more?"

"Oh, King, I would have wept all the tears in my head over those **unhappy Bretons** whose **detestable** druid **idolatry** condemns them to the everlasting flames, as our holy bishop used to say: unhappy blind men who shut their eyes to the divine light of the faith! unhappy rebels, who dare turn their arms against our good seigneurs and masters, the Frankish Kings, whom our blessed bishops order us to obey in the name of the Church! Oh, Prince, I repeat it to you, but for that the eyes of an old man are stingy of tears, mine would flow in torrents at the thought of the damnable error of those unhappy heretics!"

"Mountebank, you are a pious man," said Cautin; "kneel down and kiss my hand."

"Holy bishop, blessed be the favor you grant me."

"Rise, my son, and preserve your faith in our Church; have also confidence in the future; the accursed idolators and rebellious Bretons will not much longer escape the just punishment that is in store for them."

"Oh, no! As true as scissors have never touched my hair, I, Chram, son of Clotaire, King of France, I shall never rest so long as those Armorican demons are not crushed and drowned in their own blood. Too long have they resisted our arms. We shall soon make short work of them."

"May the Almighty hear your vow, great Prince, and may He grant me, a poor old man, enough days to witness the submission of that Brittany that has so long remained stiffnecked and indomitable."

"Now, mountebank, let us return to your bear; we had almost forgotten all about him, the wild fellow who was born in one of the lairs of the accursed Vagres."

"Nothing strange in that, glorious King! Are not those accursed fellows wolves? Have not bears and wolves the same dens? Come Mont-Dore, up my lad, show your skill to our holy bishop, who is present, and to the illustrious King Chram; also to the very renowned count and the noble audience. Take this cane—it shall be your mount; get on horseback and gallop around this table as gracefully as you can, and with the gentlest

airs that you can put on. Come, Mont-Dore, to horse, the
courser will not run away with you. Make room, there, make
room, there, noble seigneurs—above all, do not approach the
animal too closely. Come, Mont-Dore, start galloping, my daring knight!"

The lover of the beautiful bishopess straddled the cane which
he held between his two fore paws, and led by the chain which
Karadeucq held he commenced to prance with grotesque clumsi-
ness around the hall amid the loud laughter of the assembled
leudes.

As he led him, the Vagre said to himself:

"I came dangerously near betraying myself when I heard
the Frankish King speak of the bravery of the Breton race; my
heart beat with pride fit to crack my ribs; then, besides, I
thought of good old grandfather Araim, who used to call me his
pet! I thought of my father Jocelyn, of my mother Madalen—
both no doubt dead in the country that I ran away from more
than forty years ago, and where my brother Kervan and my
dear sweet sister Roselyk still live. At these thoughts tears
came to my eyes despite myself. Oh, my sons! Ronan! Loysik! here I am near to you, but shall I manage your delivery!
Hesus! Hesus! inspire me."

The Master of the Hounds pranced all along astride of the
cane, encouraged in his antics by the laughter that it provoked in the Franks. Remembering the success that had crowned his efforts during the nights of the calends of January, he
indulged in gambols that delighted the blockish leudes and that
carried their hilarity to the pitch of hysterics. Above all the
count held his sides and laughed and laughed, fit to burst his
dalmatica of silver cloth. Suddenly he checked his laughter
and said to Chram:

"King, would you see still better sport?"

"Yes, count, what have you to propose? Your face is red
to suffocation. You breathe like an ox. What new thought has
just sprouted in your head?"

"It is this: I have a plan—we have in the burg enormous and ferocious mastiffs that we use to hunt wolves and wild boars with. We shall chain the bear to one of the beams of the hall."

"And let loose some of your mastiffs against him? The idea is delicious."

"Yes, Chram; I want to offer you a royal treat."

"Long live Count Neroweg! Come, fetch the dogs! The more ferocious they are and sharp their teeth, all the more amusing will be the sight."

"Yes, yes," cried the Franks with shouts of joy; "the dogs—the dogs—a combat between the bear and the dogs."

"Hello! my master of the hounds, Gondulf! fetch in Mirff and Morff—if they leave a shred of skin and flesh on the bones of the bear I wish this goblet of wine may be poison to me."

"Seigneur, I shall run to the kennel and bring the mastiffs Mirff and Morff."

When he heard the count's proposition, which was received with universal acclaim by the leudes, the lover of the bishopess, who, faithful to his role, was riding lustily on his cane around the table suddenly interrupted his antics and was on the point of expressing with some compromising gesture his refusal to serve as quarry for the fangs of Mirff and Morff. Fortunately by means of a gentle tug given at the chain, Karadeucq recalled the Vagre to prudence and the latter continued his gambols with the most indifferent air in the world; but his conductor, without letting the chain slip from his hands, threw himself at the feet of Neroweg and said:

"Seigneur count, illustrious seigneur!"

"What would you of me, old mountebank?"

"My bear is my bread winner—you will have him killed."

"And I, do not I also run the risk of seeing the best two dogs of my pack hugged to death—or torn to pieces by your bear's claws? You said yourself, your animal was ferocious."

"Seigneur, you do not earn your living with your dogs; but my bear is my bread winner."

"Dare you resist my will?"

"Oh, great Prince," said Karadeucq on his knees, but turning towards Chram: "A poor old man addresses him to your glory; one word from you to this illustrious seigneur, who respects you as the son of his King, and he will renounce his project. I swear to you by my salvation, the other tricks of my bear which I have not exhibited will amuse a hundredfold more than the bloody combat that will deprive me of my bread winner."

"Come, rise old mountebank, I shall not hinder you in the making of your living."

"Thanks to you, great King, my bear is saved!"

Chram's words provoked violent murmurs from the count's leudes; not only did they see themselves deprived of a spectacle that was to delight their eyes, but they imagined themselves humiliated anew, now in the person of the master of the house, their count. The murmurs grew louder.

"Chram is not King in this burg, Neroweg," cried Sigefrid, one of the principal starters of the quarrel that was allayed just as Karadeucq entered the hall with his bear. "No, King Chram cannot by a word deprive us of an amusement that it pleases you to afford us. Neroweg is King in his burg."

"No, no," loudly chimed in the other warriors of the count, "we want to see the fight with the bear. The dogs! the dogs! Neroweg alone commands here."

"Yes, and to the devil with the King!" cried Sigefrid.

"The devil take Chram if he opposes our enjoyment! We are masters here."

"Only brutes of rustics send their guest to the devil when he is the son of their King," put in the Lion of Poitiers with a threatening air. "Is that the example in courtesy that you set to your men, Neroweg? It seems so, judging by the conduct of your steward, who is hastening now, when the banquet is hardly over, to carry away your gold and silver vessels out of fear, I suppose, lest we steal them."

"My sons! My dear sons in Christ! Are you about to start quarreling anew? I order peace, my sons—in the name of heaven, keep the peace!"

"Bishop, you are right to preach peace; these brave leudes who fear that I am interfering with their amusement did not understand me. I told the mountebank that I would not hinder him from earning his living."

"Thanks again, thanks again, great King."

"How much is your bear worth?"

"He is priceless to me."

"Whatever sum you may fix will be counted out to you, in case your bear is killed."

The King's words were received by the acclamations of the Franks, and allayed the quarrel that was on the point of breaking out. Karadeucq, however, without rising from his knees, cried:

"Great King, no sum can repay me for my bear; mercy, beg the count to desist from his project."

"The dogs! Here are the dogs!"

"In all my life I have not seen such mastiffs!" exclaimed Chram with admiration. "Count, if your whole pack is similarly fitted out, it will rival mine, which I considered matchless."

"What flanks! What enormous paws! Ha, Chram, if you only heard their voices, the bellowing of a bull is like the song of a nightingale beside their barking when they are on the tracks of a wild boar. I am justly proud of my dogs."

"I wager that one of them will be enough to kill the bear as truly as my name is Spatachair."

"Come, tie the bear to one of the beams, old mountebank, and let us begin. "I told you, if your beast is killed, I shall pay whatever sum you may say, royally and without chaffering."

"Illustrious King, have pity on a poor man."

"Enough, enough—chain up the bear to one of the beams, and be done."

"Seigneur bishop, in the name of your blessed hand which you give me to kiss, be charitable towards my poor animal."

"Is he perchance a Christian that I should exercise charity towards him? Oh, mountebank, mountebank, had you not shown yourself a minute ago to be a pious man, I would consider this last request an outrage."

To insist any longer would have been to risk losing everything. Karadeucq understood this, and addressing himself to Chram, said:

"Glorious King, let your will be done; but allow me to make one last request."

"Hurry up."

"The spectacle will only be a butchery; my bear being chained he will not be able to defend himself."

"Would you perchance leave him loose, old idiot, and have him devour us!"

"No, King; but if you would wish an amusement that would last some time, then at least equalize the forces; permit me to arm my bear with a club."

"Has he not his nails?"

"For the sake of prudence I have filed them off—you notice how smooth his paws are."

"Very well, he shall have a club—but do you think he will know how to help himself with it?"

"Alas, the fear of being devoured will force him to defend himself as best he may; in all your life you will not have seen such a spectacle."

"And you, Neroweg," said Sigefrid, more than any other of the leudes a stickler for the count's dignity, "do you allow the bear to have a club? You alone have the right to say here: 'I will.'"

"Yes, yes, I allow the club—I think that the bear striking at the dogs with a club will be a wonderful spectacle. And yet, I would have greatly preferred to have seen the beast killed by Mirff and Morff. But that would have ended the sport too quickly. Come, let the slaves blow the horns, and you others, who beat the drums, blow and beat at your loudest, or you shall have your own backs drummed upon; and you, torch-bearing slaves, draw near the circle that is to be formed. Hold high your torches that we may see the combat well. Strike up, you drummers! blow on the hunting horns in order to excite the dogs well."

"To the beam; tie the bear to the beam!"

Karadeucq led the lover of the bishopess to a corner of the hall, chained him to one of the beams of the colonnade, put between his paws the knotty club on which he had been riding and said to him:

"Come, my poor Mont-Dore; courage; you will have to defend yourself well, seeing that you have to fight against two dogs for the amusement of the noble seigneurs; show yourself worthy of your race."

A wide circle was formed, lighted by the torch-bearing slaves. In the front rank of the audience stood King Chram, his three favorites, the count, the bishop and several leudes; all the others mounted the table. In the center of the circle, clad in his ample jacket, which had fortunately been left to him, stood the Vagre-bear; he preserved an intrepid countenance; he naïvely sat down on his haunches, like a bear who expects no evil, and nonchalantly held his club between his fore paws; occasionally he leaned the club against his body in order to scratch himself with a movement of graceful and easy abandon. Suddenly the hunting horns struck up their deafening uproar. Gondolf, the count's master of the hounds, stepped into the circle holding the two monstrous mastiffs by the leash. From their enormous necks a dewlap similar to that of a bull dropped

down upon their chests; their large bloodshot eyes were half
hidden under their long and drooping ears; black, white and
yellow streaks ran over their shaggy skin which bristled up on
their backs the moment they perceived the bear. Instantly they
barked furiously, and dashing forward wildly they broke the
leash that Gondolf still held in his hand. In two bounds they
precipitated themselves upon the lover of the bishopess.

"At him, Mirff! At him, Morff!" cried the count clapping
his hands. "At him! At the quarry, my wild fellows! Leave
him not a shred of flesh on his bones!"

"Unless a miracle of strength and skill takes place, my companion will be torn to pieces, our strategy discovered, and the
last chance of my sons' escape will be lost; if so, I shall swiftly
stab both the King and the count at their hearts," said Karadeucq to himself, and as he did, his hand reached under his
blouse, for the dagger that he had there hidden. His hand firmly
seized it, ready for immediate use.

Seemingly unaffected by the sight of the dogs, the Vagre-
bear continued to perform his role with unaltered presence of
mind, bravery and skill; he made a momentary movement of
surprise, but immediately backed up against the beam and held
himself ready, with uplifted club, to repel the attack of the dogs.
Mirff was the first to dash forward, aiming at his belly, but that
very instant the Vagre-bear struck him so violent a blow over
the head that the club broke in three, and Mirff dropped as if
struck by thunder, and emitting terrible howls.

"Malediction!" cried the count. "There goes a mastiff that
cost me three gold sous! Here, my men, have that ferocious
bear immediately disemboweled with your boar spears and iron
bars!"

The count's imprecations were drowned by the frantic
shouts of the rest of the audience, who, themselves more disin-
terested than Neroweg in the course that the combat was taking, applauded the bear's valor and awaited the issue of the

struggle with anxious curiosity. The Vagre bear, now disarmed
and wholly exposed, was at close quarters with the other mastiff,
that, the moment the club was broken, seized his adversary in the
thigh with his formidable fangs and threw him down with the
impetuosity of the shock. The blood of Karadeucq's companion
flowed copiously and reddened the leaves with which the floor
was strewn. Twice did the bear and the dog roll over each
other; at the third time, pinning to the ground with the full
weight of his body the mastiff, that, like Deber-Trud, did not
loosen its teeth from its enemy, the Vagre clutched the brute
by the throat and held him in such a tight clutch between his
vigorous hands, that the animal was strangled. During this
doubly terrible struggle not only did the mastiff's bite cause the
Vagre an intense pain, but he ran at every instant the risk of
being cut to pieces, together with Karadeucq, if, by the slightest
accident, he but betrayed himself;—the lover of the bishopess
remained true to his ursine role; he emitted no sound other
than a few muffled grunts. The combat being over, the worthy
animal crouched down in a lump at the foot of the beam between the corpses of the two mastiffs; with his head between his
fore paws he seemed patiently to lick his bleeding wound, while
Chram, his favorites and several even of the count's leudes vo-
ciferously acclaimed the triumph of the bear.

"Alas, alas!" murmured old Karadeucq as he approached
his companion. "My poor bear is wounded, mortally perhaps.
I have lost my bread winner."

"Fetch boar spears and axes!" cried the count foaming at
the mouth with fury. "Let the ferocious brute be cut to pieces
on the spot; he has just killed Mirff and Morff, the best two
dogs of my pack! By the Terrible Eagle, my ancestor, I order
that the cursed bear be cut to pieces instantly! Did you hear
me, Gondolf?" he added, addressing his master of the hounds
and trembling with rage. "Take down one of those hunting
spears from the wall—kill that bear, kill him on the spot!"

Gondolf hastened to arm himself as he was ordered, while Karadeucq, kneeling down again, cried to Chram with outstretched arms:

"Great King, my only hope rests with you. I implore mercy from you. I place myself under your protection and under the protection of your royal suite. Oh, redoubtable and invincible warrior! Oh, ye other valorous warriors of the King's suite, as terrible in battle as you are generous after victory, you surely will not want to see this animal killed; he vanquished, but was wounded in the struggle and fought fairly! No, no, ever following the example of your glorious King, your refined and courteous honor will revolt at such brutal cowardice, even if committed towards a poor animal! Oh, warriors who are as brilliant by your armor and military grace as you are terrible by your valor, I place myself at the mercy and under the protection of your King. He will demand the life of my bear of the seigneur count, who can refuse nothing to such a noble guest!"

The Frank is vainglorious; his pride delights in the most exaggerated praises of himself; Karadeucq was aware of this; moreover, by addressing himself exclusively to the royal bodyguard, he expected to throw once more the apple of discord between them and the count's leudes. His words were favorably received by the warriors of Chram, who, stepping towards Neroweg, said:

"Count, we demand of you grace for this brave animal, and we do so in the name of the old German custom, according to which a guest's request is always granted."

"King, the custom to the contrary notwithstanding, I shall avenge the death of Mirff and Morff, who cost me six gold pieces. Gondolf, fetch the spears and axes; the bear shall be cut to pieces instantly!"

"Count, the poor mountebank has placed himself under my protection. I may not forsake him."

"Chram, whether or not you protect the old bandit, I shall revenge the death of my magnificent dogs Mirff and Morff."

"Listen, Neroweg, I have a pack that is worth fully as much as yours. You saw it hunt in the forest of Margevol. You may send the master of the hounds to my villa, let him pick out six of my best and handsomest dogs to replace the two that lie dead at our feet."

"I said I would revenge Mirff and Morff," yelled the count furiously, grinding his teeth. "Gondolf, the spears! the spears! death to the devilish bear!"

"You savage rustic, you fail in all the duties of hospitality by denying the request of the King's son," bellowed the Lion of Poitiers at Neroweg, "just as you insulted us, your guests, by keeping your wife from the banquet, and by having your gold and silver vessels removed from the table even before the banquet was over! You are more of a bear than that animal, which you shall not kill. I forbid you—the mountebank has placed himself under the protection of Chram and of us, his men."

"Companions!" cried Sigefrid, "shall we tolerate the heaping of insults upon our count?"

"Just listen to the rustic brutes!" observed aloud one of Chram's warriors, "listen to them, barking as ever, without daring to bite."

"I, Neroweg, king in this burg, as any king in his kingdom, I shall kill that bear! And if you say another word, you whom they call Lion, I shall knock you down at my feet with a blow from my axe, insolent palace cub!"

"You dare insult me, you smut-covered boar!" screamed the Gallic renegade as, pale with anger, he drew his sword with one hand and with the other seized the count by the collar of his dalmatica. "You seem to want me to turn your throat into a sheath for my blade! Ask for mercy, or you are a dead man!"

"Ha, you double thief! You wish to steal my gold necklace!" cried Neroweg, thinking only of defending his jewelry, and concluding from the gesture of his adversary that the latter's purpose was to rob him. "I was right to place my gold and silver vessels out of the clutches of all of you thievish palace cubs."

"He calls us all thieves! To your swords, men of the royal bodyguard! Let us avenge our honor! Let us slash these rustics!"

"Ha, bastard dogs!" cried Neroweg between whom and the Lion of Poitiers Sigefrid had thrown himself. "You speak of swords—here is one for you, and of good temper; you will taste it, profligate blasphemer, who have of a lion only the name! To me, my leudes! they have raised their hands against your count! Let us slash the royal bodyguard!"

"Neroweg!" cried Chram interposing, as his favorite, who had shaken himself loose from Sigefrid, rushed at the count with upraised sword, "are you all fools to quarrel in this manner? Lion, I order you to put up your sword."

"Oh, great St. Martin, blessings upon your name for giving me the opportunity to chastise the sacrilegious whelp who had the audacity to raise his switch at my holy bishop, and who has never ceased sneering at both the holy man and me since he stepped into my burg," cried the count, deaf to the words of Chram, and striving to reach his adversary, from whom he had been again separated in the midst of the uproar.

"Boys, let us defend Neroweg!" Sigefrid called out to his fellow leudes of the count. "This is a good opportunity to prove to the braggards that our rough-looking swords are better than their parade weapons! To arms! Down with them to the last man!"

"And we also to arms! let us settle accounts with these dogs of the basement! They think they are strong, because they are on their own dunghill. Death to the clowns. Let us defend the favorite of King Chram, our King! Swing your axes!"

"My dear sons in God," screamed the bishop in a vain endeavor to dominate the tumult and the increasing uproar, "I order you, all of you, to put up your swords! It is an affliction to the Lord to see His sons quarrel over trifles. Obey your father in God!"

"My friends!" cried Chram in his turn but without being able to make himself heard, "it is folly, it is stupidity to slay one another in this wise. Imnachair! Spatachair! calm our men; and you, Neroweg, calm yours instead of exciting them!"

Vain words; they dropped unheard; neither Neroweg nor the rest of the leudes did or cared to listen to words of conciliation. As to Neroweg himself, a mass of combatants had again thrown themselves between him and the Lion of Poitiers, to whom he called in an enraged voice and struggled to reach. The warriors of Chram and those of the count soon passed from insults and threats, hurled at each other from a distance, to a hand-to-hand conflict. At the first blow the engagement became general—maddening, furious, maudlin and all the more terrible because the torch-bearing slaves, who alone lighted the hall, fearing to be killed in the brawl, fled away precipitately, some throwing their torches to the ground and thus extinguishing them, others carrying the lighted torches with them in their distracted flight. In an instant the banquet hall was deprived of its living illumination; the battle continued in the dark with blind ferocity.

And Karadeucq and the lover of the beautiful bishopess, did they remain quietly in the midst of the butchery? Oh, by no means! Vagres know better than that. After having skilfully thrown the firebrand in the midst of the leudes of the King and the count, Karadeucq saw with pleasure the flames of angry rivalry between the two sets of barbarians flare up a third time, after twice having been appeased; and it was with delight that he noticed it rage in such manner that both he and his bear were lost sight of. As soon as the conflagration which he had kindled was well under way, the old Vagre rushed to the bear, and unchaining him, said at his companion's ear: "Follow close at my heels and do as I do."

The melee was at its height; the torch-bearers had either fled or were fleeing, leaving the banquet hall in almost perfect darkness. Followed by the Master of the Hounds Karadeucq threw himself under the wide and massive table which, although now broken in parts, was not upset by the combat, being, contrary to the habit of the Franks, fastened to the floor. Thus under shelter for a moment the old Vagre unfastened the chain from around the neck of the lover of the bishopess, whereupon continuing to grope their way under the table by the flickering light of the extinguishing torches on the floor, they reached the door of the banquet hall, which was free from the combatants, and rushed out. As they issued from the banquet hall the Vagres found themselves face to face with two slaves who, having fled through another issue, were running distracted with their torches in their hands. Each Vagre seized one of the slaves by the throat.

"Extinguish your torch," said Karadeucq, "and lead me straight to the *ergastula,* or you die this instant."

"Give me your torch," said the lover of the bishopess, "and take me straight to the hay lofts, or I stab you to death."

The two slaves obeyed; the Vagres parted company; one ran towards the hay lofts and barns, the other to the *ergastula,* both guided by their conductors.

CHAPTER IX.

THE RESCUE.

The prisoners in the *ergastula* had drawn as close as possible to the iron railing. Little Odille, who had fallen asleep on the knees of the bishopess, awoke with a start, saying:

"Ronan, are they coming to take us to the place of execution? I am ready for everything."

"No, little Odille! it is barely midnight; I know not what may be happening at the burg; all the Franks who were watching us left their posts before our prison and followed one of their men who came after them; all ran towards the burg brandishing their arms."

"Ronan, my brother, listen in the direction of the seigniorial mansion—it seems to me I hear an odd noise proceeding from that direction."

"I hear tumultuous cries—the clash of arms."

"Ronan, the Vagres must have come to our deliverance, the burg is on fire!"

"The fire spreads—look—look—it is as clear as day in front of the prison."

"A man is running this way—why, it is Karadeucq, our father!"

"Loysik! Ronan! Oh! my sons."

"You here, father?"

"Ronan, Loysik, all of you within, join me to break down the iron railing."

"Alas! we cannot budge—our feet are all sore—we have been put to the torture!"

"To see my two sons and yet not to be able to save them—malediction! This way, Master of the Hounds! my brave fellow, this way—let us free my sons!"

"My beautiful bishopess, are you there? Come, give me a kiss across the railing!—Your lips have pressed mine. I now feel stronger. We two, Karadeucq, will have to tear down this railing. I have set fire to the four corners of the burg—stables, barns, lofts, all is aflame. The count's main building that is now full of Franks, who are mutually slaying one another, and which is built of frame, has also taken fire; it is beginning to burn like a faggot stuck into a furnace."

"Woe is us! it is impossible to break down the railing!"

"Free us, father!"

"Oh, my sons, I shall die of rage before I fall under the axe of the Franks, if I cannot set you free."

"Come, old Karadeucq, one more effort; the Franks who guarded the *ergastula* are now thinking of nothing else but to extinguish the fire; let us dig a hole under the railing with our poniards, with our nails."

"The Franks! There they are—they are coming back to the *ergastula;* they are running this way."

"I can see their weapons glistening by the light of the conflagration."

"Father, there is no hope left! You are lost! Blood and death, lost! And here we are, sore and incapable to defend you!"

About a score of men at arms and several leudes ran with their arms in the direction of the *ergastula;* one of them was heard to say: "A part of these dogs of slaves are profiting by the fire in order to revolt; I heard them say that they were going to set the chief of the Vagres and the rest of the prisoners free. Quick, quick, let us put them all to death—we shall afterwards see to the slaves. Who has the key to the railing?"

At the very moment when Sigefrid was handing the key to the Frankish warrior his eyes fell upon Karadeucq.

"What are you doing there, old vagabond?"

"Noble youth, frightened by the fire, my bear has escaped; I am running after him—he has crouched down yonder not far from the railing. Alas, what a misfortune this fire is!"

"Sigefrid, 1 have unlocked the railing," said one of the Franks; "shall we begin with the men or the women?"

"I shall begin with the men!" cried Karadeucq, planting his dagger in the breast of Sigefrid.

"I also!" cried the Master of the Hounds, stabbing another one of the Franks."

"Vagrery! Vagrery! To us, all brave slaves! Death to the Franks! War upon the seigneurs! Liberty to the slaves! Long live all Gaul!"

"The Vagres!" cried the thunder-struck Franks, dumbfounded at the death of the two leudes. "The Vagres! These demons seem to rise from underground and from the depth of hell!"

"This way!" cried Ronan in a thundering voice. "This way, my Vagres! Kill the Franks!"

The cry was addressed to the Vagres, whom Ronan saw pouring in. Attracted by the light of the conflagration, the signal that was agreed upon, the good, brave Vagres had crossed the fosse; but how? Was not that fosse filled with such deep slime that a man would be swallowed up in it if he attempted to cross it? Certainly, but Ronan's Vagres had, since nightfall, been prowling like wolves around a sheep fold, and carefully sounded the fosse; after which the clever lads hewed down with their axes two large ash trees that stood straight as arrows nearby, stripped off the flexible branches and with them bound the trunks closely together. The long and light improvised bridge was thrown across the fosse, and nimble as cats they crept one after another over the two trunks and reached the opposite side. During the aerial perilous passage two of the Vagres fell off and immediately disappeared in the bottom of the fosse; they were Wolve's-Tooth and Symphorien, the rhetorician—may their names live and be blessed in Vagrery! Their companions had no sooner arrived on the other side of the fosse, than they met, running towards the *ergastula* to liberate the prisoners, about thirty revolted slaves armed with clubs, scythes and forks. After the warriors of Chram and those of Neroweg had long fought in the dark in the banquet hall, they suddenly dropped their quarrel, and leaving the dead and wounded on the field of battle, gave no thought but to the fire—the men of the count to extinguish it, the men of Chram to save the horses and baggage of their master and take them out of the burning stable. The Franks who had hastened to the *ergastula* in order to put the prisoners to death were only a score at the most; they were surrounded and cut to pieces by Ronan's Vagres and by the slaves, after offering a desperate resistance. Not one of these Franks escaped; no, not one! Two of the slaves took Ronan upon their shoulders, two others raised Loysik on theirs, and at the request of his bishopess the Master of the Hounds took up little Odille in his vigorous arms as one might raise a child from its cradle, the young girl being too weak to walk. Old Karadeucq followed his two sons.

The struggle that took place in front of the *ergastula* and which was crowned with triumph for the Vagres consumed less time than it takes to describe it; but there was still much to be done in order to leave the fortified enclosure of the burg. It was necessary to reach the bridge, the only practicable issue, by reason of Ronan, Loysik and Odille, all of whom were unable to walk. It was necessary in order to reach the bridge to follow the inside wall of the embankment under the trees that lined one side of the parade ground; and the parade ground itself, wholly exposed and in plain view of the burning buildings had then to be crossed. Wise and prudent in counsel, old

Karadeucq made the troop halt where it was screened by the trees from the eyes of the enemy, and said to them:

"To attempt to leave the burg in a body would be to invite being slain to the last man. The moment we are seen, some of the Franks in their fury will stop trying to extinguish the fire and will fall upon us. There is only one chance of escape. The moment we reach the open ground, which you must traverse, let us separate and mix up boldly among the frightened Franks, who are seeking to save all they can from the flames. Let us throw ourselves in among the frightened crowd and seem to be engaged in some work of salvage, going, coming, running hither and thither. We shall thus be able to clear the dangerous passage and shall separately reach the bridge—our general *rendezvous.*"

"But, father, carried as we are by these good slaves, how could Loysik and I avoid being detected?"

"That matters not; the slaves will be thought to be transporting some wounded men taken from the ruins; conceal your faces somehow and moan as loud as you can. As to the Master of the Hounds, who has prudently stripped himself of his bear skin, he can boldly run through the crowd carrying the little slave in his arms as if he had saved some young girl from the flames in the women's apartment. The bishopess can wrap herself up in the coat of the Master of the Hounds; she will have no difficulty in safely crossing the crowd in the midst of the general tumult."

The wise advice of the father of Loysik and Ronan was carried out successfully from point to point.

By the faith of a Vagre, beautiful was the spectacle of the vast Frankish burg enveloped in and consumed by the flames! At every turn were heard roofs tumbling in with a crash and throwing upward toward the starry vault of heaven large jets of flame and sparks of fire. The northern wind, blowing fresh and strong, drove towards the south large sheets of flame that surged, like the waves of an angry sea, over the crumbling buildings below. At the moment when, carried on the shoulders of the two slaves, Ronan passed before the seigniorial mansion, which was entirely built of frame and shingled with oaken laths, he saw the flaming roof, which had for some little time been supported by large charred beams, fall in with the rattle of thunder and dash itself against the foundation of volcanic rocks. Nothing remained standing of the count's once proud residence but a few huge beams, whose blackened and smoking sides were brought out into strong relief by the curtain of fire before which they seemed to tremble. The casques and the cuirasses of the leudes of Chram were seen glistening in the light of the conflagration; they were running hither and thither in a joint effort with the men of Neroweg to save the horses and mules from the burning stables.

What an infernal tumult, and how sweet to the ear of a Gaul! By the bones of our fathers the music and the sight were magnificent! The neighing of horses, the bellowing of cattle, the imprecations of the Franks, the cries of the wounded leudes whom the flaming ruins burned, or rolled down upon and crushed! And what a beautiful illumination lighted the tableau—a ruddy flamboyant light!

The two sons of old Karadeucq whom the slaves were carrying on their backs, as well as little Odille, in the arms of the Master of the Hounds, finally crossed the bridge over the fosse, closely preceded and followed by all the Vagres and the revolted slaves who joined them. They had all successfully threaded their way through the crowds of scurrying Franks around the burning buildings. After the troop of Karadeucq was safely on the other side a vigorous shove threw the keeper off the bridge down into the fosse, in the bottom of which he disappeared.

"Are we all outside of the enclosure of the burg?" asked old Karadeucq.

"Yes, all—all!"

"Now let us cut down the bridge; I have broken down the chains that hold it on the other side; if the Franks take it into their heads to pursue us we shall have a long lead over them. Once we reach the forest, then, good bye Franks! Long live the Vagrery and old Gaul! Oh, my sons, you are now free from danger! Ronan, Loysik, one more embrace, my sons!"

"By the sacred joy of this father and his two sons, beautiful bishopess, you are my wife. I shall not leave you unto death!"

"Loysik, you said to me this very night in the prison, 'Fulvia, if you were free to-day and met the Master of the Hounds, also free, what would you answer if he asked you to be his wife?' Being now free," added the bishopess turning towards the Vagre, "I shall be your devoted wife and a true mother if God should grant us children."

"And you, little Odille, you have neither father nor mother left, will you have Ronan for husband, if you survive your wounds?"

"Ronan, even if I were dead, the hope of being your wife would raise me from my grave!"

CHAPTER X.

COUNT AND VAGRE.

With Loysik and Ronan on the shoulders of their companions and little Odille in the arms of the Master of the Hounds, the Vagres and the revolted slaves hastened to reach the forest. The rear of the fleeing troop was brought up by four Vagres, panting for breath and bent down by a heavy bundle that they carried between them. It was a large coarse cloth wound around a gagged and firmly bound man, whose head was additionally wrapped in a jacket.

"Who is that man, my brave Master of the Hounds? Do you know?" asked Ronan.

"It is Count Neroweg, whom your father dexterously kidnapped from the very midst of the leudes with the aid of two of his comrades."

"Neroweg in our power! In the power of Ronan, Loysik and Karadeucq, the descendants of Schanvoch! Heaven and earth!"

"Hello, old Karadeucq, come this way—Ronan will not believe that we kidnapped the Frankish wild-boar."

"Yes, my sons, that fellow whose head is concealed in a jacket, and whom our men are carrying, is Neroweg—it is my share of the booty."

"It is your share, Karadeucq—but we, the count's former slaves, demand to have his skin and bones."

"What a pity that we have not the bishop also—the feast would be complete."

"The Lion of Poitiers killed the bishop."

"Father, are you sure that infamous bishop is dead?"

"Yes—I saw him fall under the sword of the Lion of Poitiers. The blow almost clove him in two."

"But how did you manage to capture Neroweg?"

"I kept my eyes upon you and Loysik from a distance, as you were carried towards the bridge by our Vagres who shouted: 'Room there, room for the wounded leudes whom we have saved from the ruins.' Mixing in, together with three other of our men, among the distracted crowd of leudes and loyal slaves, who were running about helter skelter, I suddenly saw the count running all alone at a distance, and carrying in his arms with great difficulty two heavy skin bags, probably filled with gold and silver; he was running towards a dry well. Neroweg was at that moment alone and a considerable distance away from the burning buildings. The thought struck me to seize the man. Together with two of our men I crept behind the bushes around the cistern into which the count threw one of the bags, fearing, no doubt, that their contents might be stolen from him in the general turmoil. The three of us fell upon him unawares, and threw him down; I planted both my knees upon his chest and both my hands over his mouth to keep him from crying out for help; one of our men took off his jacket, gagged Neroweg and wrapped the jacket over the Frank's head, while our other companion tied his feet, legs and arms firmly, took a large piece of rough cloth that lay near and wound it around the seigneur count. The bridge lay not far away; we could see it from where we stood— and that is the way in which I captured my booty. We are now far enough away from the burg; the count's voice could not be heard there. Remove the jacket from his head and the gag from his mouth. Hurrah for the Vagrery!"

As soon as Neroweg was uncovered and ungagged Karadeucq said to him:

"Count, your hands will remain bound, but I shall now free your legs. Will you walk to the forest with us?"

"You mean to kill me there! Let us walk, accursed mounte-bank, you will see how a Frank marches with a firm step to death—you Gallic dogs, race of slaves!"

The outskirt of the forest was reached at the peep of dawn—a flitting moment in the month of June. At the distance a ruddy glamour was seen struggling against the approaching light of day—it was the conflagration that still raged over the ruins of the burg.

Ronan and the hermit laborer were laid upon the grass, with little Odille seated beside them. On her knees near the young girl, the bishopess tended her wounds. The Vagres and the re-volted slaves stood in a circle around. Neroweg stood pinioned, but savage and resolute of countenance—those barbarians and thieves, however cowardly in their vengeance, are, it must be admitted even by us, their enemies, endowed with a certain sav-age bravery—he cast an intrepid look at the Vagres. Old Kara-deucq, who had preserved his vigor, looked youthed by fully twenty years. The joy of having saved his sons and of having Neroweg in his power seemed to impart new life to him. His eyes sparkled, his cheeks were aflame, he contemplated the count with greedy looks.

"We shall be revenged," said Ronan, "you will be revenged little Odille."

"Ronan, I ask no vengeance for myself; in our prison I often said to the good hermit laborer: 'If ever I should be free again I shall not return evil for evil.'"

"Yes, sweet child—as sweet as pardon. But you need not fear, our father will not kill that man unarmed," answered Loysik.

"Will he not kill him, brother? Aye, by the devil! Our father will kill the Frank as sure as he put us both to the tor-ture, and that he beat and violated this poor child! Blood and massacre, no mercy!"

"No, Ronan, our father will not kill a defenseless man."

"You are long about killing me!" put in the captured count. "What are you waiting for! And you, accursed mountebank, the chief of these bandits, why do you look at me in that way in silence?"

"Because, Neroweg, in contemplating you as I do, I am thinking of the past. I am conjuring up family recollections in which one of your ancestors, the Terrible Eagle, is mixed."

"He was a great chief," answered the Frank proudly; "he was a great King, one of the bravest warriors of my lineage. His name is still glorified in Germany—my shame remains hidden at the bottom of my grave—if you dig a grave for me, cursed dogs!"

"It happened more than three hundred years ago; a great battle was delivered on the banks of the Rhine between the Gauls and the Franks. One of my ancestors fought with yours—the Terrible Eagle. It was a desperate struggle; it was not merely a fight between soldier and soldier, it was a conflict between two races that were fated foes! My ancestor had a presentiment that the stock of Neroweg would be fatal to ours, and he sought to kill him in order to extinguish his family. Fate willed it otherwise. Alas, my ancestor's forebodings did not deceive him. This is the second time that our two families meet across the ages. You had my two sons put to the torture, and to-day they were to be executed upon your orders. Now you are in my power; you are about to die, and your stock will be extinct."

A flash of joy lighted the Frank's eyes, and he answered with a firm voice: "Kill me!"

"My Vagres, this man belongs to me—it is my part of the booty."

"He is yours, old Karadeucq—you may dispose of him at your pleasure. Say the word and we will strike him down dead."

"I wish him to be unbound; I wish him to have the full use of his limbs—but make a strong circle around us two, so that he can not run away."

"Here we are—a strong circle of swords' points, axes, pikes and sharp scythes—he will not be able to break through."

"A priest!" suddenly cried the count in accents of anguish. "I do not wish to die without the assistance of a priest! Will you assist me, hermit laborer?"

"Father," cried Loysik, "do not kill this man in that manner!"

"I do not ask you for my life, Gallic dogs! Slaves! But I do not wish to go to hell! I ask the absolution of a priest!"

"Take this axe, Count Neroweg; we shall be equally armed; the combat between us is to be to the death."

"Father, in the name of your two sons, whom you have just saved, desist from this combat."

"My sons, this axe does not weigh heavy in my hands—I shall extinguish in this Frank the stock of the Nerowegs."

"I, a man of an illustrious family, do battle with a beggar, a Vagre, a revolted slave! No! I shall not bestow such an honor upon you, bastard dog—you may slay me."

"Seize him, and shave his head smooth like a slave. Shame upon the coward!"

"I, shaved like a vile slave! I, undergo such an outrage! I prefer to do battle with you, vile bandit; give me the axe!"

"Here it is, count. And you, my brave Vagres, widen the circle—and long live Gaul!"

Neroweg precipitated himself upon the Vagre; the combat was engaged; it was frightful, stubborn. Loysik, Ronan, little Odille and the bishopess followed trembling and with anxious eyes the events of the struggle. It did not last long. Karadeucq spoke truly. The axe did not weigh heavy in his vigorous hand; it swung in the air and fell with a crash upon the forehead of Neroweg, who rolled down upon the grass with his skull cleaved in twain.

"Die!" cried Karadeucq with a triumphant air. "The stock of the Terrible Eagle will no longer pursue the stock of Joel!"

"You lie, Gallic dog! My stock is not extinct. I have a son of my second wife at Soissons—and my present wife, Godegisele, is with child. My stock will live!"

And with a feeble voice, the dying man added:

"Hermit laborer, give me paradise—my good Bishop Cautin, have pity upon me! Oh, I am going to hell! to hell! the demons!"

And Neroweg expired, his face contracted in diabolical terror.

Missing the count, his leudes must have concluded that he lay buried under the smoldering ruins; some feared that the revolted slaves captured and took him with them. If they searched for him, they must have found the count's body at the outskirts of the forest, with his skull cleaved in twain by an axe blow, and stretched out at the foot of a tree, with the outward bark ripped off and on the bare trunk of which the following words were engraved with the point of a dagger:

"Karadeucq, the Vagre, a descendant of the Gaul Joel, the brenn of the tribe of Karnak, killed this Frankish count, a descendant of Neroweg, the Terrible Eagle. Long live Gaul."

PART IV.

GHILDE.

CHAPTER I.

AT THE HEARTH OF JOEL.

Two years have passed since the death of Count Neroweg. We are now in winter; the wind moans, the snow falls. It was on the day following a similar night that, nearly fifty years ago, Karadeucq, the grandson of old Araim left the paternal roof, under which the following narrative takes place, in order to run the Bagaudy, seduced thereto by a peddler's story.

Old Araim died long ago, never ceasing to sorrow over the loss of Karadeucq, his pet. Jocelyn and Madalen, Karadeucq's father and mother also are dead. His elder brother Kervan and his sweet sister Roselyk still live and inhabit the same homestead situated near the sacred stones of Karnak. Kervan is over sixty years of age; he married late; his son, now fifteen years of age, is called Yvon. The blonde Roselyk, sister of Kervan, is nearly as old as her brother; her hair has turned white; she has remained single and lives with her brother and his wife Martha.

It is night; out of doors the wind blows and the snow falls.

Kervan, his sister, his wife, his son and several of their relatives, who cultivate with them the identical fields that more than six hundred years ago Joel cultivated with his family, are engaged near the fireplace at several household tasks, the favorite pastimes during the long nights of winter. A violent gust of wind blows open the door and several windows. Kervan remarks to his sister:

"Good Roselyk, it was on such a night as this, many long years ago, that a cursed peddler came to our door. Do you remember the incident?"

"Alas, I do! The next morning our poor brother Karadeucq

left us forever. His disappearance gave so much pain to our grandfather Araim that he died of a broken heart, and shortly after we lost our mother, who was almost crazed with grief. Our father Jocelyn alone withstood the bereavement. Oh, our brother Karadeucq was but too heavily punished for wishing to see the Korrigans!"

"The Korrigans, aunt Roselyk!" cried Yvon, Kervan's son. "The little fairies of olden times, of which good old Gildas, the shearer of the sheep, often talks? They have not been seen in this country for a long time, neither the Korrigans nor the other little dwarfs, called Dus."

"Fortunately, my boy, the country is now free from those evil sprites—but for them your uncle Karadeucq might now be in our midst by the fireplace."

"And did you never hear from him, father?"

"Never, my son! He surely died in one of those civil wars, those disasters that continue to rend old Gaul under the reign of the descendants of Clovis."

"May our Brittany be ever spared the ills that so cruelly afflict the other provinces!"

"Our old Armorica has until now been able to preserve her independence and repel all attempts at invasion from the Franks. Why should we be any less able to hold our own in the future? The chiefs of our tribes, whom we choose ourselves, are brave. The chief of the chiefs whom these have chosen, old Kando, and who keeps watch at our frontiers, is an intrepid and experienced man. Did we not triumphantly repel all the attacks of the Franks until now?"

"And already three times have you been called to take up arms, Kervan, and were forced to leave me, together with your sister Roselyk and our son Yvon, in mortal fear," exclaimed Martha, Kervan's wife.

"Come, come, you poor timid Gallic woman. Remember our family legends—Margarid, Joel's wife; Meroë, the wife of

Albinik the mariner; Ellen, the wife of Schanvoch—did they ever exhibit such weakness when their husbands took the field to fight for the freedom of Gaul?"

"Alas, no! And Margarid as well as Meroë met death on the battlefield, together with their husbands."

"While I have been only once wounded in battle against the accursed Franks, whom we cut to pieces on our frontier."

"But you seem, brother, to forget all about the danger that you ran during the last vintage. That was an odd vintage! It had to be garnered with the sword on the side and the axe ready in hand."

"Nonsense! Those were mere pleasure parties. We sallied forth gaily, and went beyond our own borders to harvest the crops of grapes that the Franks make their slaves raise in the region of Nantes. By the beard of Joel! He would have laughed a hearty laugh at the sight of our troops recrossing our frontier gaily escorting our large carts full of red grapes! What a pleasing sight! The yokes of our oxen, the bridles of the horses and even the iron of our lances were festooned with green vine leaves. And we marched to the rythmic measure of the chant that we sang in chorus:

> " 'The Franks, they shall not drink it,
> This wine of our old Gaul—
> No, the Franks, they shall not drink it!
> We make our vintage, sword and pruning-hook in hand.
> Our chariots, used in war, are our rolling presses.
> It is not blood that crimsons deep their axle-trees,
> It is the purple juice of ruddy grapes.
> The Franks, they shall not drink it,
> This wine of our old Gaul—
> No, the Franks, they shall not drink it!' "

"Father, I shall be sixteen years old next vintage in the country of Nantes—will you not take me with you?"

"Keep still, Yvon! Make not such requests. They frighten me," cried the boy's mother.

"Roselyk, dear sister, do not my wife's words remind you of our mother scolding our brother Karadeucq because he wished to see the Korrigans? She used to say: 'Hold your tongue, bad boy!' "

"Alas, brother, all mothers' hearts are alike."

"Father, I hear steps outside—it must be old Gildas. He promised to come this evening and teach us a new chant that he learned from a traveling tailor. Yes, it is he! Good evening, old Gildas!"

"Good evening, my boy; good evening to all."

"Shut the door, old Gildas. The air is cold; come near the fire."

"Kervan, I am not alone. A stranger accompanies me. He knocked at my door and asked for the house where Kervan, the son of Jocelyn, dwells. The traveler comes from Vannes, and even further. He wishes to see you."

"Why does he not step in?"

"He is shaking off the snow that covers him from head to foot."

"Good God, Gildas! Is the man a peddler?"

"Roselyk, Roselyk, does not that also sound like mother? You are right, all mothers' hearts are alike."

"No, Martha; the young man does not look like a peddler to me. Judging by his resolute mien, he would sooner be taken for a soldier. He carries a long dagger in his belt—here he is himself."

"Step in, traveler. Did you ask for the dwelling of Kervan, the son of Jocelyn? Do you wish to see Kervan? I am Kervan."

"Greeting to you and yours, Kervan. But why do you look at me so wonderingly?"

"Roselyk, look well at this young man—look at his eyes, his forehead, his bearing, his face."

"Oh, brother, one sees strange resemblances at times. One

would think that our brother Karadeucq himself stood before us—that is how he looked at the time that he ran away."

"Roselyk, do you not notice that the stranger seems strangely affected? There are tears in his eyes. Say, young man, are you the son of Karadeucq?"

The answer of Ronan the Vagre was to throw himself on the neck of his father's brother, after which he embraced no less effusively Martha, Roselyk and Yvon. After the tears were dried and the first emotion appeased, the first words that simultaneously parted from the lips of Kervan and Roselyk were:

"And our brother, our beloved Karadeucq? What tidings do you bring us from him?"

At this question Ronan the Vagre remained silent; his head drooped and tears again suffused his eyes.

Deep silence reigned hereat among the descendants of Joel. All eyes wept.

Kervan was the first to overcome his grief, and broke the silence, addressing his nephew:

"Is it long since my brother Karadeucq died?"

"Three months, dear uncle."

"Was his end peaceful? Did he remember me and Roselyk, who loved him so dearly?"

"His last words were: 'I die without having been able to fulfill my part of the duty imposed by my ancestor Joel upon his descendants. Promise me, my son Ronan, you who are familiar with my own life and that of your brother Loysik, to fulfill that duty in my stead, and to write down, without concealing aught, both the good and the evil that we have done. When you have done that, promise me that you will proceed to the cradle of our family, near the sacred stones of Karnak. My father Jocelyn and my mother Madalen are certainly dead by this time. You shall deliver the narrative that will have been written, either to my good brother Kervan, if he survives our aged parents, or to his eldest son. If Kervan should have died without posterity, ask his heirs or his wife's to deliver to you, obedient to the orders of our ancestor Joel, our family's legends and relics, and you are then to transmit them to your descendants. If, however, my brother Kervan and my sweet sister Roselyk still live, tell them that I die with their names upon my lips and dear to my heart.' Such were the last words uttered by my father."

"And have you the account of your own and my brother's lives?"

"Here it is," answered Ronan opening his traveling bag.

And he drew from it a parchment which he handed over to Kervan. The latter took the scroll with deep emotion, while, taking from his belt the long poniard with an iron hilt that Loysik and after him the Master of the Hounds had worn, and on the hilt of which were engraven the Saxon word *Ghilde* and the two Gallic words *Friendship, Community,* Ronan passed the weapon to his uncle, saying:

"It was my father's wish that this poniard be added to our family relics. When you will have read this narrative you will admit that the weapon deserves being placed together with the other articles that our ancestors have bequeathed to us—pious relics, that I must ask you to show me and which I shall contemplate with veneration. It is now getting late. I must leave you again day after to-morrow morning. I must, therefore, request you to read this very evening the narrative that I have delivered to you. I shall relate to you to-morrow what remains to be said and that I have not had the time to write down. I, on my part, have a strong wish to read our family chronicles, the principal incidents of which my father often narrated to me."

"Come," said Kervan taking up a lamp.

Ronan followed him. The two stepped into one of the chambers of the house. On a table lay a small iron coffer, the gift of Victoria the Great to Schanvoch. Kervan took from the coffer the gold sickle of Hena, the Virgin of the Isle of Sen, the little brass bell left by Guilhern, Sylvest's iron collar, Genevieve's silver cross and the casque's lark of Victoria the Great. He deposited all these articles near the poniard of Loysik. Kervan also produced from the little coffer the several family parchments, ranked them in order before Ronan, and then rejoined his family.

That long winter's night was spent by the Vagre reading the legends of his family.

On their part, Kervan, his wife and sister prolonged their reading until it was almost dawn. Contrary to their wont, they did not rise with the day. With the impressions of his family history fresh upon his mind, Ronan visited next morning the environs of the house. He found at every step mementos of his ancestors—the wide field on which his ancestor and his two sons, Guilhern and Mikael, indulged in the virile exercises of the *mahrek-ha-droad* still spread before his eyes; the living spring, at the edge of which Sylvest and Syomara had in their infantine games built their little hut to protect themselves from the heat of the sun, still babbled along its course.

The Vagre was drawn from his revery by the voice of his father's brother.

"Ronan," said Kervan, "the frost has hardened the ground and the cattle can not be let out to-day. We shall have wheat to pound in the house. Let us go in. While we are at work you can narrate to us the events that complete your narrative. I promise you that I shall faithfully transcribe them and append them to the narrative that you wrote.

CHAPTER II.

ON THE HILL NEAR MARCIGNY.

The family of Kervan are reassembled together with Ronan in the large hall of the farmhouse. After the morning repast the women take up their distaffs, or some other domestic work. The men pound the wheat, which they pour out of one set of large bags and then drop into another. Huge logs of beech and oak burn in the fireplace, seeing that outside the cold is intense. While each pursues his work in silence they cast from time to time inquisitive looks at Ronan, the Vagre son of the Bagauder.

"Uncle," says Ronan, "did you read through the narrative that I gave you yesterday?"

"Yes, and all the rest of us here assembled heard it read. But there is no mention made of my poor brother's death."

"Before broaching that subject, uncle, I should inform you of what happened after the burning down of the burg of Neroweg.

"The complete success of our raid threw the Franks and bishops of the region into consternation. All the slaves who were not too besotted, the colonists whom the seigneurs rack-rented, in short, a considerable number of determined men joined our band. From day to day its numbers swelled and it became more redoubtable. With good or evil grace the seigneurs felt themselves forced to improve the condition of their slaves.

"My brother Loysik proved himself faithful to the principle of Jesus of Nazareth that it is the sick who stand in special need of a physician. He remained with us, and soon he had a decided ascendency over our troop. His good-heartedness, his courage, his eloquence, his love for Gaul, his horror of the Frankish conquest gained him all hearts. One day he took it into his head to undertake a journey the destination of which he kept a secret. Shortly after that we had letters from him urging us to draw near to the confines of Burgundy; he was to join us in the neighborhood of Marcigny, a town situated at the extreme end of that province. Before his departure he made us promise that we would set no more burgs and episcopal villas on fire; pillage, however, continued unabated and was distributed among the poor. Thus we administered strict justice upon the Frankish seigneurs, the bishops and abbots who enjoyed a reputation for cruelty."

"But did not the Franks take up arms against you? Were they terrified to that extreme?"

"King Clotaire ordered a levy of men, but the beneficiary seigneurs feared that, if they parted with their leudes, their burgs would remain unprotected and either at the mercy of the slaves or exposed to attacks from our band. They sent but few men in answer to the King's summons. And so we were given fresh opportunities and twice we beat the Franks in pitched encounters. All the time we drew nearer and nearer to the frontiers of Burgundy as requested by Loysik."

"And what of little Odille, Ronan? What became of her, poor, dear victim of Frankish brutality?"

"I took her to wife; the dear girl never leaves me; she is as sweet as she is brave, as devoted as she is tender."

"Dear girl—and the bishopess, who interested us all, despite her errors?"

"Fulvia has become to the Master of the Hounds what Odille is to me."

"And that Prince Chram, who was scheming a parricide, did he carry out his projected treason towards Clotaire, that other monster who stabbed his brother's son to death?"

"Three days ago, on my way hither, I saw Chram and hi
father on the frontier of our Armorica."

"The father and son on our frontier?"

"Aye, and they approved themselves worthy of each othei
Oh, Kervan, I have run the Vagrery in my boyhood; I hav
witnessed frightful scenes during that period; but by the fait
of a Vagre, I never was so terrified—I still shudder with horro
when I think of what, only a few days ago, took place under m;
own eyes, when Chram and his father met.

"It was a horrible spectacle—I shall presently describe i
to you, but I must first return to our own affairs. Faithful t
our promise to Loysik, we drew nearer to the boundaries o
Burgundy. That region, one of the first that was conquered be
fore Clovis by other hordes of barbarians that preceded him fron
Germany and were called Burgunds, was full of heroic souvenir
of old Gaul. It was there that, at the voice of Vercingetorix, th
Chief of the Hundred Valleys, the people first rose in arm
against the Romans. Epidorix, Convictolitan, Lictavic an
other patriots of that province joined with their several tribe
the Chief of the Hundred Valleys, all anxious to join him i
doing battle for the freedom of Gaul."

"And I suppose that once so brave region has undergone th
fate of the others?"

"There, as elsewhere, Kervan, the bishops undermined th
mental virility of the people, besotted them, and rendered ther
submissive prey to the conquerors."

"But here in our Armorican Gaul, both the Christian an
the non-Christian druids preach to us the love of country an
hatred for the oppressor."

"And, consequently, Brittany has remained free. It har
pened otherwise with the unfortunate province that I am speak
ing of. Since the year 355 its population began to degenerat
visibly. Two chiefs of barbarian hordes, Westralph and Chnoc
omar, invaded the region; other barbarians, Burgunds by nami

who came from the region of Mayence, in turn drove away the first invaders and established themselves at about the year 416. These Burgunds, who gave their name to the region, were a pastoral people and less savage than the other tribes that poured in from Germany. The larger number of the original inhabitants were either cut to pieces or led into slavery at the time of the first conquest in 355. Although held in slavery by the Burgunds, the lot of the surviving portion of the population was less wretched than that of their brothers in most of the other conquered provinces. Gondiok, Gondehaud and his son Sigismond succeeded one another as kings until 534. In that year, Childebert and Clotaire, sons of Clovis, fell upon the Burgunds, and, although these were of their own Germanic race, laid their country waste, enslaved both Burgunds and Gauls, and attached the territory to the domain of the Frankish kingdom."

"What devastation! What bloodshed!"

"Those were horrible times, but by the faith of a Vagre, we rendered them frightful to many a conqueror himself. Well, agreeable to the request of Loysik, we drew near the confines of Burgundy and arrived in the vicinity of Marcigny early in autumn. In that happily located region the fall of the year is as mild as summer. The sun was going down, we had been on the march almost all day; the region, once so thickly populated and teeming with wealth, now lay fallow and deserted. Some more slaves joined us, others, however, fled into Marcigny, and threw the place into alarm. We expected the return of Loysik at every moment. As a matter of precaution we camped on a woody hill whence we could observe the city, lying at a goodly distance away, and hardly protected by its crumbling walls. Towards evening we saw our brother proceeding out of the town. He hastened to us, having been notified of our arrival by the fleeing slaves. It seems to me I see him now climbing the hill; he walked hurriedly; his face beamed with happi-

ness. After answering to the affectionate greetings of our delighted troop who surrounded him, all being eager to express to
him their delight at his return, Loysik made a sign that he
wished to speak. He stepped upon a mound under the over-
spreading branches of a chestnut tree. We gathered in a semi-
circle before him; many of the women who joined us in running
the Vagrery sat down at his feet on the grass. Odille and the
bishopess were foremost among these. On that day Loysik
wore a robe of coarse white wool; a ray of the westering sun
that penetrated through the foliage above his head seemed to
surround with a golden aureole his serious and sweet face, on
both sides of which, parting from his slightly bald head, fell his
long blonde hair of the same color as his slight beard. I know
not for what reason, but as I then looked at Loysik, the young
man of Nazareth occurred to me, as he preached to the vagabond crowd that ever surrounded him. Profound silence reigned
among our troop. Loysik held an address to us which I shortly
after transcribed in full, together with all that happened on the
occasion, upon a parchment lest I should forget it."

Taking a scroll from his pocket Ronan the Vagre proceeded:
"Here it is—I shall read it textually to you:

"'My friends, my brothers, all of you who hear me, I return to your midst with good tidings. Until now, you have,
by means of frightful acts of reprisal, returned evil with evil
to the Franks, the abbots and bishops. These wicked folks so
willed it—violence invites violence, oppression invites revolt,
iniquity invites vengeance. The threatening words of Jesus
have been verified—*They that take the sword, shall perish by
the sword; Woe unto you, Scribes and Pharisees, for ye bind
heavy burdens and grievous to be borne, and lay them on men's
shoulders; but ye yourselves will not move them with one of
your fingers; Woe unto you that are rich, for ye have received your consolation.* To the poor who lacked the necessaries of life you gave the goods that you took from the con-

quering plunderers, or from the modern princes of the Church. Struck with terror, many a hard-hearted seigneur and prelate felt forced to relax his severity. You have administered justice; but, alas, an adventurous, merciless justice. It could not be otherwise. In these days of tyranny and civil war, of slavery and revolt, of atrocious misery and criminal opulence, people are hurled from the paths of morality. The innate sense of justice and injustice, of good and evil is beclouded in the popular mind. Some, besotted with terror, undergo unheard-of ills with abject and degrading resignation; others, a prey to headlong vertigo, mix actions of greatest nobility with deeds that are most reprehensible. Your vengeance fatedly begets incalculable misfortunes. No doubt there is now many a seigneur, who, merciless until recently, does now conduct himself with less cruelty towards his slaves, as a consequence of the terror with which you inspire him. But the next day? You will then be far away, and the butchers then resume their murderous propensities. You set the homes of the conquerors on fire; but those buildings are speedily raised again, and it is our brothers, the slaves, who are forced to rebuild them. You distribute among the poor a part of the tribute that you levy upon the seigneurs and the prelates; but after a few days of abundance, misery weighs anew upon the unhappy population, and, by contrast, it is more painful than before. The coffers that you rifle must all be refilled by our brothers, the slaves, by dint of fresh and crushing labors. What floods of tears! What floods of blood are shed! How many ruins mark your tracks, how many irreparable disasters!'

"A voice cried out from the crowd: 'Have not our conquerors shed the blood of our race in torrents? Let the world perish, together with the iniquity that racks us! Death to the oppressors! Death to the seigneurs and the priests!'

"My brother then proceeded:

"'Perish iniquity! Aye, perish slavery! Aye, perish misery

and ignorance! Like you, I hold the barbarian conquest in
horror; like you, I hold subjection in horror; like you, I hold
in horror the false priests of Jesus, who keep their fellowmen
in bondage; like you, I hold in horror the degradation of our
country. But in order to overcome barbarism, ignorance, mis
ery and slavery, they must be combated with civilization, with
intelligence, with virtue, with labor, with the awakened Gallic
patriotism that lies torpid at the bottom of so many hearts!'

" 'Hermit, our friend,' the interrupter cried again, 'how
else can we fight our enemies than arms in hand? Are we no
"Wand'ring Men," "Wolves," "Wolves' Heads"?'

" 'What is it that has turned you into Vagres, ye men of al
conditions? What is it that drove you to revolt? Is it no
spoliation and misery, and a determination to be free rathe
than submit to slavery? If you were to be told: "Renounce
your wandering lives, and your labor will supply you ampl
with the necessaries of life, and your courage will guarante
your safety and tranquility. You who regret having lost the
joys of the hearth and of family life or who desire to partake
of them—yours can be those pure delights, while you other
who prefer austere seclusion can be free to indulge your bent
and you can live happy and peacefully;"—if you were to b
promised that, would you not prefer it to your present life?'

" 'Hermit, are such prospects possible? You are not of th
number of false priests who pretend to have the power of per
forming miracles.'

" 'Ah, had they only willed it, the bishops could have per
formed such miracles every day in the name of the human fra
ternity preached by Jesus. Aye, had they all acted like the bisho
of Chalon, a path of pacific emancipation would have been
opened to Gaul.'

" 'And what did the bishop of Chalon do?'

" 'Upon leaving you, I proceeded to yonder little town o
Marcigny, which belongs to the diocese of Chalon and where th

bishop owns a villa which he occupies in summer. He is not a wicked man, although he does keep his fellowmen in bondage. He has spent his days in quiet, idleness and opulence. He is a great friend of King Clotaire. I proceeded to that bishop. I shall narrate to you the conversation that took place between us:
" 'I said: "Did you ever hear about the Vagres?" "Alas, yes! Those people commit grave crimes in other regions. But, thank God, the Vagrery never entered Burgundy." "Well, bishop, I wish to inform you that bands of Vagres are approaching your diocese." "Oh, woe is me! Woe is all of us! What will become of us all? My diocese will be ravaged, my treasury pillaged, my palace in Chalon sacked, my villa burned down! Monk, what desolation!" "Bishop, is not the Valley of Charolles located in your diocese?" "It belongs to glorious King Clotaire, like all the rest of the lands of Gaul that have not been distributed as benefices either by himself, or by his father, King Clovis, to the chiefs of the leudes and the Church." "Are you not a friend of Clotaire's?" "That great King shows me a good deal of kindness." "Demand of him in my name the gift of the Valley of Charolles; I shall found there a community of monk laborers. Around the monastery a lay colony will be established, open to the Vagres. A portion of the lands shall be reserved for the monk laborers, the rest shall be left to the colonists. But the gift must be absolute, hereditary and free from all taxes, fees or imposts. The colonists are to be recognized as free in fact and by right, they and their descendants. Obtain the donation for me from King Clotaire, and the troop of Vagres, instead of becoming a source of terror to the region, will be a source of security to your diocese." Such was the conversation. The bishop hastened to forward my application to King Clotaire; and yesterday a royal messenger brought the King's answer. Here it is, I shall read it to you.

" 'It runs thus: "Clotaire, illustrious warrior, King of the Franks. The function and duty of a King is to come to the help of the servants of God and to receive their prayers favorably. Moreover, seeing that we sojourn but a short time in this life, it is important that we hasten to store up wealth in heaven. We can easily store up such wealth through generous donations to the bishops and the Church. Therefore, we receive favorably the request of our venerable father in Christ, Florent, bishop of Chalon-on-the-Saone, and we hereby inform all our loyal subjects, now and in the future, that a certain monk named Loysik has asked us through the intermediary of the said Florent, our venerable father in Christ and friend, a tract of land where he may live freely, pray and implore divine mercy for us. He has added that he is followed by a large number of men whom he wishes to withdraw from the disorders and the miseries of the century. Those men have promised to settle down near him, and to devote themselves to a peaceful and industrious life. Whereas, we consider the monk's request wise, and whereas furthermore we are of opinion that if we receive it favorably we shall be performing a work agreeable to God and meritorious for the remission of our sins, we hereby grant to the said monk the possession of the Valley of Charolles, situated in the diocese of Chalon, bounded to the north by the mountains known as the Balue Rocks; to the south by the river Charolles, an arm of which crosses the said valley; to the west by the ravine known as Goats' Forest, which is contiguous to the lands of the church of Marcigny. We cede to the said monk all that he may find on said territory—slaves, domestic animals, buildings, vines, cultivated fields, meadows and woodlands. He shall have the free use of them all, without anyone whosoever having the right to hinder him, to build or to plant. We exempt him and those who may settle with him in the said Valley of Charolles, of all contributions to our fisc. We forbid all our leudes, bishops, dukes, counts and all others to exact, either for themselves or their suites, whether moneys, presents, quarter or rents from the said monk Loysik, or from those who may settle down upon the territory that we have ceded to him, they being held and recognized by us as free men. Let no one be audacious enough to violate our commandments. We will it that the said monk

Loysik, his companions and their successors live free and un-
disturbed under our protection. And in order that these presents shall have greater force, we have willed that they be signed
by our own hand and sealed with our seal. CLOTAIRE."

"'As he placed this charter in my hand the bishop added:
"Now, monk, make good use of this donation and prevent the
Vagres from ravaging my diocese."

"'While the bishop was saying these words to me, some
fugitive slaves rushed in and announced to him the approach of
your troop. The prelate thereupon said to me imploringly:
"Go, run, monk, I am ready for any sacrifice in order to live
in peace with those redoubtable neighbors."

"'It now, my friends and brothers, rests with you whether
you will live happy and free. Those of you who are willing to
enter our community of hermit laborers will be admitted; those
who, preferring family life, may wish to join a woman of their
choice shall be settled upon the hereditary lands. I have visited
the valley in all its parts; a river, well stocked with fish,
crosses the meadows, magnificent woods shade it, vines and
cereals flourish on its slopes, the cattle on its meadows are numerous. The poor slaves who were either born upon the place or
transported thither will be set free; the lands that they have
hitherto cultivated for the royal fisc will henceforth be theirs
as hereditary property. The valley is immense. Even if we
were ten times more numerous than we are, the soil's fertility
will supply our wants. The lands that King Clotaire restores
to us in the form of a gift have been violently conquered more
than two centuries ago by tribes of barbarians, they were sub-
sequently invaded by the Burgunds, and finally conquered over
again by the Franks. Portions of the land are not cultivated;
the race that owned them more than two hundred and fifty
years ago, before the invasion, has long been extinct. The people who once inhabited them have been either cut to pieces during the successive conquests or have been led far away into

slavery, or have died under the yoke working for others on their own ancestral domains—they are no more. By occupying this portion of the soil of Gaul we dispossess none of our own race. But, at an emergency, we must be able to defend the territory from aggression. In these days of civil wars, donations, however perpetual, are not always respected by the inheritors of the royal power, nor by the seigneurs and the bishops. We must, accordingly, be ready to repel force with force. The valley is protected towards the north by almost inaccessible rocky cliffs; on the south by a deep river; on the west by rugged ravines, and to the east by a dense forest. It will be an easy thing for us to fortify ourselves in our possession and maintain our rights.' "

Kervan followed closely the Vagre's narrative and asked him with deep interest whether his companions took the advice of Loysik.

"Yes, dear uncle, almost all the Vagres accepted Loysik's offer; few only preferred to continue their life of adventure. They left us with the promise, however, not to enter Burgundy. We never since heard of them. Among those who now people the Valley of Charolles, many have adopted the rules of the monk laborers under the direction of Loysik. The large majority of our companions, however, have organized a lay community around the monastery; they married either women who ran the Vagrery with us or daughters of neighboring colonists. I wedded little Odille, while the Master of the Hounds took the bishopess for his mate. The artisans whom slavery and want had driven to the Vagrery, resumed their former occupations, and now work for the colony; others tend the fields, the vines and the cattle. As to myself, I have become a good husbandman, and my little Odille, who since her childhood was accustomed to tend flocks of sheep in the mountains where she was born has turned to that occupation. The bishopess works at the distaff, spins and weaves like a skilful housekeeper, and also

)versees the hospital which we opened for sick women. Loysik
⹂uperintends the hospital of men in the monastery."

"Ah, Ronan! Why did not the bishops act like your father,
ⅼeeing they did not follow the·example of our venerated druids,
ɪnd preach a holy war against the Franks? Why did not the·
Ͻhurch restore to their former owners the vast domains that they
ɹnd it so easy to wheedle from the credulity of the Frankish
Kings and seigneurs? Or, in cases where the former owners
ɪre no more, why does not the Church distribute the land among
ʈhe slaves that cultivate it?"

"Alas, the prelacy has preferred to reign over a brutified
people; they did not like to live a simple life among a free people. Oh! It will be done for our old Armorica if she ever falls
under the yoke of the priests!"

"May it please heaven that such a fatality may never befall
ɔur beloved region! Let us put aside such sad thoughts; let us
rather talk of the peaceful and industrious life of the colony
of Charolles."

"Yes, we live happy in our beloved valley, where we cultivate our fields in common and share the fruits of our labor,
agreeable to the words that you saw graven on the hilt of the
poniard that I delivered to you—*Friendship, Community.*"

"But what is the meaning of that other word—*Ghilde?*"

"It is a Saxon word; it means association, fraternity. In
the northern country where the word comes from there is a
custom, the origin of which is lost in the remotest ages, according to which all the members of a *ghilde* pledge to one another
with a mysterious oath friendship, mutual support and solidarity in all things. If the house of one of the associates burns
down, all the others help him in rebuilding it; if his crops are
destroyed by a storm or any other accident, all the associates
contribute their share to indemnify him for his loss; likewise if
his vessel is lost at sea. Is anyone of them afraid to undertake
a long voyage alone, one, two or several of his associates accom-

pany him; is any member of the *ghilde* the victim of some iniquity, all the others take his part in order to secure justice;
is he insulted, all the others rally around him to aid him in ob-
taining reparation or vengeance. Our community has put into
practice the virtues of that custom. We say there, as once we
said in Vagrery: *All for each, each for all."*

"And my brother Karadeucq, did he long enjoy that peaceful
life after a life of so many hardships?"

"He lived happy in my house unto the day of his death, and
he was able to bless my first-born child."

"Tell us the circumstances of my brother's death."

"From the written narrative that I delivered to you, you
must have seen what kind of a man was Chram, the son of King
Clotaire. His projects of revolt having failed in Poitou and
Auvergne, he made a raid into Burgundy at the head of a few
troops in the expectation of raising the country against his
father. The counts and dukes of the reign considered it in
their interest to take the field against Chram in this new civil
war. Nevertheless, he laid part of the country waste. One of
the bands of Chram arrived near our valley. Foreseeing the
need thereof in these disturbed times, my father and Loysik
had the unprotected accesses of the valley fortified with fosses
and entrenchments made of felled trees. Our colonists and the
men of the monastery took turns in mounting guard at these
places the moment the invasion of Burgundy by Chram was
known. My father was in command of one of the advanced
posts when Chram's warriors approached our valley for the
purpose of ravaging it."

"I presume an armed encounter took place between Chram's
soldiers and the inhabitants of Charolles, and my poor brother
Karadeucq—"

"Was mortally wounded as he drove the Franks back at the
head of his men. My father died after giving me the orders
that I stated to you. He wore during the combat the Saxon

poniard that belonged to Loysik, and which the Master of the Hounds had picked up as he fled from the field of carnage at the fastness of Allange. The Master of the Hounds returned the poniard to my brother after our flight from the burg of Nero-weg. Loysik afterwards presented the weapon to my father. He wore it on the day of the encounter with the Franks. He ordered me to bring it to you, in order that it be joined to our family relics."

"My brother's death was brave, like his life. A curse upon that Chram, son of Clotaire! Had he not raided Burgundy, my brother Karadeucq might still be alive!"

"Like you, Kervan, I say a curse upon Chram! But, at any rate, he met on the frontiers of our Brittany the merited punishment for his criminal life."

CHAPTER III.

THE DEATH OF CHRAM.

"Oh, Kervan," Ronan the Vagre proceeded after a short respite, "it almost looks as if these Frankish Kings and all their family are predestined to become the subjects of horror to the whole world. I shall now narrate to you the manner of Chram's death.

"My father had made me promise him at the last moments of his life that I would repair hither, to the cradle of our family, so soon as I wrote the chronicle that I delivered to you, but which I could not finish for the reasons that I shall state.

"There is nothing more difficult or more perilous than a long journey in these disastrous days. The traveler runs at every step the risk of being captured on the road and led away a prisoner by the armed bands of the dukes, the counts, the seigneurs or the bishops who are in perpetual feuds with one another, plundering or raiding one another's domains, ever intent upon enlarging their possessions. As a consequence, whoever is compelled to undertake a journey never ventures outside of the cities except with considerable numbers, so as to be in condition to repel the armed bands. I learned that a company of travelers was to leave the city of Marcigny for Moulins. That was exactly my route. I left the valley and joined the caravan. We left Marcigny in a body of nearly three hundred persons— men, women and children—some on foot, others mounted, all bound to Moulins as the first station. At that city other travelers were expected to proceed to Bourges. At Bourges I counted upon being able to join a third body and reach Tours, and in that way to proceed upon my journey to Saumur and then to Nantes, which would bring me to the very frontier of Brittany. On the stretch between Marcigny and Tours, our troop of travelers were repeatedly compelled to drive off marauding bands of armed men. In one of these encounters I was wounded, but only slightly; but several of my traveling companions were killed, while some others were captured and carried, together with their families, into slavery. The bulk of our troop, however, myself included, were fortunate enough to arrive safely at Tours, and there to rest in security."

"What horrible days these are! It would not be any more dangerous to travel in a hostile country."

"Oh, Kervan, if you could see the ravages of the conquest! Ruins everywhere, fresh and old ones. Our former Gallic roads and highways, so beautifully wide and carefully kept, with their relays of post horses and inns, are now all wild and heaps of ruins. Communication, once so easy from one end of Gaul to the other, is now wholly broken up. In one place the road breaks off because it crosses over the domain of some Frankish seigneur or of some abbey; at another place the bridges have been broken down by some armed band, that, being closely pursued, sought to protect its retreat. Thus we were compelled to make wide detours in order to arrive at our journey's end. Several nights were spent on the open fields. We were at times compelled to fell trees near the banks of a river and build a raft to effect a crossing, there being none other practicable.

"Upon my arrival in Tours, I learned that King Clotaire was there gathering troops in order to march in person against his son Chram, who had just crossed Touraine and was moving in the direction of the frontiers of Brittany. I thought the chances favorable to finish my journey in safety. I followed in the wake of the royal troops, which consisted of leudes and soldiers, the latter of whom were furnished to the King by the beneficiary seigneurs, and also of impressed colonists. When

the King's army put itself in march, I followed. Alas, Kervan!
The enemy's forces themselves could not have been more merciless towards the people than were the royal troops. Upon their
arrival in a town the Franks would drive the residents from
their houses, they would then take possession, consume the provisions, beat the men, outrage the women, and destroy everything that they could not carry with them. Clotaire joined his
troops with his bodyguard at Nantes. It was there that I saw
the monster for the first time. He wore a long blood-colored
dalmatica embroidered in gold; over the costly vestment he
had a hooded fur jacket, with the hood half drawn over his
forehead. From under his coif his eyes glistened like those of
a wild cat. The King's cadaverous visage was set in long locks
of grey hair that reached almost to his waist. He rode a large
war steed, black of coat and caparisoned in red. At his left
rode his constable; at his right the bishop of Nantes.

"Being left with only a few troops, Chram had fled before
the superior forces of his father. His plan was to enter Brittany. But he found Kando on guard at the frontier."

"Kando is one of the bravest and alertest warriors of Armorica."

"Accompanied by his worthy friend Spatachair—the Lion of
Poitiers, the renegade Gaul of whom mention is made in the
written narrative that I delivered to you, died insane—Chram
proceeded to Kando's camp and proposed to him that he join
his Breton troops to the Franks in order to make head against
his father, Clotaire.

" 'I am always delighted to see the Franks cutting one another's throats,' Kando answered Chram; 'nevertheless the horror that your parricidal projects inspire me with is such that, although your father himself is a monster after your own kind,
I refuse to enter into any alliance with you. My own troops are
enough to fight Clotaire if he should take it into his head to

invade our territory, which, until now no Frank has attempted with impunity.'

"Feeling at least certain of Kando's neutrality, but nevertheless crowded into a corner at the frontier of Armorica, Chram now stood at bay and prepared for a desperate combat on the morrow. He imagined that if the worst were to befall him, his escape would in any event be certain, seeing that he had taken the precaution of keeping a vessel ready to embark in near the little port of Croisik.

"I had arrived safely at the boundary of Brittany; I cared little for the issue of the impending battle. I had met two Bretons by accident near Nantes. The two Armoricans were bound for Vannes. From that city to the sacred stones of Karnak I knew the distance was short. We three departed before sunrise on the morning of the battle that Clotaire was to deliver against his son. In order to shorten our route and also to avoid finding ourselves entangled in the pending melee, we walked to the seashore intending to proceed to the bay of Morbihan.

"We had walked a good portion of the day, and were skirting the shore in the neighborhood of the port of Croisik when we noticed a fisherman's hut raised against a projecting rock. We turned towards it, intending to rest a few hours, when, to my great astonishment I saw near the hut several traveling mules and richly caparisoned horses in charge of some slaves. Three of the animals, one of which was a palfrey, bore women's saddles."

"A strange spectacle in that solitary place. And to whom did the mounts belong?"

"To Chram. His wife and two daughters were in the hut. A boat was moored at the shore, and at a distance of about three bows' shots, a light vessel rode at anchor, ready to set sail."

"You mentioned before the means of escape that Clotaire's

son had prepared in case his troops were beaten—the vessel, I presume, waited for him and his family?"

"My two companions, as well as myself, hesitated whether or not to enter the hut, when its door opened and a richly dressed young woman stepped to the threshold; two little girls were with her. One of them, a child of about five or six years of age, clung to the folds of her mother's robe, while the latter held another girl of about twelve by the hand. The young woman looked depressed; her eyes were in tears; behind her I saw a warrior, whom I readily recognized as one of the three favorites of Chram, Imnachair, the identical warrior who witnessed the torture to which I was subjected at the burg of Neroweg."

"Were that woman and children Chram's family? It has always seemed strange to me that such monsters should at all have families."

"Those were my very thoughts, Kervan, when the young woman, noticing our traveling bags on our shoulders, asked us with marked anxiety whether we came from Nantes, and whether we had any news of a battle that must have been fought there."

" 'We can give you no information upon that, madam,' we answered her, 'we did not even know that there were any armies drawn up for battle.'

"Suddenly one of the slaves who must have been stationed on the lookout over the crest of the rock, ran towards the hut crying: 'Horsemen! We see far away, in a cloud of dust, a number of horsemen riding at full gallop in this direction!'

" 'Death and fury!' cried Imnachair stamping the ground and growing pale. 'It is Chram—the battle is lost!'

"At these words the poor young woman fell down upon her knees, clasped her two daughters to her heart, and I could hear but the moans and sobs of the mother and her children.

" 'Quick! Quick! To the boat!' shouted Imnachair. 'Slaves,

unload the mules; take to the boat the cases that they carry; and you, madam, hold yourself ready to embark!'

"The precipitate tramp of galloping horses was heard approaching, also the clank of armors, and even voices, that, although confused, sounded furious.

" 'It is my husband!' cried Chram's wife, growing deadly pale. 'But his father is pursuing him! Do you not hear those cries of death?'

"Imnachair listened. 'Yes,' said he; 'it is the voice of King Clotaire! Flee, madam; flee, you and your children! Let us run to the boat—we shall soon row ourselves out of danger. It will soon be too late!'

" 'Flee without my husband—never!' answered the young woman convulsively pressing her two children to her heart.

"Cries of 'Kill him!' 'Kill him!' 'Death!' 'Death!' grew more distinct every instant. Those who uttered them were now no more than three hundred paces from the hut. King Clotaire headed the pursuers.

" 'Come, madam!' shrieked Imnachair seizing the young woman by the arm.

" 'No!' she answered resolutely.

" 'If you are determined to wait for Clotaire, I must leave you!' cried Imnachair. 'Adieu, madam!' saying which he ran to the boat.

"Neither I nor my two companions being anxious to meet Clotaire and his bodyguard, we rushed towards the granite boulders that strewed the beach and hid ourselves completely from view among them. Both the hut and the sea were in sight from the place of my concealment. A minute later I saw the boat, now loaded with the cases that were taken from the pack-saddles of the mules, and which undoubtedly contained the treasury of Chram, row swiftly towards the vessel, the sails of which were at the same time being loosened to the wind."

"And the woman—the two children?"

"Imnachair left them all behind. He sat in the stern of the boat with the tiller in his hand; the slaves rowed and accompanied the King's favorite in his flight."

"The heavens would be unjust if such men as Chram could find devoted friends. This wretch of a favorite no doubt gave Chram over to a deserved death; but that wife—those innocent children—"

"As I was saying, Kervan, from my place of concealment I had the sea, the hut and its surroundings in plain view. Despite the distance that separated me from the horrible scene that I am about to describe to you, I could distinctly hear the voices of the Franks, who were drawing nearer and nearer. Almost at the same instant that Imnachair pushed off from the beach, I saw Chram's wife take a few steps, dragging her children after her. Her strength failed her; she again dropped down upon her knees; I saw her and her two little daughters raise their arms imploringly, with terror-stricken countenances. An instant later, bare-headed, livid, with his armor in disorder, Chram appeared in sight near the hut; he leaped off his horse, and was moving backwards, sword in hand, parrying the blows aimed at him by three warriors. Suddenly the thundering voice of King Clotaire was heard, and these words reached my ears:

" 'Lord, look down upon me from Your throne in heaven, and judge my case, because I have been most unworthily wronged by my son! Look down upon us, Oh, Lord, and judge us equitably, and let Your judgment be that which You pronounced between David and Absalom!'

"Clotaire finished this invocation as he came within my view near the door of the hut, and he then addressed the three members of his bodyguard who were still closely pressing Chram:

" 'Stop your attack! I want to see the traitor alive!'

"The warriors lowered their swords. Chram, whose face was bathed in blood, staggered a few steps forward and fell into the arms of his wife, who had rushed towards him, and now held him in a close and consoling embrace. Her two little daughters remained on their knees with their arms outstretched towards Clotaire, who descended from his foam-flecked horse. In his hand he held his long sword. His warriors made a circle around Chram and his family. Clotaire then sheathed his sword, folded his arms over his breast, and for an instant contemplated his son in silence. Chram fell on his knees; with clasped hands he implored his father's pardon, and then bowed down his head to the ground; his wife and two daughters sobbed aloud. Clotaire looked upon the group long in silence. Finally he issued his orders to one of the men in his suite. Chram, his wife and his two daughters were bound fast despite their frantic cries for mercy and desperate resistance. All the four were then dragged into the hut. Their piercing cries reached my place of concealment, distant though it was. A few minutes later Clotaire's warriors came out of the hut and closed the door.

" 'We bound them all firmly upon the bench, as you ordered, seigneur King,' one of them reported.

"At the same moment I saw another warrior draw near the hut with a burning brand."

"But what was the death that Clotaire reserved for his son and his son's family?"

"The hut was constructed of wood and thatched with reeds. The three warriors of the King heaped around it bunches of dry seaweed and dead tree branches."

"Oh, I can guess what is to come. Oh, Ronan—that is horrible. The father is going to burn his son, granddaughters and his son's wife!"

"When a sufficient mass of these combustible materials was heaped up all around the hut, Clotaire made a sign. The warrior who held the burning brand blew upon it, and soon as it was in flame held it to the heap of dry wood and weed. In an instant the hut disappeared behind a roaring sheet of fire. The cries of the unfortunate beings who were about to perish in the flames became heartrending. I turned my head away in involuntary horror, and, as my eyes fell upon the high sea, I saw the light vessel speeding away under full sail and vanishing in the distant horizon—it carried away Imnachair, together with the treasury of Chram.

"Clotaire has four sons left to him—Charibert, Gontran, Sigebert and Chilperik. It is said that the last of these seems to have inherited the ferocity of his father Clotaire and his grandfather Clovis!"

EPILOGUE.

On the morning after the day when Ronan, my brother Kara-deucq's son gave us this account, he left us. These were his last words:

"Kervan, I leave this house happy at having fulfilled the last wishes of my father and the orders of Joel."

Ronan the Vagre left, accordingly, early in the morning to return to his beloved Valley of Charolles. My nephew promised that, in the event of any matters of importance, he would inform us if he finds a traveler bound for Brittany. He would address any further narrative either to myself or my son Yvon, should I have left this world.

May Ronan, my brother's son, arrive safely in the Valley of Charolles and find his family happy and peaceful.

If before my death I should have nothing to add to these chronicles, I bequeath them, together with our family relics, to my son Yvon.

* * * * * * *

I, Yvon, son of Kervan and grandson of Jocelyn, enter at this place the date of my father's death in the month of June of the year 561.

From travelers we have learned that King Clotaire died this year at Compiegne in the fifty-first year of his reign, and was interred in the basilica of St. Medard at Soissons with the blessings of the bishops.

I have received no tidings from Ronan. May he still be alive and happy and free in the Valley of Charolles, as we are here in Brittany, which still remains free from the Frankish yoke. May it please Hesus never to allow our beloved province to experience such a calamity.

THE END.